The Vail Family Series

To Forgive the Past

D. K. Taylor

FinnLady Press

FinnLady Press

ISBN-10: 1727671694
ISBN-13: 978-1727671698

Library of Congress Control Number: 2018959991

Printed in the United States of America

Acknowledgements

My deepest thanks and appreciation to the members
of the Kent County Library Writers' Critique Group
for convincing me I could write,
and encouraging me to publish.
Thanks guys!

Thanks to my extended family
who never doubted that I could write a book,
and who supported me all the way.

And to my editor,
Janet Scott McDaniel of FinnLady Press,
who always knows exactly how I want things to be
before I even voice the thought, thank you.

To love

means loving the unlovable.

To forgive

means pardoning the unpardonable.

Faith

means believing the unbelievable.

Hope

means hoping when everything seems hopeless.

~ Gilbert K. Chesterton

The Vail Family Series

To Forgive the Past

D. K. Taylor

Chapter 1

Mark Vail came awake slowly, reluctant to let go of the dream, a dream starring Jane Brewer, whom he hadn't seen in five years—until two days ago. *And with whom he was having dinner tonight! This was better than the dream—this was real life.* He sat up and swung his long legs off the bed, planting his bare feet on the smooth wooden floor.

He thoughtfully rubbed his hand over his whiskery face and shook his head, unable to believe she had actually agreed to go out with him. She didn't trust him; he'd seen that in her hesitation. Why would she? Still, she had said yes—so maybe she didn't hate him. Maybe, just maybe, Fate was giving him a second chance . . . and if so, he knew for damnsure, *this time he wouldn't throw it away.*

His conscience reproached him, and he ran his hands through his short hair and flopped back on the bed, overwhelmed with memories. He'd known Jane Brewer all his life. His sister Kit's best friend, she'd been like another kid sister—*until that Christmas.* He'd been able to get leave, and the whole family had gathered at Matt's home in Alabama. Kit had begged Jane to join them. The two of them had still been at Montana State. It was the first time he'd seen Jane since joining the Air Force two years earlier. In that time, she'd grown up— *transformed into a real beauty*—a fact that had hit him like a ton of bricks. During his two-week leave, they had been inseparable, and on his last night, he'd taken her to the lake to say their private goodbye . . . *and ended up making love to her.* It had been wonderful, unforgettable—*and stupid.* He'd never forgiven himself. Jane deserved better, *a whole lot better.* That one night could have changed both of their lives irrevocably—it had definitely changed him.

She'd thought she was in love with him—and he'd known it. He clenched his fists as everything came back. *She was Kit's best friend for God's sake*! He hadn't meant for anything to happen. He'd just thought they'd do some heavy making out, say their goodbyes, and he'd leave the next morning. Instead they had walked the path that led to the lake . . . *and she had joyously given herself to him, body and soul.* He had been blown away . . . by her love, by her passion, and by the sheer wonder of the experience.

Arriving back at Matt's house, they had paused in the hallway outside the study to talk, then headed upstairs to her room where they shared one last kiss before Jane said good night and slipped inside.

He knew she expected to see him in the morning; thought he'd call her when he returned to his Base. *She'd had every right to think that. Hell, he'd meant to.* But it hadn't happened that way. He'd stayed up all that night, unable to put her out of his mind, or to figure out what

10

to do. Looking back now, he realized that the young Mark he was then had been scared out of his mind, filled with emotions he had no idea how to handle.

In the end, he had chickened out. That was the only way to put it. He'd thrown honor and courage out the window and woke Matt at 0500 to say goodbye and tell him he had to get back to duty early. He didn't explain, and Matt hadn't questioned him, although he'd obviously wanted to. When Matt asked, "Have you said goodbye to Jane?" he'd only replied, "Yes."

He breathed deeply. *Not his finest hour, not by a long shot.* Since then, whenever he thought of her, and it had been often over the years, he'd always envisioned the same scene—her rising the next morning expecting to see him and her shock at learning he was gone. He'd planned to call her, write her. But things had happened. Things always happen . . . that's not an excuse. In his case, he'd been deployed to Iraq. The more time that passed, the harder it got for him to call and explain the indefensible; he'd <u>never</u> been any good at writing. Eventually he just gave up and tried to put the whole incident—and her—out of his mind.

Angry and frustrated by the memories, he let out a groan and slowly sat up. He'd neither seen nor talked to her for almost five years—until Kit had lost her leg in Iraq, and then disappeared from the hospital without a trace. Desperate to find her, Jane was the first person he thought to call. He'd expected her to hang up on him, but to his relief, not only had she not hung up, she'd been exactly the same as always—his sister's best friend—expressing only concern for Kit. He'd wanted to apologize, to say he was sorry for being such a jerk that last time, but the words refused to form. Instead, he had

11

simply thanked her for helping to find Kit . . . and hung up, making no reference to their past.

Then came the wedding; he was Hawk's best man, and Jane was Kit's maid-of-honor. Knowing she'd be there, he'd still been broadsided when he saw her for the first time at the wedding rehearsal. She was gorgeous, every man's dream.

Unable to get her alone for even a minute until after Hawk and Kit had left for their honeymoon, he'd known she was avoiding him. He'd finally managed to catch her coming out of the ladies' room, and blurted out a request for her to have dinner with him tonight. He could tell she didn't want to—she'd almost said no—but the gods had smiled on him, and she had agreed.

Soooo! Here he was, having dinner with her tonight. He still didn't know how to explain his unforgivable action—or why it had taken him so long to try. He picked up his watch and looked at it—*exactly ten hours to figure it out, to plan a campaign that would get Jane Brewer back in his life . . . and keep her there.*

The window of Jane's hotel room looked out over the parking lot three floors below. It was filled with cars and people, but she saw neither, her mind totally absorbed with thoughts of yesterday's wedding.

Four weeks ago Kit had called to tell her she and Hawk were getting married, and to ask her to be maid-of-honor. Their marriage was no surprise; she'd seen them together. She and Kit had been best friends since fifth grade, so being asked to be her maid-of-honor wasn't a surprise either.

There was no way she could have refused to be in the

wedding, not without telling Kit why—*and she couldn't do that.* She had agreed, knowing it would be difficult to see Mark again—*and it was.* She had gotten through the rehearsal and wedding—with Mark as Hawk's best man—on sheer nerve and resolve.

Now, Hawk and Kit were married, and on their honeymoon in Cancun. The wedding, in the Luke AFB Chapel, had been beautiful and as romantic as military weddings usually are, giving no hint of the difficulties the two parties had endured to get there. Only four months ago Kit had called from the Walter Reed Army Medical Center—where the Army sent her when she lost her leg in Iraq—and now she was Mrs. Hawk Hawkins, married to Mark's best friend. The same Mark she, Jane Brewer, had had a crush on in high school and fallen in love with in college. The same Mark Vail who had never even noticed her . . . until his leave five years ago, when he'd finally seen her as someone other than his kid sister's friend.

They'd had a wonderful week—which ended with their making love on the shore of the lake. She had never been so happy; it was the culmination of all her dreams . . . *until she arose the next morning and found Mark gone.* He'd just walked away—no goodbye, no 'I'll call you,' just—nothing. She'd told herself it would be all right, that he would call, or write . . . but he hadn't. Mortified, she'd never let anyone know, although his family might have suspected something since she and Mark had spent every minute of the two weeks together. She'd cursed herself for being a fool, and forced herself to get on with her life. Six weeks later, when she'd found herself pregnant with his baby, the hurt was so deep she never even tried to contact him. She *knew* he would have

13

assumed responsibility, but if he didn't care enough about her to keep in contact with her, she definitely didn't want him to come to her because he thought he *had* to.

Now, her worst fears were realized—*Mark was here*—and she wasn't over him, couldn't hate him, and still wanted him. Hearing his voice on the telephone when he had called about Kit, had been bad enough, but seeing him—*ahh, seeing him.* The memories had come flooding back—loosed from the locked box in her mind, and she couldn't cram them back in. She'd been so sure she'd put it all behind her, but she hadn't. *Oh God, she hadn't . . .*

Squeezing her eyes tightly shut, she tried to turn off the scenes playing out in her head, but the images continued to play. She stumbled to the bedside chair and slowly folded herself into it.

She'd barely gotten through the rehearsal and wedding. When she had put her hand on Mark's arm as they prepared to exit the chapel, she'd felt the shock through her entire body—while he seemed unaffected.

In the car on the way from the chapel to the officers' club for the reception, he had been driving, with her beside him, and Hawk and Kit in the back seat. Afraid to look at him, she'd stared out the window. Thankfully, Kit and Hawk only had eyes for each other.

They had almost reached the Club when Mark leaned toward her and whispered, "Do you still hate me, Jane?"

Startled speechless, she'd stared at him. *He thought she hated him! My God!* Thankfully, she was saved from having to answer by their arrival at the reception site.

As Hawk helped Kit out of the car, her own head was

14

spinning. *All these years, he'd thought she hated him . . . and she'd thought the same thing about him.* As Mark had come around to help her out of the car, she'd lowered her eyes to prevent him from seeing the panic in them.

He'd opened the door and reached for her hand, then leaned down until his head was close to her ear, and whispered, "Jane, we need to talk." His voice was rough with emotion, and she could only nod.

It was all happening again, Jane thought. Mark had been gone; now he was back and noticing her again. She should have blown him off, told him to get lost when he'd asked to take her to dinner tonight. But she hadn't —she couldn't. *How stupid was that, giving him another chance to break her heart?*

She dashed angry tears from her eyes with the back of her hand. At least he didn't know how bad it had been for her—and she would *never* tell him. Inhaling a deep breath, she huffed it out in anger and frustration. *Why in the world had she agreed to have dinner with him tonight?* She was flying back to Montana in the morning, and she'd never see him again—just like before. *Lord, she could see this train wreck coming . . . why couldn't she stop it?*

She shrugged her shoulders. What was done was done. In the words of her sainted mother, it was time to "get up and get on with it." He'd be here shortly. She stood and walked over to the closet. *What to wear? It had to be something that would knock his socks off, that's for sure.* Whatever happened, she wanted to be able to walk away with her pride intact.

15

Thank goodness, she'd thrown "the dress" in her bag at the last minute. It was one she'd seen in a store window over a year ago and bought because everyone should have at least one "little black dress." It wasn't really her—it was more what she *wished* she were—and it wasn't exactly appropriate for Sunday night at the Club . . . but it was that or slacks. She raised her chin. *The dress it was.*

Already showered, she brushed her short blond hair until it shone like a golden halo around her head, donned the dress, looked in the mirror—and swallowed. *The dress did everything she had hoped it would.* It looked perfectly plain on the hangar, but the way it was cut made it look oh so different once she put it on. It showed off every line and curve of her body. She almost looked glamorous, but . . . *could she carry it off?* The trick was to make him see what he had lost—make him want what he couldn't have. She felt a slight twinge of trepidation. *Was she sure he couldn't have her? No!* She tossed her head. She was <u>not</u> going there. Once was enough. This was about getting her pride back. Proving she wasn't just Kit's little friend, available for the taking. Right!

She was still dithering when the knock came. Taking a deep breath, she smoothed out the clinging lines of the dress, then opened the door. He wore tan slacks, a dark brown sport jacket, and a cream-colored shirt, open at the neck. The man was even better looking than he'd been five years ago, no trace of the unsure youth he'd been. This Mark was all man—hard-muscled, lean hipped, broad-shouldered, and confident. His dark eyes, however, were the same deep, velvety brown, with long, dark lashes that any girl would die for. For just a second,

16

there was a flare of some emotion in them, but it was gone before she could read it. Then his gaze swept her from head to toe, and his eyes widened in awe.

"*Jane?*" He swallowed as if he couldn't believe what he was seeing.

She refused to look away. When his eyes returned to hers, she lifted her chin and looked right back at him. *Yes! Exactly the reaction she had hoped for.*

Mark just stood there, looking at her and shaking his head.

What was the matter with him? The dress was perfectly respectable—even if it wasn't what she usually wore. Pleased with his reaction, she grinned. "I'm ready, just let me get my wrap." She peeped over her shoulder at him as she slowly turned around. The dress, while high in the front, dipped into a sweeping curve in the back, baring her neck and upper back.

Mark swallowed again.

"What's the matter Mark? Don't you like my dress?" she teased, a smile hinting at the corners of her mouth.

"Is that what you call it, a dress? More like a stealth weapon," he muttered under his breath.

"What did you say, Mark? I couldn't hear you."

"I said it's . . . you're beautiful. Actually, you take my breath away." *He was so in trouble. His little sister's friend had turned into a bombshell.* "I was planning to take you to the Club for dinner, but we can forget that."

"Why?" she said innocently. "What's wrong?"

"No way am I taking you to the Club looking like that," Mark said as he looked her over. *She was enjoying this!*

"Why not? I don't want to embarrass you. Should I change into something more . . . casual? Slacks maybe?"

He gritted his teeth. *She was enjoying this—and he had to admit she probably had the right.*

"I am not ashamed of you. Don't change a thing. But I'm not about to let those wolves get their eyes on you." *Not when I intend for you to be mine*, he thought.

"Oh. I was looking forward to meeting your friends."

Instead of answering, he took the dark cape she held in her hand and carefully wrapped it around her shoulders, swallowing hard as he took in the creamy white expanse of her bare skin. He wanted to lean down and touch his lips to the vulnerable neck and the soft curls lying close to her head . . . but he knew he couldn't. Gritting his teeth, he placed his hand lightly on her waist, and felt a warmth in his groin.

He opened the door for her, then followed her into the hall. When they reached his car, a black Jaguar, she raised her eyes to his and mouthed the word, "Wow!"

He had a sheepish grin when he answered. "My one luxury. I always promised myself that I'd buy one."

"I'm glad you did. You deserve it, Mark."

He started to ask what she meant, but changed his mind and helped her into the luxurious car. He handed her the seat belt and watched her fasten it before shutting the door.

Once he was in the driver's seat, she took a deep breath and exhaled slowly to settle herself. "So, where *are* we going then?"

Deep in thought, he looked over at her in confusion.

"You said, 'No way am I taking you to the Club.'"

"Oh. Do you really want to go there?"

"It would be nice to meet your friends . . . but if you don't want to—"

"I was *kidding*, Jane." *In a pig's eye*, he thought,

18

realizing, *he really <u>didn't</u> want to share this woman.*

She turned toward him and smiled, and he knew—he couldn't, absolutely couldn't, let her go again. Several minutes later, he realized Jane had apparently asked him another question, and was waiting for his answer. "I'm sorry, what did you say?"

"I asked about your job. Is flying everything you dreamed it would be?"

"More! I love the feeling I get when I'm soaring up there, surrounded by nothing but blue sky. It's peaceful—most of the time."

"You mean, except when you're in combat?"

"Yeah."

"Were you in Iraq?"

"Yes."

"I'm glad I didn't know."

"Why?"

"Oh, no reason." *That was close. She was going to have to guard her words more carefully if she didn't want him to know how much she still cared about him.*

"So, tell me about you."

"Well, I got my nursing degree, and I work in the emergency room at the local hospital.

"Do you like it?"

"I do, except . . ."

"Except what?"

"Sometimes I feel as if I'm the only one who never went anywhere or did anything. When Kit came to stay with me after she lost her leg, I realized how boring my life is. She's—you've all—been so many places, while I'm still living in the same town where I was born."

"I wouldn't call working in the ER a boring job."

"It isn't, exactly. It's just—oh, I don't know. I'm fine."

19

"There's that word again."

She laughed. "Kit told me what happened when she kept telling you she was fine—that she and Hawk met when you asked him to check on her while they were both in Iraq."

It was his turn to laugh. "Yeah. She was really ticked at me for sending him to check on her, but she got over it."

"I'd say so! They make a perfect couple. Do you think she'll stay in the Army?"

"I don't know. I don't think *she* knows. Kit's going to meet with the board and see what they say. If they agree she can remain on active duty, then she and Hawk will have to make some decisions. It would be easier if they were both in the same service. Then the government would try to keep them at the same installation. It's not so easy with him in the Air Force and her in the Army."

Jane was surprised when Mark stopped the car, until she realized they had arrived at the officers' club. She had worried about finding something to talk about, but their conversation had flowed as if they had never been apart.

Chapter 2

Mark stopped in the foyer. "Do you want to check your wrap?" He could see the mischief in her eyes.

"I don't think I'll need it, do you? It seems warm in here."

Oh yeah, it was that. "Probably not," he said, reaching to take the wrap. *This woman is killing me.* He handed the cloak to the woman behind the counter, accepted the receipt, and stuffed it in his breast pocket. "Okay, let's go."

"You sound like a man going to the gallows! We *could* have gone somewhere else."

"No, no. I'm fine. It's not often a man can make an entrance like we're going to."

Smiling to herself, she noted that his grin looked more resigned than humorous. They had no sooner entered the room than one of the men at the bar looked up and saw them. He nudged the man next to him. Pretty soon the whole row had turned on their stools in order to watch their progress.

"<u>Hello</u>, Bronc." Before the man finished speaking he was sliding off the bar stool and approaching them.

21

Mark took a deep breath, anticipating what was coming. "Hello, Roger. I might have known you'd be here."

"I'm not flying, am I?"

"Unfortunately not."

By this time, they were surrounded by five other men, although there were still a number of men at the bar. *At least his whole outfit wasn't here. Thank God for small favors.*

"Well, Bronc, aren't you going to introduce us to your friend?"

"Jane, this rowdy bunch of wolves are my squadron mates. I'm not sure I want to dignify them with the title of *friends*."

"Aww c'mon, Bronc. You know we'd do anything for *you*."

"Yeah, right. Jane, meet Roger, Left Wing, Coop, Jocko, Merlin, and Jimbo." As the six men stuck their hands out, Jane smiled and gracefully shook hands with each of them, laughing as she did so.

"I'm so happy to meet some of Mark's friends."

"Aww, Bronc, she calls you *Mark*."

Mark raised his eyebrow at Roger, who let it go for the moment.

Jocko pushed forward, smiled at Jane, and motioned toward the bar. "Won't you join us? We can make room for two more."

Mark had had enough. "Thanks guys, but I don't think so. Jane and I came here for dinner, so we'll see you later." Without waiting for further comments, he put his hand on her back and steered her toward the dining room.

"Hey, Jane! If this guy starts to annoy you, we're right

here. All you have to do is call. Bronc here can be a wild man."

Jane was amazed to see a flush move over Mark's face. *If she didn't know better, she'd think he was embarrassed. What was that all about?* She laughed and waved at the teasing men. "Thanks, guys; I think I can handle it. I've known Mark for a long time."

A look of surprise came over every face.

Mark sped up, putting ground between them and the men. Once they were out of earshot of his friends, he stopped and turned to her. "Why did you have to tell them that?"

"Tell them what?"

"That you'd known me for a long time?"

Now it was her turn to be surprised. "Why wouldn't I? We've known each other since I was ten and you were thirteen. I'd say that qualifies as a long time."

"Not what I meant."

She bristled. "Then perhaps you'd better tell me just what you <u>did</u> mean."

He could see he was digging this hole deeper and deeper. "Forget it. Doesn't matter."

The steward approached. "Table for two, sir?"

Mark nodded. "Somewhere out of the line of traffic, if possible."

"Yes, sir. Right this way."

The man headed toward the back of the room, ending up at a table in the far corner, partially hidden by a large rubber plant. He looked at Mark for approval, and when he got a nod, handed them two menus before disappearing. Mark seated her with her back to the room, and took the seat against the wall for himself.

"Your friends seem nice. I like them."

23

"You just met them."

"I know, but I could see they all like you. Have you known them a long time?"

"Most of them, and I guess you could say, they are good friends. They just don't know when to lay off."

She laughed at him. "And if it were one of them coming in with a new woman, and you were one of the men at the bar?"

This time his grin was real. "Point taken. I would have done the same thing, have done, in fact."

She laughed again, and the sound of her laugh made him feel happy.

"Why do they call you Bronc?"

"It's my call sign—you know, when we're flying."

"But why, Bronc?" Suddenly her eyes lit up, and she smiled. "Because you used to be a bronc rider!"

He returned her smile. "You got it."

"Do all their names mean something?"

"Most of them. Some of them are just derivatives of their given names—Jimbo is James Wyatt; Coop's full name is Marvin Cooper. Left Wing got his handle in flight school when the instructor said to dip his right wing—"

"And he dipped his left wing."

Mark nodded. "The instructor and everybody in the flight rode him about it for weeks."

"And the rest?"

"Jocko's small and as agile as a monkey; Merlin is a wizard when it comes to fixing anything."

"What about Roger?"

"I think we'll skip his for right now."

"Why?"

"Let's say it's not for publication." She frowned, and

24

he thought she was going to pursue her question. He was relieved when she picked up her menu, but she immediately laid it down, tilted her head, and studied him. He was totally surprised at the question she did ask.

"I hated seeing the "For Sale" sign on your old house. Are you sorry about selling your family home?"

Now where did that come from? "I guess, sometimes. But I really don't think about it all that much. It seemed the only thing to do after we all left the area. Now, when we can all get together, it's usually at Matt's house. "

"But what happened to all your furniture, your memorabilia, your . . . *things*?"

"I hired a realtor to sell the house, and a service to go in, pack up everything and put it in storage. Someday, all of us will have to go back there, go through the stuff and decide what to do with everything, but . . . not now."

"All of you were always so close. I envied you that."

"We still keep in touch. We call each other a lot, and we always try to get together for Christmas. Matt and Elaine have plenty of room, and their two little ones make Christmas fun. Some years we don't all make it, but most of us usually do. We have some wild times, trying to catch up on everything that's happened in the previous year. But we still miss Mom and Pop. You're lucky your parents are still with you."

"I know, but I really miss having your family right next door. Growing up . . . I guess I always felt it was my family, too."

He reached across the table and gripped her small hands with his large ones. "We considered you family, Jane." His expression clouded, and she was startled at the sadness in his velvety eyes as he continued.

"Jane . . . I need to tell you . . ." He inhaled a deep

25

breath. "I need to tell you how sorry I am for leaving like I did that last time; for never getting in touch with you. I didn't mean for it to be like that. I thought I'd call you . . . but then I got deployed right after I got back from leave. I could have—*should have*—called you, but . . . I just never figured out what to say . . . and the more time that went by the less I could think of how—"

"Forget it, Mark." She shook her head vigorously. "It's done, the past is over."

"I did worry—"

"Stop it, I said! Don't."

He could see in her eyes how much he had hurt her—and that the pain was still there. He castigated himself anew. *I wish I could have a do-over, but like the line from The Rubaiyat, "the moving finger" has written and moved on.*

Fear surged through her. Her fierce statement had only roused his curiosity. *Stupid!* She had to distract him, derail his train of thought. She changed the subject.

"I was stunned when Kit called me and told me she was in Walter Reed, that she'd lost her leg. I hadn't heard from her in a while, and then to hear like that. But I'm glad I was the one she chose to ask for help. It was wonderful to see her—even though it was for such an awful reason. I missed her so much when she left for West Point."

He could see what she was doing, and he'd let her get away with it, for now. "You two were like sisters when you were growing up."

"We were. I never had another friend like her, not one I could tell *everything*."

"Yet you never told her about us?"

Darn it all! He just wasn't going to let it alone.

26

"Jane?"

She dropped her gaze. "No. No, I didn't."

"Why not?"

She jerked her head up, and there was anger in her eyes. "I didn't tell _anyone_. You never told her either! Did _you_ ever tell anyone?" She tried to keep her anger in check. "Hawk maybe?"

He remained silent for so long she instinctively reached out and touched his arm.

"Mark?"

"No, I . . . it was . . . private . . . just between us. I should have talked to you before I left, but I didn't, and then I never felt right about calling you later, not after leaving the way I did." He looked down at their clasped hands.

"Oh Mark, _why_?"

"I guess I didn't think I had the right."

He looked up, his face pale and strained. As she watched him, she felt something release within her. She reached up to touch his tormented face. "It's all right. It's in the past, over." _And as suddenly as that, she realized it really was._

Mark reached up and took her hand in his. He was thankful for her words, but it wasn't all right. It would never be right, and he knew it. _In that moment, he promised himself—somehow, some way, he would make it up to her._ "I don't deserve your forgiveness, but I'm glad to have it. We won't discuss it any more . . . for now."

The way he said it, she knew it would come up again, and she was glad when the waiter appeared to take their order. After he left, Mark leaned forward on his elbows, and smiled at her.

"How are your parents? I remember they moved to Florida when you started college."

"That was always their dream. My mother never liked the cold weather, and Dad promised they'd move as soon as he retired. I was happy they were able to make the dream come true."

Mark propped his chin in his hand and looked at her thoughtfully. "You sounded unhappy before when you said you were still living in the same town."

"Not just the same town—the same house!

"You're still living in your parents' house, next door to where I grew up?"

"Actually, it was my grandmother's house."

"I remember, she used to live with you."

"Umm hmm. When she died, I was only ten, and although I didn't know it at the time, instead of leaving the house to my Dad, she left it to me, but gave my parents the right to live in it. I would never have asked them to leave, of course. I actually like living in the house—but sometimes I can't help but wonder what it would be like to travel, to live where no one knows me, to have to make it totally on my own. I don't know . . . look at you and your family. All of you have traveled, lived places, seen and done things I can only dream about."

"Not Matt."

"No, not Matt. But he seems very happy in his chosen vocation. Being a minister suits him. I can't imagine him pulling up roots and moving on. But the rest of you— look at you! You're flying jets! And Kit—she's a West Point graduate—and she was a company commander in Iraq. Jon is a Navy SEAL, and his life is one adventure after another. Luke's a Marine helicopter pilot . . . I

28

guess what I'm trying to say is . . . seeing all of you at the wedding made me realize how ordinary my life is."

Mark smiled. "Somehow I don't believe that."

"Now you're laughing at me! I suppose I do sound like a whiner, and I'm not . . . at least I don't mean to be. I know I'm really lucky not to have the expense of rent or a mortgage, and I have a job I actually like . . . right, I am a whiner. Sorry." Her fingers were twiddling with the silverware, and he reached out and covered her hand with his. His fingers long and slender, the hand itself lean and well-shaped, pilots' hands. She looked up at him and shrugged, and he cocked an eyebrow.

"Jane Brewer! You're the last person in the world I would ever call a complainer or a whiner. I was smiling because you're only voicing what we *all* feel at times."

"What do you mean? You're doing exactly what you *always* wanted to do. You were into airplanes as far back as I can remember; all you ever wanted to be was a fighter pilot!"

"True, but that wasn't what I meant. There comes a time in everyone's life when he wonders what his life would have been if he had taken a slightly different turn somewhere along the path."

Now, he was absently stroking her palm with his thumb, causing her heart rate to increase. *I'm not over him! Nope. Definitely not.* She pulled her fingers free. "What do you mean? What kind of detour would you have made?"

Abruptly, he removed his elbows from the table and sat back in his chair. It was his turn to shrug, and she realized he'd let her see more of himself than he intended.

"Nothing, just rambling I guess."

29

She knew he wouldn't say any more about himself, so she changed the subject. "Tell me about your family. I know Kit and Matt are the only ones married. Is anyone else contemplating the idea?"

He laughed. "No, at least not yet. It's a big decision to get married when you're in the military. It's hard for a wife, always having to pull up stakes and move somewhere else, never having your husband home when you need him, never being able to plan on anything."

"Kit and Hawk don't seem to have any doubts. And you might say Kit has an added problem."

He nodded. "I guess love must make the difference."

"Of course it does! How can you doubt it? That's the *whole* difference! Love is everything. You can conquer anything if you love each other."

He put his hands up in surrender, laughing. "Okay, okay. I'm sorry I said it. It's not like I don't believe in love. It's just—"

She raised her eyebrows. "Just what?"

He looked at her for several very long seconds, their gazes locked, before he answered. "It's just that I haven't found that type of love yet, I guess."

He saw the quick shadow in her eyes—he'd hurt her again. He'd always known in his heart that she would never have let him make love to her unless she at least believed she was in love with him. And him? *Had he loved her?* He might have . . . just not enough. On the other hand, he'd never been able to forget her. True, he'd dated lots of women—the key word being "lots." No one else had ever gotten close to him like she had. He'd dated some of them for a while, but none of the relationships had been memorable. She was quietly studying him. There was no expression in her eyes now.

It was as if she were waiting. *What did she expect him to say?*

When she spoke, her voice was soft. "Were you even looking for it, Mark? Sometimes we can walk right by something, completely overlook it, if we're not searching for it."

"You might be right. You probably are; I don't know. But I think I might be ready to look now." *Why in the hell had he said that? It had never even entered his mind before. Damn!*

Jane's eyes widened in surprise, but all she said was, "Then maybe you'll find it."

He was relieved when the waiter approached with their food, followed by the wine steward. *This conversation had taken a turn that was making him nervous. He needed to get things on a different track.*

The steward handed him the wine bottle, and he glanced at the label and nodded. As the man opened the bottle, poured a small amount into the glass, and handed it to him, he struggled to come up with a topic of conversation that wouldn't lead him back into the swamp of troubling thoughts. Obviously, she was having the same problem because they both spoke at the same time.

"Mark . . ."

"Jane . . ."

They laughed, and he knew he had escaped, for now. "Do you have a ride to the airport tomorrow?"

Jane looked up in surprise. "Kit said <u>you</u> would take me, but . . ."

"I will—I can—I was planning to."

"Thank you."

What time does your plane leave?"

"Not until 11:00 a.m., but I have to be there two hours

31

ahead, 9 a.m."

"0900, got it."

"You don't have to wait—with the new regulations, you can't go past the screening area anyway—just drop me off in front."

"I have plenty of time. Too bad you have to go back so soon. Are you sure you can't stay another day or so?" *Darn, she was shaking her head before he even finished.*

"No. I was lucky to get Friday off. I have to be back at work on Tuesday. The hospital is already short staffed."

"I feel as if we're just getting to know each other again, and now you're leaving."

She looked at him warily. "You could always call me . . . if you wanted to."

"Do you want me to?"

"Only if you want to."

He laughed. She was so cautious, but he couldn't blame her; his record <u>was</u> pretty bad. He was lucky she hadn't told him <u>not</u> to call her—but this time he <u>would</u> follow up. He made a vow to himself: *He'd call her often, as often as it took.*

Watching his mouth draw into a stern line and his brown eyes flash, Jane wondered what was going through his mind. "What's the matter, Mark?" He looked up, and several seconds passed before he shook his head.

"Nothing. I was just . . . um, thinking." She smiled back at him, and nodded.

"Ahh. Thinking is good."

"Now you're laughing at *me*."

The waiter returned to clear the plates and ask if they wanted dessert. Mark looked at her and tipped his head in a question. "Do you?"

32

She considered. She really didn't want dessert . . . but neither was she ready for the evening to end, so . . . "I think I will have dessert." She looked at the waiter. "Something light, if you have it."

"Yes, ma'am. How about chocolate mousse? Or a dish of sherbet? We have raspberry, orange, and lemon."

"I'll have the lemon sherbet, please."

The waiter nodded and turned to Mark. "You, sir?"

"No dessert for me, but I will have a cup of black coffee."

"I'll be right back," the waiter said as he turned and left them alone.

"I'm glad you ordered dessert."

"Why?"

"I'm not ready for the evening to end yet," he said as he looked deeply into her eyes.

She took a deep breath, and felt her heartbeat quicken. "I'm not either, Mark."

He found himself wondering if there was a way he could prolong the evening . . . and if he dared to kiss her when it finally did end.

The waiter returned with dessert and coffee. She picked up her spoon, but instead of eating the light confection, she let her mind wander, her curiosity about Mark growing by the minute. *What had he been doing in the last six years? Besides flying fighter aircraft, of course. Had he had a girlfriend—lots of them? Had one of them hurt him? Broken his heart even? Was that why he had never married?* She brought herself up short. *Why should she care after the way he had hurt her? She should be glad if he got hurt the same way.*

Are you going to eat that. . . or just look at it?"

His question interrupted her thoughts, and she looked

up, a blush covering her cheeks, as she quickly spooned a mouthful of sherbet.

"Where were you just now?" he asked softly.

She shook her head. "Uh, nowhere."

He arched an eyebrow and tilted his head. She knew he didn't believe her, but she couldn't explain.

All too soon her dessert dish was empty, and despite the slowness with which he drank his coffee, his cup was empty too.

"Would you like coffee before we leave?" He asked hopefully, knowing she would probably say no.

"No, thank you. I couldn't eat another bite, not even coffee."

"Well, I guess we're ready then."

He stood and walked around to pull her chair out, and she warmed at the gesture.

As he stopped to pay their bill, he was thankful to note the bar was empty of anyone he knew—his friends had left.

Jane felt the warmth of his hand the minute he placed it on her back. The heat flowed throughout her body. It was becoming increasingly difficult to pretend she no longer cared about him—but she had to do it. She'd already made a couple of blunders tonight. No more. She'd gone out on a limb by telling him he could call her. It was up to him to prove he had changed. *If he called . . . if he did . . . then . . . maybe.*

Mark was also affected by the feel of her smooth skin beneath his hand. He <u>had</u> to be careful. He knew she was not ready to forget the past, and no matter how much he wanted to rush ahead, he couldn't. *A good night kiss? Maybe . . . if he could rein himself in enough to keep from kissing her the way he wanted to.* She probably wouldn't ask him in . . . but again, he hoped she would. *What was wrong with him?* He'd never lacked confidence when it came to women, any woman—but it was definitely lacking with this woman. He was scared to death of making a mistake that would turn her totally against him—a possibility he knew would devastate him. His buddies—the same guys who had taken such delight in taunting him earlier tonight—wouldn't believe such caution in the man they called fearless. *He felt as if he were feeling his way in the dark, although come to think of it, even that didn't usually give him a problem!* The thought brought a rueful grin to his face. Keeping Jane in his life had suddenly become very important to him, and he realized he would do anything—whatever it took—to accomplish that. It also occurred to him that neither of them had said a word since they left the club parking lot. *What was she was thinking about?*

"A penny for your thoughts, Jane."

"Only a penny! Hmmm."

"Okay. How about a dollar?"

"Big spender."

"That's me. So, what were you thinking about?"

"Hmmm. I was thinking . . . I was thinking how much I enjoyed tonight . . . and how different you seem."

He was taken aback. *Different? Was that good or bad? Did he want to know? He did.*

"Different how?"

"I'm not sure. Just different. Older maybe."

"Well, I am that. Five years older, in fact."

Again, he had surprised her. *So he had kept track of the time. That was interesting.*

"Is that the only difference?"

Suddenly she wasn't sure she wanted to go there,

wished she hadn't opened the subject. "Nooo, but I don't think I can put it into words . . . just that it's a nice difference."

"Jane . . ."

They were approaching the base guest hotel where she was staying, and he reluctantly abandoned the line of conversation. Parking in front of the building, he got out of the car and walked around to open her door, as nervous as a sixteen-year-old on his first real date. *What the hell was the matter with him?*

He took her arm to help her out of the car. She turned sidewise, and her skirt rose up her thigh. His body reacted instantly. *The woman had gorgeous legs. Hell, everything about her was gorgeous.*

She slid out of the car, and he automatically curved his arm against her back as they walked up the sidewalk to the building. In front of the door to her room, he reached for her keycard, and their fingers touched. It felt as if he'd touched a live wire.

"I'm not going to ask you to come in, Mark. I have to be up early . . . and it's just better that you don't, I think. But . . . thank you for a lovely evening."

Jane leaned forward, and as her lips neared his face, he realized she intended to kiss him on the cheek—*but that so wasn't going to happen.* He reached up, clasped her chin in his hand, and placed his lips softly against hers in the gentlest of kisses. Even so, he felt a tremor of desire go through him. It was the hardest thing he had ever done to force himself to pull away, and he just barely managed it.

"Thank *you*, Jane, I enjoyed it too. Now, I think I'd better say good night."

She spoke softly, "Good night, Mark."

He turned and strode back down the walk, but halfway to the street, he turned back to say, "I'll be here at 0830 tomorrow morning."

She didn't wait for him to reach his car, but turned immediately and went into her room, closing the door softly behind her. In front of the dresser mirror, she stopped and reached up to touch her lips. She could still feel his gentle kiss. The tenderness was new—and nice.

He smiled as he drove away. *Jane Brewer was an incredible woman.* She'd refused to let him blame himself, when he knew the fault was most definitely his. She'd called him 'gentle.' Maybe he had been gentle with her . . . but only with her. He laughed. Most people thought he was hard, and he was. He'd built his cynical shell over many years, and no one ever got beneath it, except his family—and Hawk. He and Hawk were alike—at least they used to be.

Perhaps that's why they were such good friends—they understood each other. But Hawk had changed. He was different since he met and married Kit. His sister had definitely captured the Hawk's roving heart. He recalled the tears Hawk had tried to hide as he watched Kit walk down the aisle, and could only hope for a love like that in his own future.

Could such a thing happen to him? He'd never experienced it. Jane said he needed to look for it . . . *and maybe he did.*

The next morning, when she opened the door in response to his knock, he was in uniform. The light blue shirt was tailored to perfectly fit his muscular chest, and the creases in his dark blue slacks were sharp enough to cut. His flight cap sat aslant his head, angled exactly at the prescribed two fingers from his nose. He was freshly shaven, and she caught a faint whiff of pine from his aftershave. He almost took her breath away. *Not good. Not good at all.*

"Are you ready?"

She nodded, and he reached in and grabbed her bag, fitting his other hand to the small of her back, where it was beginning to feel as if it belonged.

"At least you have a nice day for your flight."

"It's lovely," she said, smiling as she took in the brilliant sunshine surrounding them.

"Have you had breakfast?"

"No. I didn't have time."

"Good. We'll stop on the way and pick up some breakfast sandwiches to eat in the car. You'll still have time to check your baggage and make check-in."

She smiled at his take-charge attitude. He had changed in the years since she had seen him—more than just going from a boy to a man; although he was definitely that and more. He exuded an aura of authority and capability that had been missing then, and she found it made her feel safe and protected—strange given their history. Her spirits lifted at the unexpected bonus of a little more time with him

Just before they reached the airport, Mark drove through a McDonald's drive-in and ordered two breakfast sandwiches and two coffees. Still refusing to simply drop her off in front of the terminal, he parked in the parking garage, opened the bag, and handed her a sandwich and coffee.

They ate in silence, neither of them seeming to know what to say. Mark spoke first, as he stared through the windshield of the car, his sandwich forgotten in his hand. "You know, it's funny. Hawk and I were talking right before he and Kit met. When I called and asked him to look her up, he mentioned that he was getting tired of the 'girl-at-every-base' thing, that maybe it was time to think about settling down. And then he met Kit, and that was it."

"And what did you say? Were you feeling the same way?"

"Maybe not then. At least I wasn't ready to admit it, but seeing Hawk and Kit married and so happy, now I think I might know how he felt."

He'd surprised her again. *It wasn't like him—at least it wasn't like the Mark he used to be—to let her see inside of his protective shell.* Still wary, her comment was flip. "So, now you're wife shopping?"

He scowled at her remark. "Hardly. Jane . . . if I email you, will you write back?"

Whatever she had expected, that wasn't it.

He added quickly, "If you don't want to, I'll understand."

She realized that he'd misunderstood her hesitation. "I'll give you my email address . . . and I'll look forward to hearing from you."

"Just don't expect too much. I already told you, I'm not the world's best correspondent, but I do try to keep up with my e-mail, as often as I can."

He had spoken gruffly, as if he had said too much, and she watched him almost angrily crumple his uneaten sandwich into the bag, glance at his watch, and open the car door.

"We better get you checked in."

"Okay." Trying to adjust to his abrupt change in tone, Jane scrabbled around for her things, and was ready when he opened her door to help her out. Mark got her bag out of the trunk and insisted on accompanying her to the baggage counter in the terminal, hanging on to her bag until he set it up on the scale for her. Once she was checked in, he took her shoulder and turned her toward him. His eyes held hers for several seconds before he spoke.

"I'd better go."

"Mark, I can't thank you enough for dropping me off, and for breakfast."

He leaned forward, and she expected him to kiss her, but he only grasped her hand and squeezed her fingers gently.

"Goodbye, Jane. Safe flight."

She reached out and touched his face softly. "Goodbye, Mark."

She turned to go and he squeezed her fingers again. Turning back, he looked deeply into her eyes and when he spoke, his words held a certainty that surprised her.

"I will call you, Jane." Then he grinned. "Bet on it."

He turned and walked away, disappearing into the crowded terminal. As she walked toward the security gate, she bit her lip. No matter how many times she told herself not to believe him, she couldn't keep from hoping, knowing her heart would be broken, again if he didn't.

Chapter 3

I hate Monday mornings, Jane thought as she drove to work the next day. Only two days since the wedding, but it seemed much longer. She was discouraged and tired and down. The wedding had been beautiful. She was happy for Kit and Hawk, but she couldn't help but envy Kit. Seeing Mark had brought back all the old memories and feelings, and changed nothing. *He won't call.* She kept telling herself that—yet still hoping that he would.

Everyone she knew seemed to be going somewhere, doing something exciting—everyone but her. She'd had enough of it. She didn't know what she was going to do, or where she was going, but she was <u>not</u> staying here— in the same place where she had been born—she was so <u>not</u>.

When she got stuck in a traffic jam, it was the last straw. She sat impatiently drumming her fingers on the steering wheel, looking at the same scenery she saw every day— and then, out of the corner of her eye, she saw it! An Air Force Sergeant was setting out a large signboard in front of the Recruiting Office adjacent to the post office. Her attention was riveted by what she saw on the sign—an Air Force flight nurse standing in front of a med-evac plane. *Suddenly, she saw herself as that nurse.* Her thoughts were interrupted by the sound of an angry horn behind her—traffic was moving again. She eased her car forward, but the image remained in her mind.

Jane pulled up and parked in front of the long, low hospital building, sighing as she got out of the car and headed for the door. An hour later it seemed as if she had never been away. She looked out over the almost-empty emergency waiting room and called the next patient, a little boy holding his left arm. Automatically trying to put him at ease, she smiled as she spoke to him.

By lunchtime, the weekend seemed light years away. The emergency room had been busy, as usual, and she'd been able to put her memories on hold. What she couldn't put out of her mind, however, were the thoughts she had been increasingly having lately that her life had fallen into a dull routine. She liked nursing, loved the challenge of the emergency room, but she kept remembering her conversations with Kit, and Mark. Both of them had done so much, seen so many different places. If not making her discontented, it was at least causing her to consider her options. The picture of the flight nurse on the recruiting poster flashed into her mind as she headed for the hospital cafeteria.

Her friend and co-worker, Ellen, joined her as she walked down the hospital corridor. "So how was your trip to Utah?"

"Oh, nice! Kit's wedding was lovely. It was the first time I ever saw a military wedding, and it was something! *Very* romantic. You would have loved it."

"All those handsome guys in uniform, hmm?"

"Mmm hmm."

"What's that supposed to mean—you aren't into handsome guys in uniform?

"No . . ." When Ellen raised her eyebrows, Jane laughed.

"That's not what I meant. You know me better than that. It's just . . . do you ever feel as if every day here is the same? That—"

Ellen interrupted her. "How can you say that? While this may not be like an inner city hospital, it's *certainly* not the same every day. There's—"

"I don't mean that, but being with Kit and Hawk and Mark—"

"Mark! Who's this Mark? I don't recall your mentioning him before." Ellen's eyes sparkled as they pushed through the door into the cafeteria.

Grabbing a tray and joining the cafeteria line, Jane filled a mug with coffee, then moved down the line where she picked up a salad.

Undistracted, Ellen continued. "Come on, Jane, who's this Mark? And what do the three of them have to do with you feeling dissatisfied with your work?"

Jane set a dish of fruit on her tray, and moved forward. "I didn't exactly say I was dissatisfied. But, you have no idea what it's like. They've been all over the world—Iraq, Afghanistan—"

"Real tourist attractions," Ellen said drily.

"You just don't get it," Jane said as she paid for her lunch.

After paying for her lunch, Jane moved through the room, acknowledging comments from co-workers. At the first empty table, she unloaded her tray, set it on a nearby cart, and settled into a chair. Ellen was right behind her, and the minute she sat down—before taking a single bite—she returned to the topic of Mark.

"So, explain it to me. What don't I get? And you still haven't said who this Mark is!"

Jane took a deep breath. *Ellen might be a good friend, but she didn't want to get into this right now, not when she wasn't sure herself why she felt the way she did.*

"You remember my friend Kit?"

Ellen nodded. "The woman who lost her leg and came and stayed with you—"

"She's the one. Well, Mark is her oldest brother—she has four—and we all grew up together. Kit and I went all through school together. Then she went to West Point, and I went to MSU."

"So how does this Mark figure in the picture now?"

"He's an Air Force Captain—all of Kit's family are in uniform, except for her brother Matt."

"You're kidding! Every one of them?"

"Yep! Mark's an F-16 pilot, Luke flies Cobras for the Marines, and her twin brother Jon is a Navy SEAL."

Ellen fanned herself with her hand. "Wow! No wonder you feel like a nobody!"

Jane bristled. "I never said I felt like a nobody! I just would like to be *somewhere* besides the place I was born and raised." The recruiting poster popped into her mind, and she debated telling her friend about it. Before she was done debating, Ellen stunned her by seeming to read her mind.

"I suppose you could always join the military yourself; I hear the Air Force Reserve is actively recruiting nurses to serve on medevac flights."

Jane ignored the skeptical look in Ellen's eyes. "Funny you should say that. On my way to work this morning I got caught in a traffic jam, right in front of the Recruiting Office."

Ellen's expression was becoming increasingly leery, but Jane kept on. She couldn't stop now. "The recruiter was moving a big signboard out to the sidewalk . . . and on it was a picture of an Air Force nurse standing in front of a plane."

"*Jane Brewer!* You're not serious! You're not actually considering joining the Air Force!"

When Jane looked back at her defensively, her friend's mouth dropped open.

"You are! You're actually thinking of doing it! What in heaven's name happened to you at that wedding? You're not the type to up and change your life at the drop of a hat. Think about this, Jane."

"I am, and I really think I am serious. And you've just confirmed why!"

"*Me?* What did I say?"

"You said I'm not the type to up and change my life. That's my whole point! I'm tired of being old, predictable, run-of-the-mill Jane Brewer."

Ellen put both hands to her head, running her fingers through her red hair. "I can't talk to you. I don't know you. Just . . . just don't do anything rash. Think about this. I mean, this is not something you can undo if you don't like it. You know, changing your life is fine . . . so long as you're sure it's for the better." She stopped suddenly and gave Jane a suspicious look. "Let's get back to Mark. Somehow, I know he has something to do with this, so stop avoiding my question and tell me what."

"He doesn't, really—not him specifically." She could see the doubt in Ellen's face as she continued. "Although

45

we do have a history."

"A history, hmmm."

Ellen's expression was definitely speculative now, and Jane quickly stood and looked at her watch. "Oh darn, I'm afraid I've got to run. I promised to be back a few minutes early so Jan could get to that briefing on the new Flu procedures."

Ellen crossed her arms over her chest, and glared. "You're not fooling me for <u>one</u> <u>second</u>, Jane Brewer. You know I'm not going to forget about this. I'm also attending that meeting, so I have to leave too. But we <u>will</u> discuss this later. I don't believe for one minute that this Mark has nothing to do with your sudden urge to join the Air Force. Not for <u>one</u> <u>minute</u>."

Jane shoved her chair under the table and rolled her eyes as her friend grinned up at her. Ellen would definitely bring the subject up again, but the truth was—she had told the truth—*Mark really wasn't the reason for her discontent with the way her life was going. And there was no way she would tell Ellen, or anyone else, about what had happened five years ago.*

At the end of the day, Jane crossed the parking lot to her car, still thinking of the lunchtime conversation. Ellen's comment that she wasn't the type to change her life had irked her. She could do whatever she had to. *After all, hadn't she done it once before?*

She drove out of the hospital parking lot, the image of the nurse in the recruiting poster still in her mind. The idea intrigued her. When the recruiting office appeared on her left, she swung into the parking lot behind the old post office building without thinking. Parking quickly, she grabbed her purse, released the seat-belt, and then just sat there, staring out the windshield.

Was she out of her mind? It <u>wasn't</u> like her to make such a sudden decision, but she refused to let herself back down. She swung the car door open and slid her legs out. *After all, she was only going in for information. What could it hurt?*

As she opened the door to the recruiting office and stepped inside, a tall sergeant came out of the back room with a mug of steaming coffee. His arm was full of stripes, and a friendly smile lit his good-looking face.

"Hello there. You thinking of joining the Air Force?"

Jane hesitated. "Um, maybe . . . that is, I just came in for information."

"That we've got. Anything specific you're interested in—nursing maybe? You look as if you're a nurse. Am I right?"

"You are. I, er, my friend, also a nurse, said that the Air Force Reserve is actively recruiting flight nurses."

"So you want to be a flight nurse?"

"I'm thinking about it."

"It's a great program. You'd enter the Air Force as a military officer. Your entry rank depends on your experience and education. Sound good so far?"

She nodded.

"Well, first of all, let's see if you're qualified. Come on back." He motioned her to follow him back to a desk at the rear of the room.

"Can I get you a cup of coffee?"

"No, thanks. I'm fine."

She sat gingerly on the chair he indicated, wondering what she had gotten herself into.

"Now, let's get right to it. To be an Air Force nurse,

you have to be a U.S. citizen, have a bachelor's degree in nursing from an accredited school approved by the Air Force Surgeon General, meet physical requirements, and be a licensed registered nurse. Are you still with me?"

"I think so. I am an American citizen. I graduated with a BS in nursing from Montana State. I'm healthy, and I am a licensed nurse, presently working in the emergency room at the local hospital."

"Okay. So far, so good. Now, suppose you ask me some questions, and I'll try to answer them."

"Well, what kind of training would I have to undergo? Would I have to go to boot camp or something?"

"Not quite boot camp, but when you first enter the Air Force, you'll be sent to Maxwell AFB in Alabama for the Commissioned Officer Training (COT) School there. It's a five-week course to ease you into military life. While there, you'll undergo physical conditioning and classroom studies that prepare you to become an officer and a leader. You'll study leadership principles, Air Force customs and courtesies, military law, officer/non-commissioned officer relationships, warfare and disaster preparedness, and the Air Force role in national security."

"Sounds like a lot to learn in a short time."

"It's a packed five weeks, I'll grant you that."

He smiled at her, and she felt reassured, as he went on. "It'll go by fast, and you'll make friends you'll keep all your life. After COT you'll know just what to expect as an officer and medical professional in the USAF, and you'll be assigned to a reserve unit close to your home."

"It sounds interesting." *Actually, it sounded wonderful*!

"I'm sure you'll find it so. Air Force nurses learn to

manage and operate air transportable hospitals, how to handle advance trauma in life support, and conduct combat medical operations in field situations. After your training you have an opportunity to select from such specialties as clinical nurse, medical/surgical nurse, operating room nurse, etc."

"I was thinking of medevac duty—is that possible?"

"There's a real need for that specialty right now, and most air evac nurses come from the Reserve component."

Her head was spinning; she couldn't think.

"Could I please have some pamphlets or something, so I can take them home to read over?"

The sergeant gave a quick nod and smiled. "You sure can. As I said, information is one thing we've got plenty of. Just hold on, and I'll put together a package."

He rose from his desk and moved around the office picking up pamphlets and info sheets from various tables. When he had what he wanted, he grabbed a large manila envelope from a basket on his desk, stuffed the papers inside, then handed it to her.

"There you go, Miss. I hope you choose the Air Force. You won't be making a mistake."

"Thank you. It all sounds wonderful. I love nursing, but I've lived here all my life—I guess I just want to see some other places."

"Well, ma'am, I think I can guarantee that. If you find you have more questions after you read through the material, just give me a call. Here's my card."

She took his card and stood. He stood too, and when he offered his hand, she shook it firmly.

"I hope I see you soon."

"Thank you, sergeant. I think you will."

★ ★ ★

Driving home, Jane found herself wondering what Mark would think if he knew she was contemplating joining the Air Force—which was strange, given that she had told Ellen just that day he had nothing to do with her decision. The realization hit her suddenly— while that might be partly true, she didn't want Mark to see her as nothing more than a quiet little nurse in a small-town hospital. She wanted to be like Kit and the rest of his family . . . *and she wanted Mark to see her that way.*

He hadn't called in the three days since the wedding. She hadn't really expected him to, even though he had said he would. Three days wasn't all that long, but still she feared he might not call .

Minutes later, she was getting out of the car inside her garage when she heard the phone ringing. Jamming her key in the door, she snatched it open and ran through the mud room and into the kitchen. She was breathing hard when she grabbed the cordless phone on the counter. "Hello?"

"You knew it was me, hmmm?" he said, sounding amused.

She felt her stomach drop. *It was Mark!* "No, of course not. Why would I think it was you?"

"Well . . . you sound as if you ran to grab the phone, so I figured you knew it was me."

She could hear laughter in his voice. "Hmph! You wish!" Thankfully he couldn't know how close to being right he was—she *had* hoped it was him, and she *had* run to grab the telephone.

"You're out of breath."

"I just got home. I was outside the door when I heard the phone."

"Did you have a good day?"

"I did, actually," she said, thinking of her talk with the recruiter. "Did you fly today?"

"Yeah, just around the flagpole."

"What?"

"You know, practice."

"Oh." This silence was uncomfortable. In his car, they'd had plenty to talk about. Now, she couldn't decide whether to tell him about her plans, or wait. Finally, he spoke.

"I heard from Hawk and Kit."

"Oh, are they having a good time?"

"<u>Everybody</u> has a good time on their honeymoon," he said wryly.

"Right, dumb question."

"What's the matter, Jane? You sound . . . different."

"Nothing . . . I wasn't expecting you to call."

"I told you I would."

"I know . . ."

"But you're remembering another time I didn't. Right?"

"I guess. I'm glad you called, Mark, really glad."

"I don't intend to break any more promises, Jane. If I say I'll do something, you can believe I'll do it. Remember that."

"I'll try. Mark, do you remember . . . do you remember me saying I was tired of being the only one who never went anywhere, the one whose life was dull?"

"I remember, and I told you that I couldn't imagine a job in a hospital ER being dull."

"Well, I'm thinking of doing it . . . making a change"

"What kind of a change?"

She took a deep breath and dove in. "I just came from the Air Force Recruiter's Office. I'm thinking of joining the Reserves."

"What!"

"I want to be a flight nurse, a medical evacuation nurse specifically."

"What!"

"Is that all you can say, *what*?'"

"I don't know <u>what</u> to say. What brought this on? You don't know anything about military life. I thought you <u>liked</u> being a nurse."

"I do like being a nurse. I don't plan to stop being a nurse. I just want to be a *flight* nurse. And I don't know why you're so shocked. I <u>told</u> you I wanted to see more of the world than Great Falls, Montana."

"I remember your saying that, but I guess I didn't think you were going to take such drastic action, or do it so quickly. Don't you think this is a bit sudden?"

"Maybe, but I've been thinking about doing something for a long time. Maybe not this, but something. I saw the sign, and it seemed right. After all, with the war, there's really a need . . . and I can help fill that need."

"Sign? What sign?"

"The sign in front of the recruiting office. I passed it on the way to work. There was a nurse standing in front of an airplane, and—"

"And that made you decide to join up?" he exploded. "What the <u>hell</u> are you thinking! You don't have a <u>clue</u> what you'd be getting into." He seemed to realize what he'd said, and stopped. "I'm sorry I said that . . . but you should give this some more thought before making such

52

a drastic decision."

That's exactly what she'd planned to do, give it some thought, but his angry comments just reinforced the way everyone thought of her.

She snapped back. "You're just like Ellen! Why does everyone think I'm some wimpy milquetoast who's too timid to leave her small-town life? Well, I'm <u>not</u>. I can, and what's more I <u>will</u>."

Mark was stunned. *Where was this coming from?* He certainly didn't think of her as a 'wimpy milquetoast.' He hadn't been able to get her out of his mind since he'd left her at the airport three days ago. *But . . . in the Air Force? Her?* He just couldn't get his mind around it.

"Jane, first of all, I definitely don't think you're "wimpy." Then his mind registered the second thing she had said. "And what did you mean by saying, I'm just like Ellen? Who's Ellen?"

Despite her anger, she almost had to laugh at the indignation in his voice. *At least he didn't think her a wimp. That was something.*

"Ellen's a friend who works with me. When I mentioned the idea to her today she said I wasn't the type to do something like this."

He couldn't help but think, *good for Ellen.* He knew that wasn't helpful, and found himself struggling for words—safe words.

"Well, that's a relief. For a minute there I thought you were questioning my masculinity."

"Don't be ridiculous!"

Well, that didn't work. He'd meant to make her laugh, but obviously she wasn't in a laughing mood. "O-kay. Then tell me, where did you suddenly get the idea to join the Air Force?"

"I just told you, I saw the sign."

"She saw the sign," he muttered under his breath. *He had to be missing something here.*

"I can't hear you, Mark. What did you say?"

He knew he was about to overstep here, but he couldn't help himself. The idea of her flying into combat areas just . . . just did something to him.

"Think about this, Jane. I . . . it's fine to make a life change . . . but not this."

Anger and disappointment coursed through her, and when she spoke, her voice was deceptively soft and controlled. "Why not? I'm a very good nurse."

He groaned. "I'm sure you are. You'd be good at whatever you do. That's not the point."

"Then what exactly is your point, Mark?"

He tried to martial his thoughts. He couldn't tell her that just the thought of her flying into harm's way—and she would be, there was no question about it—made him cringe with horror as pictures of Kit in her hospital bed flashed across his mind.

"Mark? Are you still there?'

"I'm here . . . Jane, you should check this out further. Do you even know anyone in the Reserves?"

"No. But I know people in the military, specifically *your* family."

"That's not what I mean." His frustration was beginning to show in his voice as he continued. "Why don't you talk to some of the Reserve nurses about their jobs—instead of going off half-cocked and getting into something you know nothing about?"

"*Excuse me*? What did you say?"

"Forget that! I didn't mean it the way it came out. I just meant . . . I don't know what I meant."

"I can't believe your attitude! I don't understand why you're so upset. You admit I'm a good nurse, and you know there's a real need. You're in the service. Your whole family is full-time military, including your own sister, Kit."

"Yeah, including Kit . . ." He sighed and his voice trailed off.

Suddenly, she knew. *He was worried about what might happen to her.* On one level, it pleased her to know that he cared, but her anger continued to simmer. He didn't have the right to decide her life for her. *Why did he think he had to protect her from anything unpleasant? Did he think ER nurses never saw horrifying sights?*

"Kit is fine, Mark. She and Hawk are going to have a good life together."

"I know they will, but the fact remains—she lost her leg, Jane, and—"

"That doesn't mean the same thing will happen to me! And it could happen to me crossing the street in front of the hospital. Or, the same thing could happen to you, or Luke, or Jon. Did you try to keep them from joining up?"

He took a deep breath and forced himself to stop. *She was winning this argument on logic, but dammit, logic wasn't the thing.* "You're right, of course I didn't . . . because I knew it wouldn't do any good. And before you say it, I know I can't change your mind . . . if I even had the right to try, but—"

"Mark, I appreciate that you can't help worrying about me because of Kit, but it's not the same thing. I'll probably only be flying between Germany and the States. And, I really want to do this."

55

Angry at his attitude, and disappointed that she was unable to make him see her side, she lapsed into silence. When he spoke her name softly, she knew she couldn't continue their conversation without him realizing she was near to tears.

"I have to go, Mark. Goodbye."

"Jane . . . please, Jane, wait."

He heard the click and slammed his fist into the wall in frustration. He had certainly handled that well. *How in the world was he going to get himself out of the hole he had just dug?*

Chapter 4

After a rough night spent alternately railing at Mark for being so imperious—and so male—about her considering the Air Force, and then wondering if she <u>was</u> making a mistake, considering both Ellen and Mark thought so, she arose convinced that it was the right decision for her. As she dressed, fixed a quick breakfast, and drove to work, she considered how she would tell Ellen that she had already made up her mind. It would be great if she could convince Ellen to join with her, although that didn't seem likely, given her comments the day before.

When she entered the break room, Ellen was drawing a cup of coffee from a big urn on the counter.

"Boy, have I got a lot to tell you," Jane announced as soon as she had grabbed a cup for herself from the stack on the table.

Ellen glanced over her shoulder as she added sugar to her cup. "Why, what's up?"

Jane looked at her watch again and then back at Ellen, frowning intently. "There's not time for me to tell you everything now—meet me for lunch."

"Jane Brewer! You're not getting away with a teaser like that. At least give me *something*."

Jane glanced at her watch again, then reached out and pulled Ellen out of the crowd around the coffee pot. "Oh, all right—I'll give you the short version. I did stop at the recruiter's yesterday after work—and Mark *did* call last night." She turned and headed for the door, leaving Ellen staring after her, mouth agape.

Jane pushed open the swinging door, but Ellen hurried after her, grabbing it before it could swing shut. "Now, wait just a minute. You can't make two announcements like that and then just leave me hanging. Did you tell Mark about the recruiter?

"Yes."

"Well, was he pleased?"

"No! And I really have to go; I'm going to be late."

Ellen gave a loud "humph," and stopped Jane with a hand on her arm. "Okay, I'll wait, but you better not be late for lunch. I'll save us a table."

Jane couldn't keep from grinning as she and Jane separated, Jane to the Emergency Room and Ellen to Pediatrics

★　★　★

The emergency room was busy all morning, with an accident victim brought in just as Jane prepared to take her lunch break. It was some time before she could get away and she walked into the dining room twenty minutes late. Ellen was already seated at a table, her impatience showing. She spied Jane, pointed to her watch, and rolled her eyes. Jane shrugged and hurriedly got in the buffet line, which mercifully wasn't busy since the lunch rush was over. A few minutes later she put her tray down and began setting her food on the table.

"I was about to think you weren't coming."

"Now, Ellen, you know what the emergency room is like. I couldn't get away any sooner." Grinning at her friend's obvious impatience, she sat down and took a deep breath. "Don't worry, I'll talk while I eat."

"You'd better. I've been waiting all morning to find out the details of the bombshell you dropped this morning. Start with the recruiter first."

"Hmmm, let me see—"

"Jane Brewer!"

Unable to keep from laughing, Jane held both hands up in surrender. "Well, I went there right after work, and the recruiting sergeant was nice, and very helpful and informative. If I get accepted—and I might not—and if I pass the physical, then basically, it involves one Saturday a month and two weeks of training in the summer, unless my unit is activated, or I volunteer for a tour when the unit is tasked with one. The hospital here has to let me go, and guarantee my job when I return. The Air Force will send me to COT—that's Commissioned Officer Training—for five weeks. It's at Maxwell Air Force Base in Alabama. That's where they teach you military customs and courtesies, all that stuff."

"I can see he sold you," Ellen said drily.

"It's just what I've been looking for, Ellen. A chance to do something interesting and exciting, and get to travel at the same time. And they really need medical evacuation nurses now. According to the sergeant, they almost all come from the reserve forces. I'd be filling a real need. Don't you see? I have to do this."

"You've already signed up?"

"No. I haven't. But I'm going to. I was awake most of

59

the night, and I'm going to do it, despite Mark's ridiculous comments."

"Now, we get back to Mark! Just what did he say? Did you tell him you were joining, or just thinking about it?"

"I told him I was thinking about it, and his comments were bad enough at the idea I was even thinking about it. Heaven knows what he'll say when he finds out I've actually done it!"

"Exactly what did he say that has you so fired up? I can see sparks in your eyes. Does he know he made you angry?"

"He should; I hung up on him."

"So he knows! What did he say before you hung up?"

"First, he kept repeating 'What!' as if I were voicing some outlandish thing he'd never heard of. Then, he said it was too sudden. And then . . . and then, he asked me what the <u>hell</u> I was thinking of."

She stopped for breath, and Ellen rolled her eyes and groaned. "And you exploded?"

"I guess I did, sort of. Why <u>shouldn't</u> I consider it? His whole family is in the military—except for Matt. Even his sister! I . . . I was disappointed that he didn't think I could do it, and then I got mad that he felt he had the right to all but tell me not to."

"Maybe you're not looking at this from his point of view—"

"<u>His</u> point of view! What point of view? What about *my* point of view?"

"Isn't it possible it's because his sister is in the Army? Because of what happened to her? Because she lost her leg, and he doesn't want someone else he thinks a lot of taking a chance of the same thing happening to her?"

Jane's shoulders slumped. "I know that what happened to Kit is part of it. I know that, but . . . how do you know how he feels about me?"

"Don't get so excited." Ellen spread her hands. "It only seems logical. You grew up together, you're his sister's best friend . . . you know." She shrugged.

"Maybe. I guess, but—"

"You're going to do it, aren't you? You've already made up your mind?"

"Ellen, I have to. This is right for me." She drew in a deep breath. *She couldn't tell Ellen . . . but Mark's comments had really hurt.* She blew out the breath and looked at Ellen as she bit her lip. "I can't believe he would think I'd take advice from him— that I'd let him make my decisions for me, when—" She stopped abruptly, afraid to look at Ellen after what she'd almost said.

"When? When <u>what</u>? Why did you stop? Jane, what haven't you told me?"

She couldn't believe she'd almost let out what she'd never told anyone. That showed how much the man had upset her. Thank goodness she'd stopped in time. "When we haven't seen each other in years. That's all." She shrugged, and touched the dial of her watch. "Isn't your lunch hour over?"

"Luckily for you, it is. But I won't forget; we'll get back to this." She stooped to retrieve her purse from the floor, and looked at Jane seriously. "When are you going to sign the paperwork?"

Caught by surprise, Jane hesitated, but only for a second. "Today. I'll stop by the recruiter's after work and sign on the dotted line. Maybe I won't be accepted, but I'm going to see."

"Then all I can say is good luck—both with the Air Force and with Mark. I'll see you later." She turned to leave, but Jane touched her arm to stop her.

"Ellen?"

"What?"

"You wouldn't want to sign up too . . . would you?"

Ellen stopped dead and stared at her. "You have <u>got</u> to be kidding!"

Jane's mouth tightened. "Just thought I'd ask."

Her conversations with Mark and Ellen played over and over in Jane's mind all afternoon. Every time there was a lull in the emergency room, she reheard their skeptical comments. And each time it happened her determination increased. This <u>was</u> the right thing for her to do—and darn it, it was the right time for her to do it.

At five o'clock, her mind made up, she left the hospital and drove directly to the recruiting office. Inside, she walked up to the Sergeant's desk and announced, "You probably didn't expect to see me this soon, but I've made up my mind. I'm ready to sign the paperwork now."

A broad smile lit his ruddy, Irish face, and he motioned her to the chair in front of his desk.

"Great! Have a seat, and I'll get started on the paperwork immediately."

She sat down as he booted his computer and pulled a notepad toward him. "We'll start with some basic stuff, and while I'm feeding that into the computer, you can fill out the more detailed information for me. We'll begin with your name."

Fifteen minutes later he printed out the contract and

pushed it across the desk for her signature. Once she signed, he looked it over and announced, "Well, that's it—you're in the United States Air Force Reserve . . . except for one more thing."

Startled, she sat up straighter, a frown on her face. "What else do I have to do?"

He laughed. "Don't worry—we just need you to get a physical. I'll set it up for you. The hospital at Malmstrom AFB does our physicals for us. You'll get a postcard from them within a couple of weeks telling you when to report for your physical. Once you pass, they'll notify us. It may take a while to schedule you for COT, depending on when there's a vacancy. It could take several months, but as soon as we have an opening your orders will be cut. You'll receive a copy telling you when and where to report."

He stood and stuck out his hand. "Congratulations, Miss Brewer! It's been a pleasure. And the offer still stands—you have any questions, you give me a call."

She shook his hand. "Thanks, Sergeant. You've been very helpful, and I appreciate everything."

"You're most welcome, Miss, and you be sure to call if you need anything."

She nodded and walked out of the office, a copy of the contract and a manila folder of information in her hand. *She'd done it. She was in the Air Force—assuming she passed her physical. Now came the hard part, telling her parents. She was tempted to wait until after she passed the physical, particularly given the reaction she had received from Ellen and Mark on hearing she was* <u>*thinking*</u> *about it.*

Jane opened a can of soup for dinner. As soon as she finished eating, she went into the family room, flopped down in her favorite chair, and reached for her phone. Instead of making the call, she held the phone and stared out the window. Snow had begun to fall, and she idly watching the swirling flakes float past the glass.

Her parents would be upset, no doubt about that but, hopefully, she could convince them this was right for her. *Here goes nothing*, she thought, and punched in their number.

Her mother answered on the first ring, and Jane listened to her happy voice gushing about how great it was to hear from her. She had to smile. Her mother's comments were so like her. Her effervescent personality made everyone love her. So different from her father, who was calmer, quieter, more serious, although just as caring. She did love them . . . and missed them since they had moved to Florida. When her mother yelled, "Jane!" she realized she hadn't been listening.

"Sorry, Mom, I'm excited. I guess I was daydreaming a little bit. I have something to tell you."

"What is it, Jane? Oh wait! Let me tell your father to get on the extension so you can tell us together."

She called out his name, and a minute later, her father was on the line.

"Okay, Jane. We're both here. What's your news?"

She took a deep breath, and blurted it out. "I just came from the Air Force Recruiting Office. I've signed up to join the Air Force Reserves. I want to be a flight nurse." Now that it was out, she shut her eyes and waited. It didn't take long.

"What!" That was her father. Unusual for him to speak first. She must have rendered her mother speechless. He repeated his question, "What did you say?"

"I'm in the Air Force—well, except for my physical. I actually signed the paperwork today."

Her mother finally spoke, her voice unsteady. "This is so unlike you, Jane. You never make decisions rashly. Joining the Air Force? My gosh! It's so sudden."

Her father, interrupted; his voice was serious.

"Jane, are you sure, _really_ sure, that you aren't going to regret this? You know nothing about life in the military, the regimentation, the—"

Her mother didn't let him finish. "Oh, Jane—isn't flight nurse another name for a medical evacuation nurse? For goodness sake, they might send you to Iraq . . . or even worse, to Afghanistan . . . or—"

"Mom, Dad, stop it! You sound just like Mark!" _Uh oh, that was a mistake._ She knew it as soon as the words were out of her mouth. Hoping her parents wouldn't pick up on it, she hurried on. "It's not as if I'm going to the moon . . . or dropping off the face of the Earth. I've simply decided to make a change in my life. I _do_ know something about the military. After all, Kit is my best friend, and she's been in the Army for four years— " Her mother's interruption dashed any hope that she might miss the reference to Mark; apparently she hadn't heard anything after the word Mark.

"Mark! Did you say Mark? Do you mean Mark _Vail_?"

Jane sighed. "Mom, what other Mark do we know?"

"But . . . I thought you hadn't heard from him in years?

"You're right, I hadn't. Not until Kit was injured. He called me to ask about her . . . and then I saw him at Kit's wedding."

65

Her Dad jumped in then, and she could barely stifle a groan. "You said we sounded just like Mark. What did *he* think about this idea?"

"He doesn't know I've actually signed up. I only told him I was thinking about it."

"Apparently he wasn't in favor of it."

"You could say that, Dad. You could definitely say that." She let out another sigh.

"You should listen to that boy; he always had his head screwed on straight."

She couldn't restrain the snort; it just came out. "Dad, he's not a boy! He's thirty years old! And after not hearing from him in over five years, I certainly don't know why I should pay any attention to what he thinks. It's *my* life!"

"But you're going to tell him?"

Jane could read her mother's mind, and knew where this was going. *She had to stop it right now.* "Mom, it's not as if we talk all the time. I don't know when, or if, he'll call again."

"Oh. . ."

There was a wealth of expression in that one word, and Jane knew she had just quashed her mother's romantic hopes for her. Her father spoke up.

"I can't understand why you wouldn't listen to advice from someone who knows what he's talking about. After all, Mark Vail is actually in the Air Force—"

"Dad, that's enough! I'm all grown up now. I have to make my own decisions about my life—and that's what I've done."

Her mother—who could never stand for anyone to be upset—interrupted, and her words were soft.

"Now, Jane. Your Dad didn't mean anything. It's just

a shock to hear it out of the blue like this. We never dreamed you wanted to 'change your life,' or that you'd join the Air Force, especially now."

She bristled. "What do you mean 'especially now'?"

"You have such a good job at the hospital . . . we thought you loved your work."

"Mom. Dad. I'm not quitting my job at the hospital. It'll be waiting for me when I return. I'm not going active duty. I'm joining the Reserve. I'll take my training in Alabama, and then come back to the hospital. After that I'll have one night a week and two weeks of training in the summer." Her father interrupted.

"Unless the unit gets called up. I've been reading the newspapers. I know how often Reserve troops go overseas. And, your mother's right— 'flight nurse' is just another term for med-evac."

"All right, Dad. That is possible, but I want to do this. The Air Force Reserve provides most of the air evac nurses, and that's what I want to do. My emergency room work has prepared me for that. I can really serve our country."

"But, Jane, look what happened to Kit."

"Mom! Kit met the man of her dreams, just had a beautiful wedding, and is very happy."

"She also lost her leg."

"Mom, you're not being realistic. I could get hit by a car crossing the street, or get shot by a burglar in my own house. Anything! But nothing's going to happen to me. I'm excited about training and traveling, learning new things. Please, be happy for me." A sigh escaped her lips. She couldn't believe she was having this same conversation all over again. When her mother spoke again, she sounded near tears.

67

"We are happy for you, Jane. If this is what you want to do, then we're glad you're doing it, aren't we, Dad?"

Several seconds passed before she heard his voice coming over the phone.

"Your mother's right. We do want you to be happy. But to a father, his daughter is always his little girl. It doesn't seem like any time has passed since you were crawling into my lap and asking for a bed-time story. Now, you're telling me you're going to be a military officer. I am proud of you, Jane. Your mother and I both know you'll make a great officer."

"But, we'll still worry."

"Now, now, Mother, she'll be fine."

"Mom, Dad . . . I know you're worried, but I will be fine. I love you both, and I'll call you again as soon as I have my physical and know if I pass."

"We'll be waiting to hear, honey."

"Jane, you take care now. . .and you call Mark. He could be very helpful—"

"Dad!"

"Okay, I won't say any more. You call, you hear?"

"I will, Dad, I promise. Bye."

She replaced the phone, shaking her head slowly. *Mentioning Mark had definitely been a mistake.* She knew it had raised all kinds of unrealistic hopes and expectations in her parents' minds. She had to laugh at her Dad, despite her frustration. She supposed it was generational, but he seemed determined to think she needed someone to take care of her. She'd probably never convince him otherwise.

Outside, the snow was really coming down now. She stood and walked over to the huge picture window and looked out. The ground was already covered, and it showed no sign of stopping. She'd be glad for her four-wheel drive SUV in the morning. She shook her head and smiled wryly, remembering her Dad's, "You call that boy!" She suddenly knew she wanted Mark to know what she'd done—but she couldn't call him, not after hanging up on him yesterday.

The next morning, Jane found Ellen waiting for her when she got to work.

"So? Tell me."

Unable to hold back a wide grin, Jane gave her friend a mock salute. "You're looking at a member of the U.S. Air Force Nurse Corps—providing I pass the physical."

Ellen dropped her head to her chest, then met Jane's eye. "You did it." She shook her head. "I thought maybe you'd change your mind before they got your name on the dotted line—but, you actually did it?"

"Yep! I told you I was going to, and I did."

"No regrets?"

Ellen was looking at her closely, as if she expected to see evidence of regret, and she stiffened before she answered. "No, I'm sure I made the right decision."

"Do your parents know?" When she nodded, Ellen continued, "And how do they feel about it?"

"They were upset at first. I guess shocked is more descriptive, but they're okay with it now. Still worried, but . . . accepting."

"And Mark? Does he know?"

"No!"

Ellen frowned. "Aren't you going to tell him?"

"Not unless he calls me . . . and he won't."

"How can you be so sure he won't?"

"I thought I told you, I hung up on him the last time he called." Ellen's arched eyebrows almost reached her hairline.

"Well, there is that. But if he *does* call?"

"He won't! But if he does, then I'll tell him."

"That should be interesting."

Ellen's wry grin said she knew Jane was worried about telling Mark. Thankfully, as other staff arrived, the area around them was getting crowded. Their shift would start in five minutes, and they needed to get moving.

"I gotta go, Ellen. See you at lunch?"

"Sure. I've actually got some news for *you*."

Jane tilted her head, and she arched an eyebrow. "Really? What?"

Ellen's grin was impish as she waggled her fingers in a goodbye wave. "Later. I'll tell you at lunch." She was already moving down the hallway as she spoke.

Jane headed off down the hallway to the ER and smiled. *Now I'll be the one wondering all morning— definitely, Ellen's intent.*

The ER wasn't busy, and Jane was able to take her scheduled lunch break. She and Ellen reached the cafeteria at the same time.

Jane spoke first. "Okay! I know you did that on purpose this morning, so tell me now. What's your news?"

Ellen's laughter was teasing. "I couldn't resist getting even after the way you left me hanging the other day. Come on, let's go through the line. I'll tell you while we're eating."

It was obvious from Ellen's demeanor that her news was good; she was bubbling over. A few minutes later, once they were sitting at the table, the reason became evident.

"I've been dying to tell you. Guess where I'm going for Christmas?"

"Just tell me!"

"I'm flying home. I've already asked for the time off, and got it. Since Christmas is on a Friday, I only had to ask for two days off. I'll have five days at home!"

"That's great, Ellen! Your family must be so excited."

"They are . . . but that's not my *big* news."

"Well, stop doling it out in dribs and drabs. What else?"

Ellen rolled her eyes before continuing. "Guess who's *also* going home to Texas for Christmas?"

Jane leaned back in her chair and looked at Ellen. "Stop with the guessing game, Ellen. Just *tell me*." Ellen waited a few seconds, letting the suspense build, before making her announcement.

"Dennis!" Ellen couldn't repress her grin.

"Dennis Martin! You sound excited! You always gave me the impression that he was just 'good ole Dennis.'"

"I know I did. I'm ashamed to admit I took him for granted. We grew up together, and you know how that is. After all, it's sort of like you and Mark—you grew up together too."

"I don't think it's the same." *It definitely wasn't, not that she would explain.* "But go on. You grew up together, and . . .?"

"We did. His Dad was the ranch foreman, and they lived on the ranch, so Dennis was always around. We dated, and went to the prom together, you know."

"Um hmm."

"Dennis went to Texas A & M, and then went right

71

back to the ranch to work for my father. After nursing school, I wanted something different, at least I thought I did. Dennis was angry when I took the job here. I think he thought we'd just get married and keep living right there on the ranch, but I wanted to be independent, on my own, at least for a little while."

"Like I do." Jane said, and Ellen nodded sheepishly.

"Pretty much. Anyway, we had a big argument, and I took off. After Dad bought the ranch here—"

"Where we go riding?" Jane asked.

Ellen nodded, and Jane thought she could see where this was going.

"About a year after he bought the ranch—which was coincidentally about a year after I came up here—I called home, and Dad said he had hired a new foreman. I couldn't believe Mr. Martin was leaving, and said so. Dad laughed and said, he didn't think I had to worry— Jock Martin would never leave the 'Triple W.' Mr. Martin was staying right where he was, but Dennis would be coming up to take charge of the new ranch. I couldn't believe it."

"Why? Sounds as if he had all the credentials."

"I don't know. I hadn't heard from him since I'd left home, and even though it was mostly my fault, I missed him. Mom had told me he was seeing Mary Sue Johnson—even though I hadn't asked for the information, and didn't want to know."

"Right!" Jane hid a smile.

"Yeah, well, she always did know me pretty well."

"I can't believe I never knew all this backstory—that you and Dennis had such a history. How come you never told me before?"

"I guess because I don't come off looking too great.

After all, it's stupid to blow off someone who's always wanted the best for you, and then immediately want him back . . . which is pretty much what I did."

"Ellen, I think you're too hard on yourself. After all, we all want a chance to spread our wings, and try out our own independence. I couldn't wait for my parents to retire to Florida; and what I've just done is another perfect example."

"Thanks, but I'll always feel guilty."

"What happened when he showed up here?"

"Well, one day he called and asked me if I was still mad at him, or if I had calmed down enough to come out and ride. I didn't appreciate the way he put it, but since I had been hoping he'd call, and I really did miss riding, I said yes."

"And it was all smooth sailing from there?"

"More or less. At first our dates were only occasional, and we were both careful—sort of like walking on eggs around each other."

"So, what's changed?"

"I think I grew up. I know he's the man I want to be with, and I can even see myself living on a ranch, especially since it's not the one I grew up on."

She stopped and looked at Jane, her shoulders squinched up, a wide grin on her face, and excitement in her eyes.

"I think, that is, I hope, he's going to ask me to marry him again while we're home. He's sort of hinted, you know, asked if I could see myself living on a ranch again, things like that."

"Oh, Ellen, I'm so happy for you! No wonder you look so bubbly and happy." She was surprised and delighted for Ellen. *It was really amazing how you never knew people as well as you thought you did.*

★   ★   ★

The next morning, Jane was roused from a deep sleep by the ringing of the cordless phone on the night table beside her bed. She reached for it automatically. *Who would be calling her at seven o'clock on a Saturday morning?* She couldn't help the disgruntled note in her voice as she hit accept and mumbled a sleepy "Hello?"

"Good morning, Sleepyhead."

"Mark!" She struggled to sit up in the bed, and tried to rub the sleep out of her eyes. "It's Saturday morning, for Heaven's sake! My only day to sleep in!"

"I'm sorry I woke you. Are you still mad at me?"

"Let's say I've cooled down some." *But she was afraid he was going to be mad at her once she told him her news.*

"You don't sound too sure." When she didn't say anything, he continued. "Did you think about what I said?"

"I thought about it."

"And?"

She sucked in a deep breath. "And I signed up. I just need to pass my physical, and—"

His voice exploded over the phone before she even finished the sentence. "No! Didn't you hear <u>anything</u> I said before? I can't believe you didn't even check it out! What'd you do? Sign up the next day?"

"Actually, I did."

"If you're not the stubbornest, most determined female I ever met. I can't even talk to you . . . and it's too late anyway. You've already done it."

74

Before she could staunch her anger enough to let him know what he could do with his stupid male attitude, she heard a click, then nothing but dead air. *He'd hung up on her! They were certainly batting a thousand—first she hung up on him, and now he'd hung up on her.*

She flopped back on her pillow and closed her eyes. She had been lying there for about five minutes, fighting tears of anger and frustration, when the phone rang again. She stared at it and let it ring. *If it was her parents, she couldn't talk to them now, they'd know something was wrong.* It rang until the answering machine came on.

"Jane . . . pick up, *please*. I know you're there. I need to apologize. . ."

Slowly, she picked it up and hit accept. "Hello."

"Have you been crying?"

"Why would you think that?"

"Your voice sounds funny, and . . . Jane, I'm sorry. I shouldn't have hung up on you. You just make me so—"

"Mad? Go ahead and say it."

"Well, yeah. But I shouldn't have hung up on you. Can you forgive me?"

Suddenly she saw the humor of the whole thing, and a giggle burst out of her mouth.

"Are you *laughing*?"

He sounded amazed, which made her laugh harder.

"What's so funny?"

Now he sounded irritated.

"You think my apology is *funny*?"

Doing her best to stop laughing, she answered him. "No, no I don't. I was laughing at us, the two of us. First, I get so mad I hang up on you, then you hang up on me. We've been acting like two teenagers."

"I guess."

She tried to get her breath. "Mark, thank you for calling back. I'll forgive you . . . if you'll forgive me."

"I knew as soon as you hung up on me that I was in the wrong, that I had no right to act like I did—"

"And yet you hung up on me just a little while ago for the same thing."

"I know." His voice sounded soft and unsure when he spoke. "And I want to tell you . . . I want you to know, I think you'll make a great evac nurse; you're just what the Air Force wants—smart, and independent. I know all that . . . but—"

"But you can't stop seeing Kit—"

"I can't, Jane. *I can't*! When I got the call that she had been wounded and that I should get to the hospital in Landstuhl ASAP . . . when I saw her for the first time in that hospital bed—"

"I understand, Mark, *I do*, but you have to stop treating me differently from the rest of your family. As severe as Kit's injury was, you didn't insist that she get out of the Army . . . nor did *you* think of getting out of the Air Force—or insist that Jon or Luke do so." She heard him groan.

"You and your damned logic. I can never win an argument with you." He sighed. "I know you're right, it's just . . . oh hell, I don't know what it is."

A feeling of warmth spread through her. Although he might not be ready to admit it, his anger and protectiveness meant that he cared about her. Knowing that, she could live with the rest.

"It's all right, Mark. I accept your apology. Can we start again?"

"Let's. So . . ." He sucked in a deep breath,". . . do

76

you know when they'll do your physical?"

"Not yet, I think it depends on how many people they have from this area, but I'll let you know . . . if you want me to."

"Of course I want you to! Call me as soon as you know. I have to go now, I'm scheduled to fly this morning."

"Okay, fly safe. I'll call you as soon as I hear anything.

It was almost two weeks later when she checked her mailbox and found the official-looking envelope with Malmstrom Air Force Base as the return address. With shaking fingers, she tore it open to find the notification she had been waiting for: her Air Force physical was scheduled for January 5—*a month from today*. Going to the refrigerator, she lifted the December page to see the calendar she had just hung under it. She marked the date in red ink, noting that January 5 was on a Tuesday.

She'd promised to let Mark know, but it had been two weeks since his last call—and his apology—and only one email. Still somewhat unsure about their relationship, she debated emailing him instead of telephoning. Even as she thought it, however, she was reaching for the cordless phone on the kitchen counter. She was too excited to wait—and too anxious to know how he would react. She punched in the cell phone number he had given her, wondering if he would be angry again. Before she could worry further about what she was doing, he answered.

"Mark Vail here."

"Hello, Mark—"

"Did you get your physical date?"

"It came in the mail today. I just opened it, and I'm scheduled for January 5th. You're the first person I've told."

He smiled, immensely pleased that she called him first. "I'm glad! I've been anxious to hear from you."

"You didn't have to wait. You could have called *me* you know."

"I really wanted to, but since you had promised to let me know, it seemed wiser to wait until you heard about your physical." *If only she knew how much he had wanted to call, but he still wasn't over his anger about her joining up, and was afraid to call her until he had been sure he could control his over-protective attitude. He simply couldn't risk making her angry again. How could he explain his reasons to her?*

"Oh . . ."

Mark hurried to alleviate the disappointment he heard in her voice. "Look Jane, what are your plans for Christmas?"

Taken aback by his abrupt change of subject, she stumbled. "Uh, I don't know."

"Are you planning to visit your parents?"

"No. I was off for Kit and Hawk's wedding, and I don't want to ask for any more time, not when I hope to be leaving for training soon."

"No plans with Ellen?"

"She's flying home to Texas for the holidays."

"Hmm. So you don't have *any* plans for Christmas?"

"No, I don't."

Mark took a deep breath as he considered his options. He had already made some inquiries and had a half promise that he could have a few days off around the holidays. Although he had called in all his markers and would owe favors to several of his friends, *it would be worth it—if she invited him. Time to find out.* "How would you like company?"

"You!"

"That sounds insulting! Of course, *me.*"

"Oh, Mark! That would be *wonderful*! Since Christmas is on a Friday this year—and I'm scheduled to work New Years—I should have the whole three-day weekend off. I can't believe you'll be here."

"Whoa! Wait a minute; hold up a second. I was just asking. I've done some preliminary checking, and I *think* I've got everything lined up. I wasn't sure how you'd feel, so I haven't firmed up anything yet. Things are usually slack over the two-week holiday period. If I volunteer to take all the New Year shifts, I'm pretty sure I can be there Thursday night, and I wouldn't have to leave until Sunday afternoon. I thought if you wanted to, we could drive up to the mountains, and go skiing the day after Christmas. I remember you and Kit used to love to ski."

"Oh, Mark, that's the most wonderful Christmas present *ever*! It would be perfect! When will you know for sure? I can't wait! You and skiing; it'll be per—" She stopped, suddenly realizing how much she was giving away by her exuberance.

"I take it, you think my plan is a good one," he said, smugly. He hadn't missed the pleasure and excitement in her voice, and his heart lifted. His campaign to remake himself in her eyes seemed to be working . . . *if he just didn't make any more missteps.* "In answer to your questions, I'll confirm everything tomorrow and give you a call tomorrow night. Is that soon enough?"

She giggled, unable to contain the happiness bubbling through her. "I think I can wait that long."

"Until tomorrow then . . . take care."

"I will. Goodbye, Mark." No sooner had she ended the call than she picked up one of the sofa pillows and began to dance around the room. *He was coming! Mark was coming!* And he'd told her to 'take care'—that sounded . . . oh wow! She had to call Ellen. This news couldn't wait until tomorrow.

The minute she heard Ellen's voice she interrupted, "Ellen, you'll never guess what just happened, never in a million years—"

"You heard from the Base?"

"I did, but that's not it."

"What do you mean that's not it? I thought you were waiting with bated breath to hear when you were going to have your physical?"

"Oh, I was, and I <u>am</u> excited—it's scheduled for January 5—but that's not the wonderful, great, *super* news I'm talking about."

Ellen's laughter trilled through the line. "This has to be about Mark! What's he done that has you babbling like a maniac?"

"He's coming to visit . . . for Christmas! I was so down when you told me you were going home. I mean, I was happy for you; I really was, but—"

"I understand. I would have felt the same way. Now go on with your story. I'm dying here."

"I decided to call him after I read the letter from Malmstrom telling me the date of my physical. He had asked me to let him know. At first, I wasn't going to, because I haven't heard anything from him since we

80

hung up on each other two weeks ago—except for one measly email—but, he said to let him know when I found out, and I—"

"And you wanted to talk to him," Ellen said drily.

"Uh, yeah, I did. Anyway, I called him, and—"

"Did he give you a reason for not calling?"

"You know, now that I think about it, he didn't. I think we did mention it. Well, *I* mentioned it, but then he told me he could get the weekend off, and—"

"And everything else flew out of your head. Good maneuver on his part I'd say."

"I—I guess."

"Oh Jane, *stop it*! You *know* I'm teasing. I'd say he made up for any lack of communication with this surprise."

"It is a surprise, Ellen, it really is. Luckily, I'm scheduled to work New Years, so I'll be off Christmas. Everything is working out perfectly!"

"When is he coming?"

"He thought he could get here Thursday afternoon, but he's going to call me tomorrow night after I get home from work. I hope . . . he didn't mention how he planned to get here. He'll never get a flight reservation at this late date."

"Maybe he's taking a military flight into Malmstrom."

"Maybe, but I don't think they have regular flights there from Hill, especially not this close to Christmas. Surely, he—"

"Now don't worry yourself into a snit. He's going to call tomorrow. He must have a plan for how to get here, or he wouldn't have told you he was coming."

"I guess. Well, anyway, I just had to tell you. I'll see you at work tomorrow."

81

"Okay. See you."

Wednesday, Jane was on pins and needles the entire workday. Finally, the last patient had been shown into a cubicle where he would be examined by a doctor. Letting out a sigh of relief, she rushed down the hall to the locker room. After retrieving her purse, her mind was so tuned to Mark's expected call that she almost ran Ellen down as she turned to leave the room.

"Whoa there, girl! Why the rush . . . as if I didn't know! When do you expect Mark to call?"

"I'm not sure, but I don't want to miss it."

"Like he wouldn't call back," Ellen said with a smirk, her eyes lit with teasing.

"I know I'm being silly, but I—"

"You're not silly. I'd be the same way. It's just so unusual to see the staid and proper Miss Jane Brewer all fluttery and flustered. Now me, that's my normal state, but you're always so serious and thoughtful about everything you do. I wonder if Mark knows what he does to you."

"He does not!" *Heavens! What an awful thought. She needed to get herself in hand before he called . . . and definitely before he arrived.* She could feel her face warming as she remembered almost giving herself away on the phone yesterday.

"And just *what* delicious thought is bringing that lovely shade of pink to your face? Is it possible that Mark knows more than you're admitting?"

Ellen's grin said she was teasing, but the idea didn't bear thinking about. "Stop it, Ellen. You're fishing, and I'm through biting. I've got to run, anyway. Mark said he'd call after work . . . and I intend to be home when he does. See you tomorrow." She spun on her heels and rushed down the hall.

Ellen's voice trailed after her, "I'll expect a full report tomorrow."

Jane didn't answer, but she heard Ellen's laughter as she hurried out the door.

Ten minutes later she entered her garage, and unlocked the kitchen door. After checking the answering machine, she breathed a sigh of relief when there were no new messages. *She'd made it in time.*

Tossing her purse onto the nearest chair, she headed for the bedroom to change out of her scrubs and into something more comfortable. She had just pulled on her favorite blue sweatpants and had her head in the ragged MSU sweatshirt when the phone began to ring. She yanked the shirt down and grabbed for the phone, knocking the alarm clock on the floor in her haste, frowning as it hit the floor and its face separated and slid under the bed.

"Yes, I'm here," she said breathlessly. Mark's chuckle made her heart skitter, and she flopped down on the bed.

"A man might get ideas the way you're always out of breath when you answer the telephone when you're expecting me to call."

Yep, she was definitely going to have to get herself in hand here; something that seemed pretty much impossible right at this minute.

"You still there, Jane?"

"I'm here. I just got home. I was changing clothes—"

"So, are you dressed—or not?" She heard a smile in his voice.

"I am <u>completely</u> dressed . . . except for my shoes."

83

*Heavens, so much for Ellen's "staid, serious Miss Jane."
She was so out of her depth here.* "Uh, were you able to
make all the arrangements? Are you coming?"

Mark could hear the hesitancy in her voice, knew that
she was excited but trying desperately to keep from
showing it. *She got so flustered when he teased her,
which made it irresistible.*

"It's a go! I'll be there Thursday, around 1600."

"How did you get tickets so late? I was afraid all the
flights would be booked."

"I'm not flying commercial—"

"You're not! Did you get a military hop? I can't
imagine there are many trips from Luke to Malmstrom."

"Not flying military either." *This was fun,* he thought,
envisioning her puzzlement as she tried to figure it out.

"But, you'd <u>have</u> to fly. You said you only had off the
one extra day—"

"I *am* flying. I'm taking one of the aero club planes. I
was able to get it for the weekend."

"But . . . but . . . you fly fighters. How can you . . .
you're not flying it yourself . . . are you?"

His laugh boomed over the line. "Of course I am!"

Knowing he had her totally confused, he took pity on
her and explained. "Hawk and I both joined an aero club
in Phoenix and got our private pilots' licenses when we
first got to Arizona. We used to fly a lot. Hawk hasn't
maintained his, but I still fly about one weekend a
month, whenever I have the time."

"I—I didn't know. She'd wondered what other things
he'd done in the intervening years since he'd so
unexpectedly left her. Getting a private pilot's license
was apparently one thing. *How many other things about
him didn't she know?*

84

"Jane, you sound upset. What's wrong?"

"Nothing. There's nothing wrong. I'm just realizing how many things I don't know about you."

"I know, and I want to correct that. There are a lot of things I don't know about you, either. I'm hoping this weekend we can correct a lot of that. Can we just take it one day at a time, and see how things play out?"

He sounded almost as unsure as she was, and somehow that was what reassured her. "All right."

"Good! Then I'll see you in five days. I'll call before I leave, okay?"

"Okay. Five days."

It was December 24, and festive decorations filled the hospital: Christmas trees on every floor, elves and Santas on every door, Poinsettias on tables and desks. Most of the staff was in a happy mood as they anticipated the coming holidays.

And Mark was arriving this afternoon! She felt as if she would float up in the air if she didn't hold onto something stationary. It had been five days since he'd told her he could come, days in which she'd alternated between excitement and worry. Worry about how things would go, worry that she might not be able to keep him from finding out her feelings for him, and worry over the secret that still lay between them. He was so perceptive; sometimes she felt as if he saw into her very soul. However, as the day of his arrival neared, excitement had overcome the worry, and now she just wanted him to get here.

She completed the patient information sheet she was working on and took it back to Doctor Ramos in the examination cubicle.

"Well, Miss Brewer! You look as if you have the Christmas spirit. Got big plans?"

She really liked the fatherly doctor and grinned, although she was afraid she might be blushing. "I'm expecting company from out of town this afternoon, Doctor."

"I'm guessing from that blush, this company would be male. Am I right?"

"Yes, you are." Anxious to forestall any more questions, she quickly handed him the info sheet. "I'll bring Mrs. Bushwell right back, okay?"

He glanced at the sheet and nodded. "Bring her back."

Thankful that she'd derailed his question, she hurried out of the room to get the doctor's next patient. For once, she was glad the waiting room was full. There was no time for conversation or questions from the other staff members about her weekend plans.

The day finally came to an end. As she left the hospital, surrounded by cries of "Merry Christmas!" and "Have a nice holiday!" her cell phone rang. Fumbling in her purse, she snatched it up.

"Yes?"

"Jane? Are you still at work?"

It was Mark! "I'm leaving the hospital now."

"I just landed at Malmstrom. I've called a cab, so I should get to your house about the same time you do."

"I could have picked you up."

"I know, but this way you won't have to." His voice dropped to a whisper. "I can't wait to see you. Drive carefully going home." He hung up.

He'd hung up. She stared at her phone and shook her head. Telling her to drive carefully—on a route she took every day! The man seemed to have an uncanny perception about what she was thinking. Perhaps he knew what a time she was having keeping her mind on mundane things like driving. It was a trifle inconvenient having him read her so well.

Pulling out of the parking lot a few minutes later, Mark's words still in her head, she forced herself to concentrate on the road ahead of her, and pulled into her garage fifteen uneventful minutes later. Letting herself into the kitchen, she breathed in the crisp and heady scent of the pine and cedar she had used to trim the rooms. She set her purse on the table and slowly spun around, taking in the results of her hard work. *She hoped Mark would enjoy it.* She had gone all out once she knew he was coming, getting a huge tree for the first time since her parents had moved to Florida. The giant Fir filled the corner of the living room, and she walked over and bent down to turn the tree lights on. The tiny blue lights filled the dim room with an almost magical aura, and she hugged herself with excitement. She had always loved Christmas. The thought of sharing it with Mark gave her goose bumps, despite the reminder from her inner self not to make any long-range plans. She'd done that once before . . . and look how it turned out.

She stood up, determined to squelch the inner voice and live in the present. She wouldn't let the past spoil this weekend. She looked at her watch and ran to change clothes.

She tossed her uniform in the hamper and looked longingly at the shower. She really didn't have time, but decided to take one anyway, thankful she'd washed her hair that morning.

Five minutes later, dressed, she smiled at her

reflection in the mirror as she fastened the thin, silver chain around her neck, and brushed her hair into a soft fluff around her face. She loved the new outfit; the rosy red slacks were a perfect fit, and the soft cowl neck of the sweater flattered her face. She slid her feet into black velvet ballet slippers and hurried out of the room. *Mark could arrive any minute!*

She had no sooner filled the teakettle and set it on the stove than she heard the doorbell. She quickly turned the stove off and ran to open the door, throwing it wide. *What would Mark would think of her home?*

Mark stood on the porch, bag in hand, and they stared as if needing to reabsorb each other. Finally, she reached out and pulled him inside. "Come in, it's too cold to stand out there."

He stepped into the foyer, dropped his case, and pulled her into his arms, hugging her tightly, as he breathed her in.

"You smell sooo good."

Her arms crept around his neck, and she tucked her head against his shoulder, content for the moment just to hold on to him.

He kissed her, lightly at first, then more deeply and she felt herself melting into him. At last he pulled away, almost desperately, and she felt lost and shaky on wobbly legs. Still holding onto his arm, she took a deep breath.

"Wow!" she said softly. "That was—"

"Awesome."

He grinned as he said it, and she smiled uneasily, unsure what to say. Mark didn't seem to have that problem.

"Speaking of 'wow,' that describes your outfit—and

the woman wearing it. All Christmas-y and soft and . . . awesome. I'm running out of words."

Jane realized she was still holding his arm, and she released it quickly. "Let me take your coat."

Mark walked into the living room and she shut the door and hung his leather jacket on the hall rack. When she entered the living room, she found him standing in the center of the room, turning slowly as he observed everything.

"I like what you've done here, Jane. It's homey and comfortable, but polished and sophisticated. It takes talent to achieve that."

"Thanks, I'm glad you like it." She felt a warm glow at his compliment, watching him closely as he continued to check out the room. When he got to the tree in the corner, he burst out laughing.

"How in the world did you get such a big tree in here?"

She laughed along with him. "I never would have gotten it in here by myself. Ellen and Dennis helped me cut it out at the ranch. It took the three of us to get it in here. Dennis set it up."

"Hmm. So, have they both left for Texas?"

The thoughtful look in his eyes made her heart flutter, and her voice was tremulous when she spoke.

"Yesterday morning. They'll be gone for a week."

Conversation flowed easily after that, and an hour passed quickly. Needing to start dinner preparations, Jane stood and gestured toward the stairs.

"Let me show you to your room. You can get settled in while I put the soup on to heat." She led the way, talking over her shoulder. "I have only two bedrooms, but there is a third room up here. It was always Mom's

89

sewing room, but I've made it my office. The bathroom is right there."

Too much info. She was talking too much. Could he see how nervous she was? "And here's your room." She stopped at the door and let him precede her into the room. He threw his bag onto the bed.

As he turned toward her, she met his gaze and found herself stammering. "My room is across the hall. Not that you needed to know that." She felt her cheeks flush. *If he hadn't known she was nervous before, he would now.* She backed up, desperate to get away before she said something else ridiculous. "I hope you'll be comfortable. I—I'll just leave you to unpack now. Come down when you're ready." She turned to go, but Mark stepped forward and gently took hold of her arm.

"Jane—thank you for letting me come. I need to prove to you . . . it's important to me that I . . . I need for you to know I've changed."

Her heart racing, she stood still as he leaned toward her. Expecting him to kiss her, she was surprised when, instead, he reached up and rubbed his fisted fingers across her warm cheek before quickly stepping away.

"I'll be down in a few minutes. Just give me time to wash up and stow my gear."

"Sure. Whenever you're ready."

Ten minutes later she was kneeling in front of the fireplace when she heard him on the stairs. The fire, laid the night before, needed only the strike of a match, but in her nervousness, she fumbled with the match and couldn't get it to light.

"Darned match! Why won't you light?"

"Can I help?"

Jane heard the laughter in his voice and smiled at him

ruefully. "I'm not usually so helpless. The match just won't light."

He knelt beside her and took the match. Their fingers touched, and a burning sensation shot through hers as if they'd been touched by a lit match. She looked up, but he appeared to have felt nothing. He raised an eyebrow and looked at her, before looking back at the match.

"No wonder you're having difficulty, the match is bent." He reached for the matchbook she'd dropped on the floor and tore out a fresh match. He struck it on his thumbnail and held it to the kindling. Immediately, a bright flame surged up toward the pile of logs. He sat back on his heels, resting his hands on his knees. "There! This is nice."

"It is. How about a cup of tea—or a beer?" *Of course he wouldn't want a cup of tea! Guys didn't drink tea. Damn, damn, damn.* Although the corners of his mouth turned up in a tiny smile, at least he didn't laugh at her.

"A beer would be nice."

At her sudden nod, he did grin as he raised one eyebrow.

"Although I have been known to have a cup of tea on occasion."

She rolled her eyes. *He was teasing her. And no wonder, she was acting ridiculous, like a teen-ager, not like a woman who was twenty-six years old, a seasoned hospital nurse, and future med-evac nurse.* She let out a sigh as she turned toward the kitchen. She had taken two steps when his voice halted her.

"Jane."

She didn't turn around, and he repeated it. "Jane."

She slowly turned to face him, and was surprised by the tender expression on his face and the warm light in

91

his velvety brown eyes.

"She bit her lip before speaking. "I know I'm acting ridiculous, but—Well, you make me nervous." He nodded.

"I get that, and it's understandable. A lot of time has passed since we . . . since we knew each other."

Her mouth opened slightly and her eyes studied him, waiting to see where he was going with this. Before continuing, he gave her a rueful smile, and his eyes glinted as he tipped his head to one side.

"Would it surprise you if I told you I'm nervous too?"

"You, nervous? I'll bet you've never been nervous a day in your life—"

"You'd lose—"

Her forehead wrinkled in a deep frown.

"Lose?"

"You'd lose that bet—that I've never been nervous. I might know how to cover it better, that's all."

She gave him a look that told him she didn't believe it, before grinning up at him. "Okay, I . . . I'll get that beer."

In the kitchen, she put both hands on the edge of the sink, leaned forward, and blew the fringe of bangs off her face. *Could he possibly be nervous? She didn't believe it for a minute . . . but it was nice of him to try and make her feel better. Beer, yeah that was why she was here. And tea.* She grabbed a mug from the rack on the counter and a teabag from the canister, then filled the cup with water from the kettle. While it was steeping, she got a bottle from the fridge and removed the cap.

She'd bought what used to be his favorite—*was it still?* He seemed like a stranger in so many ways. Of course, he could be—five years, almost six, it was a long time. She sighed. *He'd said he'd changed . . . so how could she know him?*

He was still sitting on the rug beside the fire when she returned with a tray holding a bottle of beer, a cup of tea, and a plate of gingerbread cookies cut into Christmas shapes. He spoke before she could set the tray on the coffee table in front of the couch.

"Don't. Let's have it here in front of the fire. He patted the rug next to him. "There's something special about a fire on a cold, winter's day. It warms the heart as well as the body." He met her gaze and smiled.

"Why Mark! I didn't realize you were such a poet—"

"I'm not! No way."

She couldn't believe the deep red on his cheeks. *He was embarrassed!* It was obviously not an image he wanted to cultivate, but the man definitely had a softer side. She didn't know him at all . . . *but, oh how she wanted to.* She knelt beside him on the soft Oriental rug, and set the tray between them. He reached for the beer, and studied it before looking at her in surprise. How'd you know my favorite beer?"

She bit her lip, and hesitated. "It's what you used to drink. I wasn't sure you still did, but—"

"I still do—but I can't believe you remembered. You couldn't have seen me drink a beer many times. "

"Maybe not, but I remembered." She didn't look at him, but he leaned in, put his fist under her chin and raised it up until her eyes met his.

"Thank you, Jane. I like that you remembered such a small thing."

His dark eyes held hers for a moment, and then as if needing to change the subject, he looked at the tray she had set in front of them on the hearth.

"Umm! Gingerbread cookies—my Mom always made them for Christmas."

"I know." A smile tugged at the corners of her mouth.

"Flavored with orange peel?" His eyebrows lifted, his eyes sparkling hopefully.

She gave him a radiant smile. "Of course. I used your Mom's recipe." She felt as if his eyes were eating her up, as he reached out for a handful of the cookies.

"You're an amazing woman, Jane Brewer. I just can't believe—" Instead of finishing the sentence, he took a bite of the cookie and rolled his eyes heavenward. "Boy, do these take me back. They taste just like Mom's."

She stared at him and frowned. "I'm glad you like them, but . . . what can't you believe" What were you going to say?"

"When?"

His blank look didn't fool her; he knew what she meant. "Before . . . you said 'I just can't believe—' but then you didn't finish. What were you going to say?"

He looked away from her and shook his head. "I don't remember, it must not have been important."

She knew it was, and she also knew he had no intention of telling her. "Fine. We can eat in about an hour. The pot of vegetable soup I made yesterday is simmering on the stove—and there's homemade bread— it's made with a bread machine, but—"

"Sounds wonderful! You obviously do a lot of cooking. I'm surprised. Isn't it hard to cook for just one person?"

"I love to cook, but I really don't do much of it during the week. I do most of my cooking on the weekend and freeze it in meal-sized portions. Then when I drag in after work all I have to do is zap something in the

94

microwave." She shrugged. "Now you know my secret."

"I think it's great. You obviously manage very well." He studied her for several seconds without speaking, and when he spoke his voice was softer.

"Are you ever lonely?"

Was he asking if she had any male friends? Would he be surprised to know that she didn't, at least not anyone important? She didn't think she wanted to let him know that, at least not right now.

"Sometimes. But I'm usually pretty busy. The hospital is small, and both Ellen and I work quite a lot of overtime. Uncomfortable with the topic of conversation, she jumped up. "I'll just go and check on the soup."

Mark watched her hurry into the kitchen, taking the tray and the empty cookie dish with her. Settling back against the heavy coffee table he stretched his long legs toward the fire, giving an unconscious nod as he studied the bottle in his hand. *A man could get used to this. Not something he better do,* he admonished himself. He needed to be careful if he wasn't going to scare Jane off. He could see she was still unsure of him, although at times the light in her eyes gave him hope. *He just had to take it slow. Not easy when she was so adorable.* He'd angered her earlier—when he'd almost let the cat out of the bag. *He'd almost said he couldn't believe he'd wasted so much time—five damned years, nearly six!* Well, those years were gone . . . but he didn't intend to let any more go by. And that was a promise he made to himself.

He gulped the last of his beer and rose quickly to head for the kitchen. Jane was humming a Christmas carol as she stirred the big pot of soup on the stove.

"Smells great, I can't wait."

Startled by his comment, she spun around. "You can't be hungry, not after all those cookies."

He lifted his hands, palms up, and shrugged. "What can I say? I'm a growing boy."

She looked at him doubtfully. "Well, we can eat as soon as the soup's hot—shouldn't be much longer."

Jane had set the table in the small breakfast nook. He smiled, glad that she didn't feel she had to impress him. He leaned against the door frame, content to watch her bustle around the kitchen.

"You know what I'd like?"

She looked up, tilting her head as he continued.

"After dinner, let's take a walk around the neighborhood. It's been so long since I've been here—not since I came home to sell the house after Mom and Dad died. I'd kind of like to see what's changed . . . what's still the same."

Jane smiled. "Actually, I'd planned to do that after dinner tonight. It will be dark then, and the lights make everything so beautiful. I don't think you'll find much has changed—it's still pretty much the same. "

"I'm glad. It would be sad to find nothing the way I remember it."

She lifted the lid on the pot of soup, and a fragrant aroma escaped into the room. Mark sucked in a deep breath.

"Now I know I'm hungry; my stomach is even growling.

Jane laughed. "Well, you don't have to wait any longer. The soup is hot, and the bread is ready to come out of the oven. If you'll fill the glasses with ice and water, I'll dip up the soup and slice the bread, and we can eat."

Once they were both seated, Jane quickly bowed her head and silently asked God to bless their food. Mark smiled as he bowed his own head, remembering that her family had always said silent grace. Curious, he'd once asked his father why they did that, and been told that everyone's traditions were different. He'd gone on to explain that their silent grace came from Jane's father's Amish roots, where it was a tradition to thank God silently.

Jane looked up and smiled at him, surprised. "You remembered?"

"How could I forget, as many meals as our families shared?"

"Still, it's been a long time . . . and I'm glad you remember—"

"I remember a lot of things, Jane. And I wouldn't change any of them . . . except—"

She raised her hand, afraid she knew what he was thinking. "Don't go there, Mark. It's in the past—I don't want to remember." She saw his eyes fill with pain, as his lips formed a straight line, and he muttered under his breath.

"But I can't forget."

He hadn't meant for her to hear . . . but she had. Choosing to ignore it, she picked up the glass of wine she had filled from the bottle he'd brought.

"To Christmas future!"

He raised his glass to touch hers. Their eyes met, and a little smile flickered on his face as he murmured, "And may we share many more of them."

Afraid to hope, she took a sip of her wine and set the glass down. "The wine is very good, Mark. I've never had it before."

97

"It's one of my favorites, and I hoped you'd like it."

She picked up her spoon and began eating, watching Mark out of the corner of her eye. The soup was one she often made for friends, and she was anxious to know how he liked it. His eyes lit up after his first mouthful.

"This is the best soup I've ever tasted. I don't want to hear any more talk about you not being a cook. You can cook for me anytime!"

She laughed, pleased at his compliment, and relieved that the conversation was on safer ground. From there on out, conversation flowed easily. She asked him about his flying, and they discussed her work at the hospital. Mark was obviously as anxious as she was for the evening to go well, for he didn't mention her upcoming physical.

After finishing his second bowl of soup and numerous slices of hot, buttered bread, Mark leaned back in his chair and let out a sigh. "That was wonderful, but I don't think I could eat another bite, not even a crumb."

"Me either. Let's load the dishwasher and go for our walk now. That way, you'll get your tour of the neighborhood, and we'll both get the exercise we need to make room for dessert. "

"Sounds good to me." He immediately stood and began picking up the empty plates. Jane put the leftover soup in the fridge and wrapped the bread, and they both loaded the dishwasher.

As they finished, Mark gripped Jane's shoulders, and his eyes met hers. "We work well together, don't you think?" He tilted his head. waiting for her response.

She nodded, recalling all the times she'd dreamed of the two of them performing similar routines, but she pulled away, not wanting him to know the direction of her thoughts. "Time for that walk. After we get back, we can have cocoa and cookies in front of the fire. "

"With marshmallows?"

"Of course! We can even make S'mores if you want—I have all the ingredients. The fire will be perfect by then."

A little later, dressed in outerwear, including boots and gloves, they opened the front door to find the ground covered with snow, and more falling. At the bottom of the steps, Jane kicked out her foot, and the snow, flew up in a cloud. "I love it when it's fluffy like this. It's not good for snowmen, but it's lovely to walk in."

Mark's smile was indulgent as he held out his arm for her to grasp. When she did so, he pulled her against his side. As they started down the walk, Jane looked up at the sky. "It's really coming down. If it keeps up all night, we may not be able to go tomorrow."

"We'll check the weather when we get back, but since we weren't planning to leave until after dinner tomorrow, the crews will have plenty of time to clear the roads."

Mark stopped in front of the house next door and stared silently at the lit Christmas tree visible through the front window. A smile lit his face, and Jane squeezed his arm.

"Sometimes I pretend you all still live there. I know it's silly, but it was such fun growing up next door to each other." He looked down into her upturned face, and his expression was so tender her breath caught in her throat.

"We did. I have fond memories of the house, and—" He stopped talking, all his attention concentrated on the house in front of them. "I can't believe the old swing is still there . . . looks as if it has a new rope."

Jane smiled at him. "It does. The family living there now has two children. Jared, the father, fixed the swing within days of their moving in. During the summer, at least one of the children was on it every day. It seems to be one of their favorite pastimes."

Mark seemed lost in his thoughts, and Jane slid her hand down his arm and into his gloved hand. "You're feeling sad, aren't you? I'm sorry, Mark."

He shook himself free of the memory and turned to face her. His eyes held hers. "It's all right; one can't go back, and I guess it's a good thing. I'm really glad to be here now. It's nice to see that the old house is well taken care of and has a happy family living in it—at least I hope they're happy."

She smiled up at him. "They are, Mark. You'd like them. He works in the aircraft sheet-metal maintenance shop at Malmstrom, and she's a stay-at-home mom."

"You sound as if you know them well?"

"I do—sometimes I babysit for Charlie and Susan. They're adorable children, and in many ways remind me of us when we were their age."

They continued walking in silence, enjoying the beauty of the night and the patterns the colored lights made on the snow. Occasionally Mark stopped to ask if a remembered neighbor still lived in a particular house. With the exception of Mrs. Knight who had moved to Florida to live with her daughter, the occupants remained the same, and the lack of change seemed to please him.

By the time they had circled the block, the snow was falling heavily, and they left a trail of deep footprints behind them. At her front door, Mark removed his Stetson, banged it against his leg to brush off the snow, and then stomped the snow off his boots. Jane unlocked the door, and once inside, they both hung their jackets on the hall rack and removed their boots, setting them on the tray she'd put there for that purpose.

"If you'll check on the fire, I'll heat up the cocoa and get the cookies."

"Don't forget—you said S'mores."

Laughing, she shook her head. "I won't forget."

Minutes later, when she entered the room with a tray holding the ingredients for S'mores and a dish heaped high with more ginger cookies, Mark looked up from the ouch where he was slowly turning the pages of the photograph album her mother had left.

"I saw this on the shelf and couldn't resist looking at it; I hope it's all right."

"Of course, but those pictures are all really old—my mother started that album when she and my Dad were first married."

"So, it's the story of your life."

"Boring." She reached for the book, but he quickly held it out of reach.

"Please don't! I really want to see. I'm surprised there are so many of my family in here. Photos of my Mom and Dad when they were young too."

"You shouldn't be surprised; our parents were good friends, used to play cards and visit often. There are photos of the rest of your family too—when we were all kids."

She set the tray on the table in front of him and joined him on the couch. He stopped and leaned in to examine one of the photos, pointing his finger at the individuals.

101

"Is that—"

"You and me."

"It looks as if I'm helping you up, and you're crying. Did I knock you down?"

"You mean you don't remember?"

When he shook his head, she laughed. "How could you forget? I was only four, and I remember it *very* well. Let's see . . . You would have been eight, and you don't remember?" Her brows knitted as she looked at him skeptically.

"I guess not. What happened?"

"Look at our clothes." She waited as he studied the photo.

"Judging by the feather headdress, I was pretending to be an Indian chief. But . . . what's that you have on?"

Jane rolled her eyes and shook her head. "You were always the chief . . . or the captain. The leader."

His grin was infectious, and she laughed with him. "Kit and I always wanted to play too. See her, there in the corner?" She pointed to his sister, half-in, half-out of the photo. "Kit had her own outfit. She always insisted on whatever Jon had—and since cowboys and Indians was your favorite game, she had a cowboy outfit. I, didn't have one, but Kit 'borrowed' Luke's cowboy hat and chaps. He must not have been home, or she'd never have gotten them."

Mark burst into laughter again. "You'd have swum in Luke's clothes—he was half a foot taller than you."

"So? Why do you think I was on the ground?" She giggled. "I had just managed to get myself into the outfit. I had to hold the pants up, and I could barely see under the hat, but Kit told me to hurry up before you all got away. I was running, and I tripped over the too-long pants and fell. My mother had seen us from the window and had gone to get the camera, so she missed my fall, but she took the picture anyway. When I started crying, you came back to help me. You stood me up, brushed me off, and wiped my tears. I've never forgotten it. You didn't want us to play with you, but—"

"But I could never bear to hurt your feelings either," he said, remembering how cute she had been back then. He leaned back against the couch and reached out for her hand. "Those were good times—we had a nice childhood."

As he held her hand, he gently stroked her palm. She shivered and tried to pull her hand away. He didn't immediately release it, *wishing he dared to do more than hold her hand.* Finally, he made himself let go of her hand, and the minute he did, she jumped up.

"The cocoa should be ready by now—I'll go and get it."

"And some more of those cookies?" Jane left the room, and a tiny smile lit his face as he turned back to the album.

It wasn't as hopeless as he had thought. He made her nervous—the feelings were definitely there. He just had to convince her to trust him again. Until then he'd have to force himself to go slowly—because if he didn't, she'd bolt like a wild filly.

When she entered the room, he was standing in front of the TV, watching the weather report.

"They're calling for it to snow all night."

"The skiing will be great—if we can get there." She handed him a mug of cocoa, set her own on the coffee table, and sat down on the couch. He settled beside her and collected a handful of cookies, biting into one

103

immediately.

"Um. What time did you say dinner was tomorrow? We don't have to leave all that early, although I would like to arrive at the ski resort before dark. That way we can get a good night's sleep and an early start on the slopes."

"I thought around noon—that way we should be able to get off by three."

"Sounds good. What are we having for dinner—besides the turkey?"

"Which is already thawing in the fridge. I got up early yesterday and made the pies—apple and pumpkin—before I went to work. There's a mashed potato casserole in the fridge, waiting to be heated up, and my Mom's Cranberry-Marshmallow Salad." She grinned, waiting for his reaction. He didn't disappoint.

"And you said you can't cook."

"I said I don't cook <u>much</u>. Actually, my mother insisted I learn, 'so I could be a proper' wife'." She made air quotes with her fingers.

"Smart woman, your mother," he said with a grin.

He set his mug down on the nearby end table. When he turned to face her, his dark eyes held a curious intensity. She squirmed under his look, wanting to look away, but unable to do so. He moved closer to her on the sofa, and she suddenly didn't know what to do with her hands.

"Mark . . ."

"Yes, Jane." The intensity in his eyes changed to humor. "Do I make you nervous?"

"Yes . . . no . . . maybe." Her hands fluttered in her lap. "Why are you looking at me like that?"

She tried to put some distance between them, but he

reached for her hands, holding both of hers in one of his. He used his other hand to pull her even closer. She trembled under his hand, and he frowned.

"Jane, you aren't afraid of me, are you? Please, don't be. I swear I'll never hurt you again."

Her eyes clouded as if she saw visions of the past, but she smiled tentatively, raising her chin slightly as she spoke softly.

"I'm not afraid of you, Mark."

With a surge of relief, he released the breath he hadn't realized he was holding. "Thank God for that," he murmured under his breath. Confusion flashed in her eyes, and he leaned close and kissed her softly. When he felt her respond, he pulled her into his arms, hugging her almost desperately. Her arms went around his neck, and her fingers raked his hair. He shivered with the emotion he felt, and leaned his head on her shoulder, shutting his eyes tightly as tears threatened to well. *He wanted, needed her so badly, but he couldn't . . .*

Jane leaned away from him and studied his face. "Mark . . ."

He drew in a deep breath and sighed. "I know—it's time we went to bed . . . " At her look of surprise, he chuckled. "I mean, our own beds."

"But it isn't all that late—"

"And we need to go before it's too late," he said with another crooked grin. He pulled her close again and kissed her lightly before pushing her away. "Now, go to bed."

She laughed. "Okay, I'm going, I'm going." As she spoke, she raised up and kissed him again. He reached for her, but she slipped away and ran lightly up the stairs, giggling. "Good-night, Mark."

105

He watched her go. *The woman was killing him . . . and he was pretty sure she knew it.* Thoughtfully, he picked up the tray, took it into the kitchen, and returned to bank the fire for the night. *He was definitely walking a fine line.*

When she awoke the next morning, snow was falling softly outside her bedroom window. Jumping out of bed, she pushed the sheer curtains wide for a clearer view—of a perfect Christmas morning! Deep snow covered the ground, and the white surface sparkled like a field of diamonds. She stretched her arms above her head and turned around. Leaning against the tall bedpost, she replayed the previous evening in her head.

It had been wonderful, one she would never forget. It was getting harder and harder not to read more into Mark's actions than was there. It was all too new—and just because he said he had changed didn't mean he had. Still . . . *sometimes there was something—a light, an emotion, something in his eyes she couldn't pin down.* Hope bubbled up in her, and she spun around the room, her arms outstretched in a dance of joy. She'd worry about tomorrow when tomorrow arrived. Today was for living.

Her wild spinning was interrupted as her hand hit something. There was a crash behind her—the picture that had stood on her chest of drawers now lay on the floor. Luckily, it landed face up. She stooped to retrieve it just as she heard a knock on her door.

"Are you all right in there? I heard a crash."

She snatched open the door, forgetting she was still in her old, flannel nightgown. "Everything's wonderful!

106

Did you see the snow? What a perfect day!"

He smiled at her exuberance while his eyes took in her outfit. "You look like Red Riding Hood's granny. I might be tempted to eat you . . . if I were a wolf." He waggled an eyebrow.

She knew he was teasing, but her face still warmed with embarrassment, and she retreated into the room. "But . . . you're not! I'll get dressed and be right down."

He was already dressed in jeans, flannel shirt, and the ever-present cowboy boots. He'd even shaved, and his short hair was still damp indicating he'd showered. Flustered, she turned to look at the clock. *She must have overslept.* "How long have you been up?"

He gave an 'I don't know' shrug. "Not long. I woke up, knew I wouldn't go back to sleep, and decided to go down and make coffee. Take your time."

She nodded, slowly backing up, her hands self-consciously holding the open neck of her nightgown together. "I'll be down in a few minutes."

He heard her close the door behind him as he headed for the stairs. *Good thing she didn't ask why he couldn't sleep.* After last night, and that good night kiss, he'd rolled and tossed for what seemed like hours before he got to sleep . . . *and dreamed of Jane* . . . then woke up, anticipating seeing her. *He was in deep trouble here . . . very deep.*

Despite that, as he filled the coffee pot, he found himself whistling, "I'll Be Home for Christmas" . . . *and home looked an awful lot like Jane Brewer's living room.*

Having decided not to take time to dress, Jane hurried down the stairs minutes later to find that Mark had already lit the lights on the tree. The room was suffused with a lovely blue glow, and she stopped on the last step to enjoy the magic of the scene, remembering Christmases past. Mark startled her when he spoke from the doorway where he'd been watching her.

"You all right?" he asked with the slight frown and tilt of one eyebrow.

"I'm great. I was just enjoying the tree . . . and remembering. Thank you for lighting it, even though we'll be leaving."

He shrugged. "It's Christmas morning. I knew you'd like it."

Her smile was bright as she came down the last step. "I do. My parents always turned the tree on before I came down on Christmas morning. Even after I was too big to believe in Santa, I would lie in my bed until I could hear them downstairs, before I got up."

"And is that what you did this morning?" He was grinning as he said it. *With her tousled hair, the crumpled collar of her nightgown peeking out of her robe, and her ridiculous fluffy slippers, that child was still visible.*

"No. This morning I overslept. The sun woke me. I smell coffee—you're spoiling me." She peeked up at him, quickly looked away, and rushed to change the subject. "Let's have it in front of the tree."

She looked at the mantel clock—it wasn't quite seven, and through the window she could see the sun just beginning to peek over the Bearpaw Mountains. "The roads—"

"Are clear, and it's going to be a beautiful day. Stop worrying."

"Okay, no worrying. Why don't you check out the weather station . . . just in case?"

He shook his head, but leaned to turn on the TV.

"While you do, "I'll get the coffee."

In the kitchen, she hummed as she poured coffee into two mugs, then opened the refrigerator and took out the wrapped cinnamon buns she had taken from the freezer the night before. They were a Christmas tradition in her family, and as soon as she'd known Mark was coming, she'd spent an evening making and freezing them. She put them in the microwave and took the coffee in the other room.

As Mark accepted his coffee, he raised his head and sniffed. "What's that I smell? It's not . . . more home-baked bread?"

"No, but you're close. Cinnamon buns."

"Wow! When did you have time to bake?"

"I made them before you came, and put them in the freezer."

"You really are awesome, you know." As he spoke, he leaned forward and kissed her lightly. The coffee she still held sloshed over the side of the cup, but she was unaware, as his gaze held hers.

"What was that for?"

"Merry Christmas, Jane Brewer," he said softly, taking the mugs of coffee and setting them down on the coffee table. He took her in his arms. His kiss warmed her from the tip of her head to the toes curling in her fluffy slippers, leaving her speechless. When she could finally breathe, her voice was barely a whisper.

"Merry Christmas, Mark."

The beep of the microwave reminded her of the cinnamon buns, and she turned slowly, brushing one hand dazedly across her lips.

She rescued the buns and slid them onto a plate,

pleased at their melting shininess. She knew they tasted as good as they looked because she'd been unable to resist trying one before she put them in the freezer. She carried them in and set them on the table in front of Mark with pride.

"Here they are! It wasn't Christmas at our house without my Mom's cinnamon buns."

As he watched, she pulled a bun apart, slathered it with butter from the dish she'd included on the tray, and handed the warm bun to him, together with a large napkin. She watched anxiously as he bit into the gooey treat.

A dribble of melted butter ran down his chin, and he swiped at it with the napkin, at the same time rolling his eyes and murmuring an "mmmm" of approval.

"These are wonderful! I could make a meal on them."

"Good! Because that's all I planned for breakfast. My mother didn't make them often. And when she did, we wanted to be able to eat our fill, so she never fixed anything else."

"Good!"

As he spoke, he was already reaching for another bun.

Jane carefully spread butter on her own bun, took a bite, and let out a dreamy sigh. "This so takes me back. I love everything about Christmas—cinnamon buns, blue lights on the tree, and packages <u>under</u> the tree—"

At the mention of packages, Mark sprang up. "Presents—it's time for presents!" He walked over, knelt beside the tree, and retrieved a small box beautifully wrapped in silver paper and shiny blue ribbon. *It looked like something from a jewelry* store. Jane gulped, and her eyes sought Mark's. *What had he done? She had a gift for him under the tree, but—"*

A wide grin lit his face as he handed her his gift. "What big eyes you have, little girl!"

He was teasing her again, and she didn't know what to say. She put down her unfinished cinnamon bun, and carefully wiped her hands on her napkin and reached for the gift. Laying it in her lap, she gently rubbed her fingers over the beautiful bow.

"It won't bite," Mark said softly. "Why don't you open it?

When she still hesitated, he repeated his statement.

"Jane—just open the package."

Looking up, she was surprised by his anxious expression. *Why was he anxious?* She slowly picked the box up and carefully examined it, then slowly slid the ribbon off and laid it on the table beside her. She slid her thumb under the tape and let the paper fall open. She'd been right! The box was from her favorite jeweler in town. When she raised her eyes, Mark was perfectly still, almost as if he were holding his breath. At his raised eyebrow, she lifted the lid and immediately let out a gasp.

"Ohhh." She raised one hand, her fingers covering her open mouth.

"Do you like it? I wasn't sure what to get, but this made me think of you."

"Oh, Mark. It's . . . it's the loveliest gift I've ever had." She touched the tiny gem in awe, then slowly lifted the beautiful necklace out of the box, where it sparkled in the lamplight.

"It's called 'Evening Star'—I think that's the one they call the wishing star."

If he only knew how many times she had wished on that very star—ever since she was in her teens . . . and

111

always the same wish.

Mark was still standing, and she rose to stand on her toes and throw both arms around his neck, letting the necklace hang down his back. He stood stiffly for several seconds as she kissed him softly. Suddenly exhaling, he encircled her with his arms, and pulled her tightly against his hard body.

"You . . . like it?"

"Oh Mark, I love it. Please, put it on for me." She handed him the delicate necklace and turned her back to him.

He felt all thumbs trying to open the tiny clasp with his big hands. Finally succeeding, he looped the chain over her head and fastened it, then leaned down to place a kiss on her nape.

She reached up to feel the tiny star against her neck and crossed to the wall mirror. The necklace was perfect, laying just over her pulse point. She spun to face Mark, her face sparkling with a huge grin.

"Now it's your turn!"

She knelt beside the tree, reached back beneath the lower branches, and withdrew a flat, square package. As she held it out, her eyes glowed like the tiny star around her neck.

As Mark accepted the gift, he felt the rapid beat of his heart and wondered, *would she always take his breath away like this?*

Jane's hands were clasped beneath her chin, as she watched him.

"Open it! It's not as exciting as yours . . . but I had fun choosing it . . . and I hope you like it."

"I will—" He stopped and looked deep into her sparkling eyes. "I will because it's from you," he said,

112

holding her eyes for a second before looking away. After snapping the ribbon, he tore the paper off, and stopped. He was speechless as he looked at the leather-framed, black and white photograph. It was one he had never seen, but he remembered when it had been taken—he'd been eighteen years old and had just won his first bronc riding event. He was holding the big trophy proudly as his sister and Jane looked at him in awe. His mouth twitched in amusement—they would have been about fourteen, and he could almost see his chest swell as he enjoyed their adoration. "Where did you get this?"

"Do you like it? It's nothing like your gift." She reached up and wrapped her fingers around the star at her throat. "I wanted to give you something special, but I couldn't think of anything—"

He silenced her with a finger on her lips. "Jane, I love it." Touching the faces beneath the glass, he shook his head back and forth slowly. "We were so young, so sure that our lives would always be as great as they were then."

"Nothing stays the same, Mark. Everything changes."

He detected the note of worry in her voice and looked up and smiled at her. "You're right of course. I do like my gift, very much. But where in the world did you get it. I can't believe I never saw it."

"I've had it a while. One time I was spending the night with Kit—after your parents had died. We found a box of your mother's things in the back of her closet, and were going through it. There were several photographs—this was one of them. I begged Kit to let me have them.

"What was the other one?"

"Just a snapshot—taken at the same time I think."

"Can I see it?"

"Ummm, It's upstairs."

She wasn't anxious to show him the picture, and he was curious as to why. "Go and get it . . . please."

She left the room, and he heard her walking around in her bedroom overhead. As she came down the stairs, his curiosity grew. She held one hand behind her back. When he reached out, she extended the small 3 x 5 frame without looking up.

He was surprised to see his own face looking back at him from the picture. She was right; it <u>had</u> been taken at the same time as the other one. Suddenly it dawned on him—she'd wanted a picture of him . . . and despite everything, she'd kept it. A surge of joy went through him at the thought. She might not want him to know it . . . *but she had kept it.*

Jane reached for the picture, and he held it out, but when she would have taken it, he held on, causing her to frown.

"Before I give it back, tell me why you wanted it . . . and why you still have it." She lifted her chin—*that defiant little movement again*—and shrugged.

"I just did. It reminded me of good times. I have one of Kit too . . ."

Her voice trailed off, and he let go of the frame. She turned and set it on the mantel. *She was embarrassed. He probably shouldn't have insisted on seeing the photo, but he couldn't be sorry. It gave him hope . . . hope that he badly needed.*

He followed her across the room, stopping just behind her. She didn't turn around, and he put his hands on her arms and whispered in her ear. "Jane . . . I'm sorry if I've

114

upset you, but it makes me happy to know you wanted a picture of me, and even happier to know that you kept it. Would it surprise you to know . . . that I have one of you?"

She turned immediately. "You do? Show me."

He released her and reached for the wallet in his back pocket. Opening it, he poked through a number of cards until he found what he was looking for and pulled out a laminated photo of her in her nurse's cap.

She took it, and her eyes widened. *It was one taken when she graduated from nursing school, and she couldn't believe he had it.*

"How did you get this?"

"Kit told me when you graduated, and I asked her to send me a picture." *He could see she was surprised.*

"Why?"

He raised his left eyebrow, and although his grin was wry, his voice was soft when he answered. "The same reason you wanted that other one?" Her cheeks turned rosy under his gaze as she watched him return the picture to his wallet and replace it his pocket. *He couldn't decide whether he'd upset her or not.* The clock on the mantel struck, and when she glanced at it nervously, he reached out and pulled her to him in a comforting hug. "I know—we both have things to do. I need to shovel the walk, and you need to get dressed and start dinner." He planted a brief kiss on her pert nose. "You know, Jane. This may have been a little bit embarrassing—for both of us—but I think it's also has been very enlightening . . . for both of us. We learned some things we both needed to know."

When she didn't answer, he slipped a finger under her chin and lifted it until their eyes met. "Don't you agree?"

She nodded, her eyes wide. *He could drown in those eyes.* Leaning closer, he touched his lips gently against hers, then turned her around and gave her a light shove. "Go! While you do your thing in the kitchen, I'll shovel off the walk."

"Let's call our families first—I'll put the turkey in while you call, and then I'll call my parents—I can get dressed afterward, and shoveling the walk can wait."

"Fine! I'll call Kit first—and then Matt. Luke and Jon will have to call me—"

"Do they know you're here?"

"No! But they always call my cell phone anyway."

Before either of them could move, the phone on the kitchen counter rang. Jane picked it up and was surprised to hear Kit say 'Merry Christmas!' "Merry Christmas to you, too."

Mark was in the doorway, whispering loudly and frantically waving his hands up and down.

"Don't tell her I'm here! Don't—" He stopped when he heard her say, "But Mark's here; wait a minute I'll give him the phone."

He huffed out a breath. Too late! The cat was out of the bag, and he knew he was in for it. He reluctantly accepted the phone, and slowly put it up to his ear.

"Hello, Kit."

"So, big brother! You're at Jane's! Care to tell me what that's all about?"

"Merry Christmas to you too. And, no, I don't care to tell you what it's all about. Jane and I are going skiing, that's all."

"Like I believe that! You needn't be so secretive about it. I think it's great. I knew you'd get around to realizing how you felt about her one of these days . . . although

116

after five years I was beginning to doubt you had any smarts at all."

"Don't be so insulting to your big brother. And you have no idea about my feelings—"

"You wish. And if you're not going to tell me any of the gooshy details, then put Jane back on."

"She won't tell you anything either." As he said it, he gave Jane a glaring look, daring her to say anything to his sister.

"Just put her on—I'll talk to you later, after Hawk gets through."

Mark handed the telephone to Jane, groaning inwardly at the grilling he could expect when he talked to Hawk. He grimaced as he heard Jane speak.

"Hey, Kit. Yes, it was a surprise to me too."

Jane talked to Kit for several minutes and then handed the phone back to him.

"Here! Hawk wants to talk to you." He rolled his eyes, but didn't take the phone.

"Wait a sec. I'll get it in the other room." He heard her replace the phone as soon as he picked up in the other room.

"Well good buddy . . ."

Hawk was in a talkative mood, and it was some time before the call ended. He went to look for Jane and found her still in the kitchen, and still in her nightclothes. He stood in the doorway silently watching her bustle around, periodically using her arm to brush a strand of hair out of her eyes. He couldn't refrain from smiling. He'd been so stupid—and being young was no excuse. Thank goodness he'd come to his senses—hopefully, not too late. Gritting his teeth, he swore to himself it couldn't be—he wouldn't let it be. She looked

117

up just then, saw his expression, and frowned.

"What are you looking so fierce about?"

She cocked her head in the little mannerism that always reminded him of a wren. "Nothing. I'm through with the phone if you want to call your parents."

"Thanks, but I think I'll get dressed first. The turkey's in the oven, and the pies are out of the fridge. There's nothing I have to do right now. Why don't you go ahead and call Matt?"

"I'll do that," he said, barely repressing a groan, knowing Matt would also be surprised to learn he was at Jane's.

His brother answered on the first ring and, as usual, after wishing him a Merry Christmas, his first question was where was he calling from? "Um, actually, I'm at Jane's. I had a few days off for Christmas, and we're going to go skiing."

After a brief silence, Matt chuckled, and his voice was full of humor when he spoke. "Took you long enough."

Surprised, Mark couldn't keep the gruffness from his voice. "What do you mean by that?"

"You always had a soft spot for that girl. And, when you left here that Christmas, you had just realized it—and it scared you to death."

"You knew that!"

"I did."

"Pastor's intuition I suppose?"

"I didn't need anything but my eyes to tell me you had fallen in love. You were the only one who didn't realize it. But I didn't think—none of us did—that it would take you this long to do something about it."

Stunned speechless, he thought about what his brother had said. *How come he'd been so blind, unable to see what had apparently been obvious to his whole family?*

"Mark, you still there?"

"Still here . . . thinking I guess."

"Mark, haven't you talked to Jane at all since then?"

Mark had to clear his throat before answering. "No. Well only once when I called her for Hawk—to see if she knew where Kit was. And then of course at their wedding."

"Ah so . . ."

"What?"

"Seeing her after all that time hit you like a ton of bricks, didn't it?"

"What are you, a prophet or something?"

"Just your brother—and I know you well."

"Better than I know myself apparently."

"You'll figure it out, just don't blow it again."

"That's not a very pastorly statement."

"That's because it's your brother talking."

When Mark got off the phone a half hour later, he was still reeling with Matt's opening salvo. He rubbed his hand across his short hair and shook his head. He'd been surprised by both Kit and Matt. He didn't know what to expect from Luke and Jon, but he was pretty sure he'd be hearing from both of them before the day was out.

He'd heard Jane come down while he was on the phone, and she was still in the kitchen. He headed that way, stopping in the doorway. She looked up when he leaned against the doorframe.

"How was Matt? They all okay?"

He nodded but didn't say anything, and she looked up from chopping Broccoli for a salad. At his expression, she scrunched up her face, and gave him that wren tilt of her head again.

119

"What's wrong, Mark? Did Matt have bad news, or—"

He rushed to reassure her, not wanting to discuss what Matt had said. "No, no. Everything's fine. How long 'til dinner? I think I'll tackle the walk. After four cinnamon buns I need to work up another appetite."

"It's only ten, dinner won't be ready before twelve, so go get your exercise."

"Okay, come get me if Luke or Jon calls."

"It must be nice to always know you'll hear from them."

"It is, but Christmas is the only time—usually we call when we can—but at Christmas everyone makes a special effort. Jon might not be able to call, but he always tries—and we know better than to ask where he is."

He was on his way out the door when his cell rang, and he unzipped his parka to reach it. Knowing it was either Luke or Jon, he said "Merry Christmas" without waiting. It was Luke—calling from Afghanistan—and he could only talk a few minutes as he was on duty. After Luke cut the connection, Mark laughed and shook his head. Luke's first comment—after "Merry Christmas—" was "How come I'm always the last one to know anything?" And then before he could even answer, Luke had continued, "It's about time, man. I never could figure out what you were waiting for." His family was amazing. They all knew now, with the exception of Jon. Doubting his brother could call, he left his phone on the hall table, re-zipped his parka, and called to Jane.

"That was Luke. He'd already gotten the word—from Kit! "Her response to his comments was a peal of laughter. "Now, I am going out and shovel the walk."

★　★　★

The snow was over a foot deep. Good thing it was a while 'til dinner; it was going to take him some time to clear the path and driveway.

Adjusting his heavy gloves, he gripped the handle of the shovel firmly as he thought over the morning's events. First the unexpected call from his sister—unexpected only in the fact that he had planned to call her. While he hadn't consciously intended to withhold the information that he was at Jane's, he knew the thought had been in his mind. He should have known better, despite his earlier denial, she knew him well.

And once Kit knew, everyone knew, or soon would. Whether she told Jon, or whether he did, would depend on who Jon called first. His family had always been close, and he was glad they still were. Jon and Kit had such an emotional bond they always knew when each other was hurt—probably a twin thing. Jon had called from the other side of the world when Kit lost her leg. Since he hadn't called yet, he was probably in some hot spot somewhere, but if he called, it would be Kit he talked to first.

At least he'd gotten to call Matt. He couldn't get his brother's comments out of his mind. Matt hadn't chastised him for leaving like he did that last Christmas they'd all been together—he'd only seemed surprised Mark hadn't contacted Jane in all those years, and he didn't know the answer to that himself. Matt's comments had been surprising—given his brother's unspoken disapproval at the time—when he'd left in the middle of the night. Disapproval which he'd deserved . . . Looking back, Matt had actually been very forbearing.

He realized that instead of being upset with Matt, he had a warm feeling in his chest.

He stopped to wipe his face, surprised to see he was half-way down the walk. He'd been so deep in his thoughts he hadn't even realized it. He went back to his work—and to his thoughts, wondering what Jon would have to say when he heard the news. At that moment, Jane opened the door behind him. *Perfect timing. He had about three more shovels to go, and he'd be through.*

"You're finished! Great! Jon is on the phone for you. You left your cell phone in the living room." She gave him a teasing grin. "The word must be out—he called my number . . . and asked for you."

Mark didn't even groan—what was the use? "Tell him I'll be right there, as soon as I kick off my boots."

He jammed the snow shovel upright in the snow and hurried to the porch and heeled off his boots. Not wanting to take a chance on Jon getting cut off, he hurried into the kitchen and grabbed up the phone. Wherever Jon was calling from, the connection wasn't good, but he could understand him well enough.

"Merry Christmas Big Brother!"

"Merry Christmas, Jon. I was beginning to think you weren't going to be able to call this year. Since you called on Jane's phone, I'm assuming you've already talked to someone in the family." He heard his brother's laughter and was glad Jon couldn't see his wry grin.

"Talked to all of them—you're the last. And I have to tell you Bro—Kit and Luke may have been surprised, but not me, Mark—not me. I saw the way you looked at Jane at the wedding. I figured your long 'winter of discontent' was about to come to an end. In fact, I can't figure out what took you so long. Did Matt tell you he wasn't surprised either? Damn, Kit and Luke must have been blind at the wedding."

Deciding not to comment on that, he changed the subject. "Are you doing all right, Jon?"

Jon laughed again. "Don't want to talk about it, huh? Okay. Me, I'm always fine. You'd hear if I weren't."

"Yeah, I know, but—"

"Don't worry!"

"Who's worrying? I just asked a question."

"Right."

"Hey man, I gotta go. And Mark, next time I'm home I expect to hear about a wedding in the offing."

The line went dead before Mark could answer. He slowly replaced the phone and rubbed his hand across his face, before going to hang up his parka. *His whole family knew about him and Jane now . . . or thought they knew. The thing was, they didn't know the real story—he and Jane were a long way from a wedding—and what if he messed up again?*

★   ★   ★

As they sat down to dinner a little while later, he admired the beautiful table, and the beautiful woman sitting across from him. It was turning out to be one of the best Christmases he had ever had. She was watching him, a slight smile on her face, and he realized she was waiting for him to say grace. As he did so, he knew he was thankful for so much more than the food on the table.

"Well, you've heard from all of your family—"

He grinned at her. "You were right. Luke and Jon had already talked to both Kit and Matt, and were already armed with questions about our relationship—"

"Do we have a relationship, Mark?"

Her eyes were serious, and her voice soft, and he pondered how to say what he wanted to say. What did she want him to say? She was biting her lip, and he knew she was anxious about his answer.

"I don't know if you can call what we have a relationship yet, Jane." He watched her go still and draw in a soft breath. "I don't know . . . but I very much hope it will turn *into* a relationship, *a long one*. I want that." He studied her face after he finished, watching her eyes light up and her lips curve up in a small smile.

She nodded her head. "I want that too, Mark."

Deciding it was time to change the subject, he asked, "When do you plan to call your parents?"

"I was thinking I should do it as soon as we finish eating, but—"

"Are you going to tell them I'm here?"

"I can't lie to them; and they'll know anyway."

"Is it a problem . . . my being here?"

She could almost believe there was hurt in his voice, and she hurried to clarify her comment. "Not in the way you're thinking." She let out a rueful laugh. "In fact, just the opposite." She closed her eyes, remembering her mother's comments the last time she had mentioned Mark's name—and all she'd said then was that they'd talked on the telephone.

She let her head fall down on her chest. *She so didn't want to get into this. How could she tell Mark that her mother's biggest dream, and probably her father's too, was for her to marry him.* Just the thought brought heat to her face, and she reached for her napkin in an attempt to disguise it.

Mark noted the lovely color suffusing her face, and wondered if her parents' reaction would be similar to that of his siblings. But why wouldn't she want him to know? He scowled.

"Perhaps you'd better explain."

His look said there was no way out of this. She laid down the unhelpful napkin and brushed her warm face with one hand, then licked her lips, before lifting her chin."

He smiled at the tell-tale movement; he loved that determined little chin.

"I told you before . . . they like you. My parents really like you. When I called to tell them, I had signed up . . . I sort of mentioned that their reaction was the same as yours." She stopped and stared at her plate. When she raised her eyes, her expression pleaded with him to let her drop the explanation.

He knew where this was going—their families were obviously just alike—but he couldn't let her drop it. She was too cute, struggling to avoid telling him her parents wanted them to get together. He struggled to contain his grin as he dipped his chin and raised one eyebrow.

"Go on Jane. Their reaction was?"

"Oh, stop it, Mark. You weren't going to tell your family you were here either . . . were you? If Kit hadn't called . . . were you?"

She looked at him defiantly, and he knew she had him."

"Maybe, I'm not sure. But we're talking about your parents. I'm interested to hear what they said. How was their reaction the same as mine? Are we talking about what I thought about your signing up in the Air Force Reserves?"

"Oh, all right! They said I should listen to you, that you 'had your head screwed on right.' My Dad told me to call you, that I should listen to you, that you could be 'real helpful!'"

Mark burst out laughing, as he stared into eyes that dared him to say anything. He ignored the look, and finally she couldn't withhold her own grin.

"Your Dad told you to listen to me, hmmm? So why didn't you? Since I'm so knowledgeable, so helpful, and all?"

"Stop laughing at me . . . and we're NOT discussing my joining the Reserves. You know where that leads."

He raised both of his hands, palms facing her, but he was still grinning. *He might be dropping the subject for now, but she had an uncomfortable feeling that her Dad's comments would resurface again, and likely when she least wanted them to.*

She stood abruptly, picking up her plate and reaching for his. "What kind of pie do you want? I'll get it if you want to pour the coffee."

"I'll have a slice of each." *Her laughter pealed out, and he felt a twinge in his heart as he realized how much he loved the sound.*

As she was putting a dollop of cream on each piece, he picked up the coffee pot, leaning over the plates of pie as he did so.

"Ummm, pumpkin. You definitely know the way to a man's heart." *Her expression told him flattery would not make her forget their previous conversation.*

By three o'clock they were on their way to the ski resort. The roads were indeed clear, and a wintry sun sparkled off the new snow. Jane settled back in her seat and let out a deep sigh of contentment.

At the sound, Mark turned toward her, "What was that deep sigh for?"

She offered him a brilliant smile. "Nothing. I'm just happy. *And we still have two more days."*

★　★　★

A day-and-a-half later they were back in the car, this time returning to Great Falls. Jane stretched her legs out in front of her and groaned softly.

"Sore?"

"A little . . . but it was worth it. I've never seen the snow so perfect. I'd forgotten how much I love skiing."

"Me too, even though it's been years since I went. I guess it's something you don't forget how to do."

"Like riding a bicycle?" She laughed. "For someone who claims he doesn't go any more, I notice you're not stiff—must be all that jogging." When he didn't comment, she looked over at him. "What are you thinking?"

"Just that it's been one of the best Christmases of my life . . . thanks to you."

His eyes warmed her, but her voice was sad when she spoke. "Except it's over . . . and I don't want it to be."

"What would you have changed?"

"Nothing, nothing at all—it was perfect."

"Then what's the problem," he said reasonably.

"I . . . I think I'm afraid."

She'd surprised him with that, and he took his eyes off the road long enough to glance over at her. "Why on earth are you afraid?"

"I keep thinking of all the things . . . all the changes . . . this coming year will bring—me in the service, you being transferred—who knows where we'll be . . . or what we'll be doing next Christmas?"

He reached out and put his hand over hers where it rested on the seat.

"What you're really thinking about is that Christmas five years ago . . . aren't you."

She looked up immediately, ready to deny it, but she couldn't. Even though she hadn't been conscious of it, the memory had been there waiting to be recognized. She looked at him helplessly, and then turned away to look out the window.

Mark kept his eyes on the road ahead, his expression grim. *Was he never going to be able to erase her memories of what he had done? Just when he thought he was making progress, something always reminded her.*

They drove in silence for several miles before Jane, unable to stand the quiet any longer, spoke diffidently. "Mark. I'm not angry with you. I . . . I know you're different. You've been . . . I can't tell you what this time has meant to me. I don't want it to end . . . and I'm . . . I'm afraid it will."

He didn't look at her, and his voice was resigned when he spoke. "I guess we'll just have to wait and see, then. I've told you, this isn't the end." He turned toward her, and his voice was determined. "It isn't the end, Jane. You will hear from me; I promise. I promise." He turned back to the road, his expression stoic.

"I believe you, Mark."

But he knew in her heart she was still afraid to believe.

128

Chapter 5

Two weeks later, Jane walked out of the Base Hospital at Malmstrom and took a deep breath. She'd taken the first step, completed her physical. Now began the waiting. Most of the tests were familiar to her from her work in the hospital, and she thought she'd passed; she'd completed everything they asked. *Still . . .*

Mark would call tonight to ask about her physical. Determined to convince her that she could depend on him, he'd called several times in the past two weeks. Although neither of them ever mentioned it, their conversation in the car on the way home from skiing was still between them. Her conscience prickled her sharply, and guilt weighed heavily on her at the secret she had kept, *and was still keeping from him.* It wasn't something she could tell him over the telephone, or in an email. She should have told him when he was here. It would be a long time before she had another opportunity, and she knew the burden of guilt would get heavier and heavier.

She forced herself to stop worrying over something she could do nothing about for the foreseeable future. It would be at least another hour before she could expect Mark's call. In the meantime she decided to call Ellen, who would also be anxious to hear how the physical had gone. She smiled as she thought of her friend who had, indeed, returned from Texas with an engagement ring on her finger, and plans to marry in June. She had already asked Jane to be her maid of honor. It would be the second time in a year that she had played that role, and the old saying, "always a bridesmaid, never a bride," went through her mind. Before she'd agreed, she had reminded Ellen that if she passed her physical, she might not be available, but Ellen had refused to accept the possibility.

Holding the phone in her hand, she remembered her comments to Mark. The year ahead loomed with unknowns—Would she pass her physical? Would Mark have to go overseas? Would she be at COT in June . . . and miss Ellen's wedding? Or even be overseas then?

She entered the number and listened to the ring.

"Hi Jane, how'd it go. Do you think you passed? When will you know?"

Laughter in her voice, Jane proceeded to answer all of Ellen's questions. "It seemed to go all right. I don't know if I passed. They said it would be a couple of weeks before I could expect to hear."

"Oh."

"You didn't really think they'd tell me today, did you?"

"I guess not . . . but I was hoping they might."

"You're just worried you might not have a maid-of-honor for your wedding."

"I am not!" Ellen laughed. "Well, that too. But mostly I wanted you to find out. I know how anxious you've been."

"I'm teasing you, Ellen. I know you're not selfish enough to worry about the wedding. And, I am on pins and needles wondering if I'll make it."

"You need to get your mind on something else. Want to go riding tomorrow? I already checked, and neither of us is on the schedule to work."

"Did you also check the weather? This is January, you know."

"I did! No more snow, and predictions are for a sunny weekend. It'll be cold, but we can bundle up. There's nothing like a fast ride in frosty weather to blow the cobwebs out of your mind."

Jane laughed again. "Okay! Okay! I'm convinced. Is Dennis going with us?"

"Maybe. Do you mind?"

"Of course not. As long as he doesn't mind me intruding."

"Don't be silly. He's not like that. It'll be fun. Too bad Mark's not here."

Jane ignored the comment, remembering she was expecting him to call. "Look, I better get off the phone. Mark promised to call this evening, but I wanted to let you know I survived the physical."

"Sure, I'll see you tomorrow. Want me to pick you up?"

"No, I'll drive. That way you won't have to bring me home. I'm sure Dennis will want you to stay a while."

Ellen didn't disagree, and Jane hung up the phone, which rang within minutes.

"So how did it go?"

"What happened to 'hello'?" she teased.

"Hello. How'd it go? I've been thinking of you all day,

131

waiting 'til I thought you'd be home. You were on the phone the first time I called."

She was surprised, and pleased, at his comments. "I called Ellen to tell her. I didn't think you would call so early, you're usually at work."

"I *am* at work, but I couldn't wait any longer. Now, tell me how it went."

"You're as bad as Ellen. But you should know better. They didn't tell me anything . . . except that I would hear in a couple of weeks."

"I know they didn't tell you anything, but you must have a feeling. I can always tell when I've passed a physical."

"Yeah, well I can't. I think it went all right. At least I completed all the tests. There were no dreadful gasps from the technicians, and the doctor didn't frown when he listened to my heart."

Mark laughed. "All right! So I'm being ridiculous. I know this means a lot to you, and I—"

"Mark, you aren't hoping I don't pass . . . are you?"

Anger shook his voice. "I don't believe you said that. I should hang up."

"No, don't . . . please. I'm sorry. It's just that you were so mad when I signed up, I . . . " She heard his expelled breath and prayed he wasn't going to hang up.

"Okay. I guess you had reason to think that. But you're wrong. I wouldn't do something like that when I know how much you want it." His voice quieted, and she could barely hear his next comment. "Even though I still hate it."

"Oh, Mark."

"I know. I've promised not to go there . . . and I won't. And for your information, I do hope you pass . . . and

132

I'm sure you will."

"Thank you, Mark. That means a lot."

"What are you doing this weekend? Do you have to work?

"No, it's the first weekend since Christmas that I don't. I'm going riding tomorrow with Ellen and Dennis."

"I wish I were there to go with you."

"I wish you were, too. Ellen even said that it was too bad you weren't here."

"Someday we *will* ride together, Jane. And that's a promise."

"I'll look forward to it."

Several weeks later Jane was driving home, struggling to see through the fiercely blowing flakes of yet another snowstorm.

She was anxious to reach home and, hopefully, find an email from Mark. He had been really good, and most days she found an email waiting when she got home. Finally pulling into her garage, she breathed a sigh of relief. Her shoulder muscles were tight from the strain of peering through the thick snow. Inside, she remembered she hadn't checked the mail. She set her purse down and went through the foyer, opened the front door and brushed snow off her mailbox. The stiff wind almost blew the door shut in her face and, looking up and down the street, she could see that her tire tracks were already filling in. Without looking, she reached in the box and pulled out several pieces of mail, then backed into the house and slammed the door. Throwing the mail casually on the small table under the mirror hanging in the foyer, she shucked her coat and hung it up in the closet, kicked off her boots and set them in the metal tray on the closet floor. She stood for a minute trying to decide whether to go upstairs immediately and change out of her uniform, or turn on the computer. Suddenly, her attention was drawn to the pile of mail. One piece had slid out of the pile, and she could see the "For Official Use Only" stamp across the front. She snatched it up—it was from the Air Force! Tearing it open, she rapidly scanned it, then threw her hands up in the classic victory sign, and let out a squeal— "I passed!"

She had to tell Mark! She started for the phone beside her favorite chair, then stopped and veered toward the computer. First, she'd see if she had anything from him.

She clicked the mail icon and stood waiting for the screen to fill. Smiling, she saw what she was hoping for. Instead of reading it from the screen, she clicked "print," and waited for the printer to do its work. She snatched the message from the machine, and happily noted it was a long one. Holding it tightly in one hand, she passed through the kitchen and grabbed an apple off the counter, then went into the den and settled in her favorite chair. Only then did she look to see what Mark had to say. *He was going to Afghanistan!* Her head sunk to her chest, and she let out a groan. *So it was definite.* He'd expected to go there, had tried to prepare her, but she'd still been hoping.

Chapter 6

Sometimes she felt as if her life was whizzing by ever since she had signed up for the Air Force, she was so busy. After her phone conversation with Mark and his assurance that she would accomplish everything she needed to do, and that he had confidence in her, she had gotten busy and checked each item off as she did it. And Mark had been right, by her date of departure for training, she was ready.

The last five weeks had flown by. Her decision to join the Air Force Reserves had been the right one. She and her fellow officers-to-be had undergone physical conditioning and classroom studies preparing them to become officers and leaders, plus warfare and disaster preparedness, as well as the Air Force's role in national security; and everything else the recruiting sergeant had told her about. Sometimes it felt as if her head were spinning with all the data. It had taken a while for her muscles to become used to the rigorous physical training, and not ache each night when she tumbled into bed.

The sergeant had also told her she would make

friendships that would last throughout her career, and she was sure he was right. Thrown together so closely, all with a common goal, they had quickly bonded, and Jane knew she would never forget some of their amazing experiences.

And now it was over; graduation was tomorrow. *She could hardly believe it.* She studied the poised and confident young woman staring back at her from the mirror. She was definitely thinner—and more toned— the result of all those early-morning calisthenics and afternoon runs. She grinned at the image. *Yep, it had definitely been worth it.*

Her grin faded. It had been so long since she had seen or talked to Mark. She had often rued their agreement not to call each other during her weeks of training. His frequent emails had been the encouragement she had desperately needed to keep going at times during the busy weeks since she had arrived here at Maxwell. But now it was over. His last email had said he'd call her tonight at 2000, and that he had a surprise. *Tonight! Only*—she figured the time in her head—*only eight more hours!*

As she stood in the center of the room that had been hers for the last five weeks, she slowly spun around, taking in each detail. No trace of her remained—it was the same starkly utilitarian room it had been five weeks ago when she had moved into it.

The formal graduation ceremony would take place in a little over an hour. Her parents had driven up from Florida to see her graduate. She'd seen them last night, and would meet them immediately after the cap-tossing ceremony. She knew they were really proud of her. They'd at last overcome their misgivings . . . or were at

136

least hiding them.

She glanced at the military watch on her arm—*still an hour before final formation. Perhaps now was a good time to call Kit.* She had planned to call several times before, but something always came up. Dragging the one straight-back chair over in front of the window, she picked up her cell phone and settled herself.

She keyed in the number and pushed send, then waited. After several rings someone picked up, and she heard her friend's voice.

"Lieutenant Hawkins here."

"Kit, it sounds great, your name I mean. Where are you? You might have let me know. Did Hawk get his transfer? Are you going to be close to each other?"

"Jane! Is that you? Where have you been? I've called your home several times. In fact, I was almost ready to call the hospital and see if they knew where you were."

Jane swallowed. *Uh oh. Good thing she hadn't waited any longer.*

"Well, maybe you better sit down. But first, answer my questions."

"Okay, but I'm not going to forget *my* questions. As to where I am—our requests for transfer came through. We didn't expect to get the same post since we're in different branches, but we were lucky. I'm at Fort Bragg and Hawk is at Seymour Johnson. We're both in North Carolina, about 65 miles apart. We have a house in-between, which gives each of us about a 35-mile commute. It's workable, and we consider ourselves lucky. We've been so busy we haven't talked to anyone since Christmas.

"So *that's* why you didn't know. I would have expected Mark to tell you."

"Know? Know what? What's going on? Is something wrong?"

Jane laughed. "Hold up, Kit. You sound like me—you're always telling me I never give you a chance to get a word in edgewise. Nothing's wrong; I've just got some exciting news. I'm calling from Maxwell AFB in Alabama—I'm graduating from COT this morning. I'm about to become a full-fledged Lieutenant in the Air Force Reserve."

"*Whaaaat?* Are you *kidding* me?"

"No, I really am an Air Force nurse, at least almost."

"But what . . . why . . . how . . . I just can't. . ."

Listening to Kit's sputtering, Jane burst into laughter. "I knew you'd be surprised."

"That's putting it mildly! You didn't say a thing about joining the Air Force when we saw you at our wedding . . . or when we talked at Christmas . . . and yet you must have joined up right after that?"

"Pretty much. Don't you remember me complaining about my dull life when you came home to recuperate after you lost your leg?"

"I remember. You kept saying I had been everywhere and you had been nowhere."

"Well, that was the start. And then at the wedding—you, your brothers, and Hawk were talking about your adventures and all the places you'd been. All of you seemed to have such interesting lives—"

"*Jane*, this is so unlike you! You <u>never</u> make up your mind without worrying the subject sixty ways from Sunday. I can't believe it."

"That's what Mark said when—" The stunned silence on the other end of the line told her she'd made a grave tactical error.

138

"Mark <u>knew</u>? And he didn't . . . wait, how long has he known? When did he find out?

"Ummm . . . actually, he knew at Christmas."

"He knew? And *neither* of you thought Hawk and I might be interested in hearing about something that big, that important? I can't believe you'd . . . I don't know what to say . . . I'm—I'm speechless."

"Kit, please don't be mad. I'm sorry. And please don't blame Mark. It wasn't his fault. It really wasn't. I had only just signed up. I hadn't had my physical or anything, and I didn't want to say anything until I was really in—"

"Uh huh. And yet you told Mark. Hmmm . . . So what does my brother think of your being in the Air Force?"

"Why does everyone want to know what Mark thinks about it? Why should he think anything about it?"

Kit laughed. "You're kidding, right? My big brother *always* has an opinion—on *everything*. If he knew—and you say he did—then I know he had something to say about it. And I bet he wasn't in favor of it."

"How did you know?"

"Ah ha! He hated the idea, didn't he?"

As Jane remembered their conversation, and her anger, she spoke without thinking. "He told me that I didn't know what I was doing. That I should reconsider, that change was one thing, but this was too much."

"Uh oh! I hope he wasn't standing in front of you when he said it."

"No, he was on the telephone. Why?"

"Because I know you, Jane Brewer. You would have knocked his block off if he was anywhere in close proximity . . . not that he didn't deserve it. I can't believe he said something so dumb, especially when all of us are

139

in the service full-time."

"Um, well actually, I think you're the reason, Kit."

"*Me*? Oh no." She sighed. "He's still upset about my losing my leg, isn't he?"

"He is."

"Oh dear. I had hoped seeing how happy we were at the wedding would have reconciled him to it and that he'd move on, as I have. After all, I didn't lose my life . . . and look at all I've gained."

"Well, you always had a positive outlook on everything, Kit. Mark, now he's another story."

"Tell me about it. What a pessimist! But that's enough about me. I can't say I'm totally surprised about you and Mark. Hawk and I both saw the sparks between you and that stubborn brother of mine at the wedding. I expected him to keep in touch with you this time—write, email, call, *something*. I always thought it was odd that he never did before."

"Odd? Why odd?"

"*Because*—despite the fact that you both deny it, I know you and Mark have a past. Something happened that time at Matt's, when we were all there for Christmas right after he completed officer training. You spent all your time together, and then he left like that—in the middle of the night—without even saying goodbye, and you wouldn't say anything. Both of you were different after that. Whatever it was, neither of you ever got over it. You can deny it all you want, but I know what I know. I always hoped, somehow, you'd get together again. When I called this past Christmas, and he was at your house, I was happy. I thought, hoped, that *finally* . . . Jane, are you still there? Oh! Is Mark there now?"

Jane was stunned at how much her friend had figured

out. *She'd thought she'd covered her feelings so well. Now she didn't know what to say.* She couldn't explain their current relationship to Kit, not when she was so unsure of it herself, and especially not since Kit was Mark's sister.

"No, no he's not here."

"I'm surprised he didn't come for your graduation—that's a big event. He's not still holding a grudge because you joined the Air Force, is he?"

"No, no he's not . . . we're not . . . it's complicated."

"Sounds like it. Just wait 'til I talk to that rat brother of mine."

Oh no! What had she done? If Mark hadn't mentioned anything to his family it had to be because he didn't want them to know.

"No, don't Kit. You can't call Mark. I'll—I'll explain . . . just not now."

A loudspeaker interrupted their conversation.

"What was that?"

"They just announced that all graduating cadets need to assemble in front of the building. I have to go." She breathed a sigh of relief. *Saved by the loudspeaker.*

"Fine! You go graduate, but I'll be expecting a call, and soon. If I don't—"

"You will, I promise, Kit. I'll call as soon as I can. Just don't call Mark. Bye."

★   ★   ★

Kit put the phone down and glowered at Hawk.

His eyebrows arched upwards. "So, what's up? Was that Jane?"

"Yes, it was."

"So . . . what?"

141

"Did Mark ever tell you about a relationship with Jane?"

Hawk shrugged. "I didn't know him until flight school."

"I know, but that doesn't mean he never told you."

"Well, he didn't. Why would he?"

Kit rolled her eyes. Men were such . . . such . . . men. "I don't know, except I know something happened in their past. You saw how they were at the wedding!"

Hawk grinned. "You mean like there was a loose electrical current surrounding them whenever they were in the same room?"

"Exactly. When we were all in high school, Mark treated Jane like another kid sister, when he noticed her at all."

"What are you getting at? Why are you bringing this up now?"

Kit's forehead wrinkled in concentration. "Well! You know how surprised we were to find out he was at Jane's when we called at Christmas?"

"Yeah. So?"

"They've been in contact ever since—frequently, from the sound of it. And, he knew she was in the Air Force!"

"She's in the Air Force! And you didn't know it?"

"She joined the Air Force Reserve, and she's graduating from COT today." Kit looked at her watch. "In thirty minutes actually, and Mark knew all about it!"

Hawk had a stunned look on his face. "I don't believe Jane never told you any of this before."

"Well, Mark didn't tell you either . . . and he's your best bud."

"But he's your brother!"

An evil gleam began to appear in Kit's eyes. "You're

right! They both owe us; and we're going to collect!

Hawk saw that look, and burst out laughing. "Look out Mark and Jane!"

Kit pulled at her chin and looked speculatively at Hawk. "Do you know how to contact Mark?"

"The same ways you know, his cell phone and email. Why?"

"I'm beginning to get an idea."

Her eyes sparkled, and Hawk realized again how much he loved this woman. "So, what's your idea?"

"Well, I wasn't going to say anything yet, and you may not want to do it, but—"

"Kit Hawkins! Stop with all the delaying tactics and spit it out. Now."

He headed for her with raised hands as if to choke her, but she giggled, and then snuggled against him, circling her arms around his waist. When she looked up at him, the laughter was gone from her face, and her expression was soft and serious.

"What is it, Kit?"

"Hawk, I've been keeping a secret, too."

He raised his eyebrows in question, then leaned away and frowned at her.

She raised her arms to his neck, leaned forward, and kissed him. "Don't get mad. I only just found out. I suspected, but wasn't really sure until I saw the doctor yesterday."

"Doctor! You went to the doctor yesterday? Is something wrong? Kit, what's the matter?"

"Hawk! Nothing's the matter! You're going to be a *Dad*, that's all."

As she said it, she peeped through her lashes at him, holding her breath for his response. He didn't disappoint.

"We're having a *baby*? When? Oh, Kit—"

"Are you pleased?"

"Pleased doesn't do it at all. I'm overwhelmed. A *baby*. . ." He picked her up and swung her around the room in circles, laughing like a madman. Suddenly he set her on her feet, leaned back, and studied her seriously. "Kit, are you all right? Are you sure you should—"

"Hawk! Surely you're not referring to the fact that I have one leg! My leg has <u>nothing</u> to do with having a baby. Do I need to teach you an anatomy lesson?"

The laughter was back in her eyes, and Hawk knew he had been foolish, but he also knew he'd never get over worrying about her, and she might as well get used to it.

He got a puzzled expression on his face, as he remembered how this had come up. "I'm afraid I don't see the connection with what we were discussing before—getting even with Mark for not telling you he was in touch with Jane—"

"Hawk, you're not thinking. You know how Mark always has to be the one in charge? The one who knows everything that's going on in the family? The one who makes sure all of us are *informed* and in touch with everyone?"

The sparkle of mischief was in Hawk's eyes now. "I'm beginning to see the light. Kit Hawkins, you're diabolical! But it would be mean not to let him know he's going to be an uncle."

"Oh, I'm not going to keep it from him. I wouldn't do that. I'm just going to let him find out from someone else."

"He'll hate it; he'll probably be mad at you."

"I'm sure he will be. But he deserves it for not telling

144

us he was serious about my best friend—"

"How do you know he is?"

"Oh, I'm sure he is. I'm not sure *how* I know—Jane was very evasive—but I know. He's serious. Now, here's the way I envision it working out. You're going to call him, and during the conversation you'll ask him how Jane is and wonder why he never told us she was joining the Reserve—and <u>that's</u> <u>all</u>."

"Not tell him our news? Kit, I don't believe you'll be able to do it. You'll be grabbing the phone—"

"No, I won't, and you won't tell him either. We have to let him know he can't do this to us."

"Uh huh. I'm beginning to see some pitfalls here. And besides, I <u>want</u> to tell him! I can't wait to brag a little. After all, it's not every day a guy finds out he's going to be a father."

"I know . . . but you can wait just a little, can't you?"

"I suppose I'll have to. But after we call—and don't tell him—then what?"

"<u>Then</u> I'll call Jon and tell him. I'd call him first anyhow, but normally I'd hang right up from talking to him and call Mark. This time I won't."

"And you figure Jon will tell him?"

"Oh, he will! He <u>definitely</u> will. I plan to ask him to wait a week and then call Mark with some trivial news, and just as he's ready to hang up, I'll tell him to casually drop it into the conversation—something like, 'Isn't that great about Kit and Hawk? I'm really happy for them.'"

Hawk slapped his forehead with the palm of his hand and groaned. "He'll go off like a grenade, and then he'll burn up the telephone wires getting to us. Man, oh man. Kit . . . are you sure you know what you're doing?"

"Yep. Positive."

Seeing her mischievous eyes and her teasing grin, he had to laugh. "Okay, but that's enough about Mark and revenge. I want to talk about us and the baby. When are you due?"

"I'm only about a month along; looks like we might have *two* things to celebrate on our first anniversary."

Hawk's grin spread from ear to ear, and he hugged her close against his chest. "So come November we'll be a real family."

When she nodded, he grabbed her hand and pulled her toward the bedroom. "Come on, let's celebrate."

"Hawk, it's broad daylight!"

"Sure is."

Though she pulled against him, her resistance was token. She wanted him as much as he wanted her, and when he swept her up in his arms and headed for the bedroom, she hung on tight and kissed the side of his neck.

The graduation ceremony had been both moving and beautiful, and afterward they had all promised to keep in touch. Realistically, however, Jane knew that they were scattering across the globe, and it might be a long time before she ran into some of her classmates again—if ever. That's just the way things were. She looked up and saw her parents coming toward her across the grassy field, and smiled and waved.

Both of them looked back, pride evident in their eyes. Then her Dad grinned. "Do I salute you, Lieutenant?"

She laughed. "No Dad, I'm still your little girl, but this time I'm not playing dress-up."

"No, you're not."

Tears came to his eyes, and she knew he was remembering the pretend fashion shows she had loved to do for him, dragging out her mother's dresses, and even on one occasion, his old Army uniform from when he was in Vietnam. He blinked the tears away and smiled.

"Am I still permitted to hug my little girl?"

She looked around and saw families all across the compound hugging and even kissing their graduates. She nodded and suddenly found herself swept into her father's arms, her mother grabbing her arm and holding on. Tears welled in her eyes as she realized how very, very fortunate she'd always been to have such loving parents.

"Come on Mom, Dad. This new lieutenant is taking you to lunch at the officers' club."

"Can you do that?" her mother asked worriedly. "After all, we're not military."

"Don't be silly, Mom. Come on. You're my guests. I want you to meet my friends."

★   ★   ★

The next morning she and her parents had breakfast in the officers' club, her mother still in awe that they could eat there. After breakfast, they dropped her off at the airport on their way back to Florida. Her flight to Great Falls left at 1300. She smiled, realizing she was thinking in military time—1300 instead of 1:00 p.m.

It had been great to see her parents, and graduation had been satisfying. Only one thing had been missing—*Mark.* She'd known he wouldn't be able to come, but he'd said he'd call last night, and he hadn't. Of course, there could be all kinds of reasons, but . . . she'd really expected him to call and congratulate her. He had kept

147

his promise and emailed her regularly all during training, but she'd missed talking to him. He'd known yesterday was graduation day, and she'd been sure he would call. She rummaged for her phone in her new Air Force purse to turn it off before boarding the plane, and discovered that it was already off. *Oh no! Mark couldn't have reached her even if he had tried!* As soon as she turned it on, she saw Mark's text message. Her heart lifted as she read his words. "Sorry I missed your big day. Tried to call you. No dice. Call me."

Approaching the security checkpoint, she hurriedly turned the phone off again, shoved it into her bag, handed the security agent her military ID card, and continued through the fenced-off lane. She had to remove her shoes and place them in the basket, along with her watch, belt and purse, but her heart was singing. She could hardly wait to get to the flight waiting area so she could return Mark's call—if he wasn't flying. She passed through the scanner without a bleep and sat down to replace her shoes and gather up her personal items from the basket.

She was early, and not many people were waiting for the flight to Great Falls. After stopping long enough to purchase a Starbucks latte, she settled into one of the seats, checking the signboard for the ETA on her flight. Still reading 1300—on time. A quick glance at her watch told her she had an hour-and-a-half, plenty of time to talk to Mark. The only people in the area were two soldiers engrossed in magazines, and a young teen thumbing an I-Pad.

She took the top off her coffee, retrieved the phone from her purse, and punched in Mark's number, crossing her fingers. He answered on the third ring, and she let out the breath she didn't realize she'd been holding.

"Congratulations, Jane! I wanted to tell you yesterday, but I had to fly all day, and then I had to go to a squadron function last night. Between times, I tried to call you, but—"

"I know, my parents came for graduation. I was showing them around, and forgot I left my phone in the room. I didn't realize it was turned off until this morning."

"So how does it feel . . . being a shiny new Air Force Lieutenant?

"It feels *wonderful*, Mark. I'm so excited! You can't imagine the pride I felt sitting up there with all my fellow graduates, watching them get their awards and their bars. And when we all tossed our caps up in the air . . . you just can't imagine—"

"I think I can. It's been a while, but I <u>can</u> still remember."

"Oh, of course you can! What was I thinking?"

"You're excited. I understand. Did you know your parents were coming? I don't remember you mentioning it."

"I didn't know. They decided at the last minute. I was surprised, but I'm *so* glad they came, and Mark, they were really proud of me. They really were."

"I'm sure they were. I'm proud of you, too."

"Oh, Mark." He didn't speak for several seconds, then he spoke so softly it was almost a whisper.

"I got my orders." He heard Jane suck in a breath.

"When? When do you have to go?"

"I have to be there May 15. The unit will leave here on the thirteenth."

"So soon?"

"Shhh! That's the bad news. The good news, at least I *hope* you'll think it's good, is my leave was approved. I have one week, starting May 1—"

She squealed in delight and was embarrassed when she saw the two soldiers and the teen look up at her. She ducked her head and held the phone closer to her mouth. "Sorry. Did I deafen you? I'm just so excited. Mark, that's *wonderful*! I never dreamed you'd be able to come visit before you left."

"I told you I was going to put in for leave—"

"I know, I know. It just seemed too much to hope for that you would actually get it." She hugged herself, trying to take it in.

"Believe it. I'm looking at the orders, and I just finished making my flight reservations."

She could hear the smile in his voice, and she smiled too. "When will you be coming?"

"Next Saturday . . . if that's all right."

For the first time, she could hear a note of doubt in his voice, which surprised her. "Oh, Mark, it's more than all right; it's *perfect*! You know I'll have to work, right?"

"I know, but we'll have your days off—and evenings . . . won't we?"

"I'll check in at the hospital day after tomorrow, and see about my schedule—I'll arrange it so we can be together as much as possible. What time will you arrive?

"My flight gets in on Saturday, at 1400."

"If I don't have to work that weekend, I'll meet your plane."

"That'd be great, but if you can't, it'll be fine. I'll take a cab . . . or rent a car. I'm really looking forward to seeing you, Jane. I've . . . missed you."

"I've missed you too."

"I have to go. I'll call you tomorrow night."

"Safe flight. Mark?" He was gone, and she'd forgotten to tell him she'd talked to Kit. *Oh well, it could wait, and it wouldn't be long now.* She turned the phone off and replaced it in her purse. Then she shut her eyes and went over everything Mark had said, wishing their conversation could have been longer. But the important thing was—*he was coming to see her!* She hadn't dared to hope they would see each other before he left for Afghanistan. Now they would. And—he had remembered . . . and tried to call her. *That meant everything!*

Chapter 7

Jane's flight home was uneventful, and at 1700 she pulled into her driveway.

Turning off the ignition, she leaned back in the seat and stretched her arms over her head, glad she'd asked Ellen to leave her car at the airport rather than meet her. They'd see each other tomorrow, but right now all she wanted to do was crash. *Lord, she was tired.* She smiled, hardly able to believe she was now in the Air Force Reserve. *It seemed another world from here—and it was.* She sighed deeply. Monday she'd be back at work in the emergency room, and COT would seem even farther away.

Opening the door, she slid out, reaching behind the seat for her suitcase. She slammed the door and stopped. *It had been four months since she'd seen Mark . . . and now he'd be here in a little over a week.*

The house smelled musty when she opened the door, but otherwise seemed okay. The room looked bare without the plants Ellen had taken to care for while she was gone. She opened a few windows and let the cold breeze clear out the dead air before turning the thermostat up to take the chill off the house. Too tired to unpack, she flopped down on the couch and stretched her legs out in front of her.

Thankfully, she had tomorrow to catch up before having to report back to work on Monday. In the morning, she'd call Ellen and run by the grocery and stock up on food. But right now, she had nowhere to go and nothing she <u>had</u> to do. She laid her head back on the couch and felt her eyes drift closed.

She startled awake, disoriented and trying to figure out where she was. The telephone beside her jangled again loudly. She snatched it up, almost dropping it in the process.

"Hello?"

"Hi. Is this <u>Lieutenant</u> Jane Brewer?"

A giggle escaped her. "It is." Suddenly a tremor of fear shook her as she wondered why Mark was calling. "Is something wrong?"

"No, I just wanted to make sure you got home safely."

In an instant, her fear changed to happiness. "I did. The flight was good, and we landed right on time. My house is fine. In fact, you woke me up. I sat down on the sofa for a minute and drifted off to sleep."

He laughed. "Relaxation after the turmoil. I know the feeling. I won't keep you. Turn in and get your beauty sleep. I'll call soon."

"Okay. And Mark . . . thank you for checking on me."

"You're welcome."

★   ★   ★

The week passed on wings. She had anticipated the time would drag as she waited for Mark's visit, but she had been right about work. Within hours of reporting

153

back at the hospital it was as if she had never left, and of course Ellen dragged her into helping to plan her upcoming wedding." Now the day had arrived—*Mark would be here in five hours.* She had been having nervous palpitations ever since she arose this morning. *Would Mark be different? Would he think she was different? Would they find anything to talk about?*

At the airport, she was unable to decide whether to wait for Mark at the baggage claim area—he might only have a carry-on bag. In the end, she went to one of the public phones and called in an announcement, "Mark Vail, your party will meet you in the baggage claim area."

Hurrying to the baggage claim area, her nervous apprehension returned. *She and Mark really didn't know each other all that well, despite their history; it had been so long ago. Both of them had changed a lot in the five intervening years. Still, his last visit had been great—*

Totally absorbed in her thoughts, she jumped at the sound of Mark's voice. He was standing right beside her, and he did have only a small carry-on bag. She'd been right to make the announcement. He started to reach for her and then backed off, and she realized he was as nervous as she was.

A smile tugged at his lips and he reached forward to brush a curl back from her forehead. "Hi. I didn't expect to see you here at the airport. You look wonderful . . . but you've lost weight." He frowned slightly.

"All those calisthenics I guess." She shrugged, wishing for this strange awkwardness to be over.

He smiled. "I'm glad you could meet me." *Glad didn't touch it. He could eat her up . . . which reminded him.*

154

Have you eaten?"

"Um, no."

"Want to stop somewhere and get something?" Her shy smile sped up his heartbeat.

"If you don't mind, I'd rather go home. I have a stew simmering in the crockpot . . . but if you'd rather stop—"

"No, that sounds perfect. I'm starved. Airlines don't serve anything but peanuts or pretzels, and I skipped breakfast so I could take care of something before I left this morning."

She looked at him, wanting to ask what was so important that he skipped breakfast, but deciding against it. "Okay. I'm in the parking garage across the street. I see you didn't bring much luggage; I wasn't sure where to meet you."

"Luckily you made the announcement. I try to avoid checking baggage if at all possible. It's such a nuisance having to wait for it."

★   ★   ★

As Jane drove, Mark enjoyed the opportunity to just look at her. *He had missed her more than he would have imagined possible.* Watching her drive, he saw that she did it the same way she did everything, competently, with no wasted motion, nor did she let herself get distracted.

He had such high hopes for this week. It would be his last opportunity for six months, at least, to convince her he wanted, needed her in his life . . . and that he wouldn't disappoint her ever again. A tall order for one week, but certainly not impossible, at least he hoped not.

Although she kept her eyes on the road, and checked the rear-view mirror periodically, Jane's thoughts were

155

on the man beside her. *What would this week bring?* She was still overwhelmed that he was here, really here.

Minutes later they were at her house, and Jane quickly climbed out of the car ahead of Mark. As she inserted her key in the front door, she called to him, "Get your bag—you can clean up while I put out lunch."

As they entered the house, Mark sniffed appreciatively. "What is that wonderful smell?"

She laughed. "It's the stew I told you about; it's been cooking all morning. It should be about ready. I'll set the table while you take your stuff upstairs."

She hurried around the kitchen: getting bowls and utensils before putting a loaf of French bread into the oven to warm. She smiled as she worked; she couldn't wait to tell Mark of the surprise she had for him. When she heard him descending the stairs, she spooned the simmering stew into bowls, and took the bread from the oven and began to slice it.

"Um, it smells good in here. I'm ready to eat the proverbial horse."

"Speaking of horses—do you still ride much?"

He looked surprised that she would mention riding.

"'Fraid not. I'd love to, but except for when I'm in Wyoming . . . no, I haven't ridden in almost a year."

"Well, guess what? You're riding tomorrow." The look of excitement on his handsome face told her she had made a wise choice.

"You're kidding! How? Where? Do you ride?"

She laughed, and her eyes sparkled. "Here. Sit down and let's eat before it gets cold. I'll explain over lunch."

Jane bowed her head as soon as they were seated, and he did the same, remembering how it was always a part of mealtime when he was growing up, and still was over meals at Matt's. A feeling of guilt touched him as he knew he seldom bothered other times. His parents would be disappointed.

His eyes lit up at his first bite of the stew. "Jane, this is incredible."

She laughed again. "It's only stew."

He swallowed a few more spoonsful and then looked at her intently. "Okay. Now, tell me about this riding you have planned. Where are we going? How often do you ride, and when did you learn to ride? You used to be afraid of horses."

"I was, sort of, but I always liked them. I guess you don't remember Kit and me attending your rodeos—there weren't many we missed. I used to hide my eyes sometimes, I was so afraid you were going to fall off!"

She blushed at the admission, and he found it delighted him. "You thought I was going to fall off? I'll have you know, Jane Brewer, I was the Montana Amateur State Champion Bronc Rider my last two years of college. *I don't fall off!*"

"Except that one time, in Kalispell—" She smiled.

"You remember that! You couldn't have been more than—"

"I was twelve, and I was scared to death. When you didn't get up right away, I thought you were dead."

He chuckled. "Of course I wasn't dead, just had the wind knocked out of me, that's all."

"Well, I didn't know that, did I?"

"So, are you going to tell me where we're going riding, or not?" The corners of his eyes crinkled as he smiled at her.

"Remember, at Christmas, I mentioned that my friend Ellen was going home to Texas?"

157

"Okay."

"She was born and raised on a cattle ranch there. Her family also has a ranch <u>here</u> where they ship cattle to grow fat on Montana's lush grass. It's about half-an-hour from here, and Ellen spends almost every weekend out there. Since she taught me to ride, I'm there almost as much as she is."

"And that's where we're going tomorrow? Way to go! I never dreamed I'd get a chance to ride. And on real horses! Wow!

"What do you mean '*real*' horses? What other kind are there?"

"You know . . . I mean not riding stable horses. Real ranch horses. Like my own—"

He stopped, but Jane had caught the last word.

"Your own . . . what?"

"Nothing."

She was curious but decided to let it go for now, even though it was the second time he had made an odd reference.

"I was worried you might not have any riding clothes with you, but I should have known better. The first thing I noticed when I saw you at the airport was the boots."

"I <u>always</u> wear boots when I'm not in uniform."

"You didn't have them on at the wedding . . . or when we went to the club."

"Well, almost always. Kit would have killed me if I wore boots in her wedding."

"I know that's why they call you 'Bronc,' but I have a feeling you never told your friends you were a <u>champion</u> bronc rider." The way his cheeks reddened told her she was right.

"Maybe not."

158

"Mark Vail! And I thought fighter pilots were the cockiest, most confident breed alive."

"I'm confident—just not a braggart!"

She laughed at the disgruntled look on his face.

Jane awoke the next morning after a night spent restlessly tossing and turning, staring into the darkness listening for any sound from across the hall, wondering if Mark was doing the same thing. *She still couldn't believe he was here. And today they were going riding together!* She sat up, anxious to start the day. The smell of fresh coffee and bacon drifted in from the hallway, and she heard sounds coming from the kitchen. Puzzled, she looked at her small bedside clock—seven a.m. Not all that late—Mark must be an early riser.

Embarrassed that he was up before her, she found her robe, rammed her arms into the sleeves, and without stopping to hunt for slippers or brush her hair, padded down the hallway in her bare feet.

Mark's back was to her, and she watched him move confidently around her kitchen. Two glasses of orange juice sat on the counter, beside plates and silverware. Bacon sizzled in the pan, and eggs sat in a bowl beside the stove, ready to be cracked into the skillet. He even had bread waiting in the toaster. He seemed perfectly comfortable in her kitchen! In fact, he looked as if he was used to fixing breakfast, and did it often.

"Good morning!" He spun around, just looking at her for several seconds without speaking. Embarrassed, she began to move backward, out of the room.

"I heard you, and I . . . I didn't think. I just came down without getting dressed." She looked down at her bare

159

feet, and put her hand up to touch her uncombed hair. She pulled the sash of her robe tighter around her waist. "I'm sorry—I'll be right back."

Before she could leave the room, he stepped forward. He knew his stare had made her uncomfortable, but he had been unable to help it. *She was lovely with her hair curling in an aureole around her head, her face fresh and rosy from sleep, and the slight look of confusion in her eyes.* He reached out and gently touched her cheek. "Don't go. You look lovely." He grasped her arm and pulled her further into the room. "Come, sit down. Breakfast is almost ready. I'll have the eggs up in a minute."

She let him push her into a chair at the small table in the window alcove, watched dazedly as he set a glass of juice in front of her. He pushed the lever on the toaster down, and deftly lifted the perfectly browned bacon, laid it on a paper towel to drain, then smoothly broke several eggs into the pan.

"I hope you don't mind my taking over your kitchen. You were sleeping so soundly, and I wanted to do this for you."

She put her hand to her mouth. *He had seen her sleeping* . . .

"No . . . of course I don't mind. It's great . . . but how come you know so much about cooking? When do you have time to cook?"

He chuckled as he set the toast in front of her and turned to scoop the eggs from the skillet and put them on a plate with the bacon.

"And who do you think has been taking care of me all these years?"

She went silent, remembering he was only nineteen

160

when his parents died, and he had become responsible for all of his siblings. "I'm sorry . . . I know you had to take over when your parents died. I just meant . . ."

He sat down in the chair across from her, reached out and put a hand on hers, and his eyes held hers as he gave her a gentle smile.

"It's okay, Jane. I know what you meant. I'd forgotten what a gentle creature you are."

She took a sip of juice and began to eat the food on her plate, stopping in surprise. "Wow! You're a great cook. These eggs are perfect, and so is the bacon. You must do quite a bit of cooking."

"Hawk and I had a house together before he and Kit got married. He's a disaster in the kitchen, so our division of duties fell, more or less, that he did the cleaning between maid-days, and I did most of the cooking. I wasn't bad—Mom made all of us learn to cook. She said being a man was no excuse not to know how to feed yourself. After she and Dad . . . after the accident, Kit and I took turns fixing the meals. At first things were pretty basic, but we both got better. By the time I left home, I could keep myself from starving. Hawk never complained."

"You must miss him now that he and Kit live on the other side of the country."

"Do I ever! I thought about getting another housemate, but decided just to terminate the lease on the house."

"But what will you do with all your furniture, your stuff?"

"There's not that much. We rented the place furnished. It's mostly just my clothes, family photos, large-screen TV—personal stuff. I rented a storage locker near the base and moved into the Bachelor Officer Quarters. Makes it simple now that I'm leaving for six months."

"But what about when you come back?"

"Depends. I may be reassigned or . . . who knows? I can always stay in the Quarters until I decide what I want to do."

"Do you mind moving around so much, not having roots, never knowing where you're going to end up?" *What a lonely life!* But of course, she was being ridiculous. What made her think he was alone? A man like him would always have women after him. She'd never dared to ask Kit if he was dating anyone, but assuredly he would have been. Had he changed? He'd left her before, with no qualms at all. He'd been really great about keeping in touch with her while she was in COT . . . and he was here now, but . . . when he left for Afghanistan, would she hear from him, see him again?

Mark noticed the cloud cross her face, the way she sat up straighter and firmed her shoulders. *What was she thinking about?* He reached out and grasped her hand. *It was so easy to touch her, and so hard not to do more than touch.* "You're here, but your mind is somewhere else. What are you thinking about, Jane? And, what caused the shadow on your face?"

Goodness! He saw way too much. She was going to have to do better at hiding her thoughts and feelings. Something she had never been good at. "Just wondering what you had been doing the last six years . . . where you had been—" She felt her face warming. *What was wrong with her? Talk about hiding her feelings . . . what a numbskull she was.* "I . . . please forget what I just said, Mark. I don't know why I said it."

162

"Why should I forget it? It's a natural question. I certainly want to know what you've been doing, and you have every right to ask the question. I don't mind answering it."

"I'm not sure I—"

"Don't be silly."

He stood and picked up the dishes, but she stopped him with a hand on his arm.

"No way are you doing the dishes, not after fixing breakfast. You're _my_ guest, remember."

"Then we'll do them <u>together</u>, and while we do them I'll tell you what I've been doing, and then you can tell me. Deal?"

She was forced to grin. *He knew exactly how to get around her, always had.* "Deal."

Several hours later they approached the turn-off for the Whitaker ranch, and she motioned to Mark. "This is where we turn. It's the lane to the ranch. We're almost there, even though you can't see the house and barns yet."

Mark nodded, anxious to see the ranch Jane had been describing with such enthusiasm. It was obvious she loved coming here, and that she loved riding even more. He felt a rush of happiness at the knowledge—he'd been afraid she might be too much of a city girl to be happy on a ranch . . . his ranch.

"There it is!" Jane sang out gleefully.

He looked out the window on his side of the car and caught his first glimpse of the ranch house. It was a sprawling, log-and-stone structure that seemed to hug the land it was built on, giving the appearance of having sprung from the landscape where it was situated. A long veranda ran all the way across the front.

Off to the right were the barns, sheds and a building that was probably a bunk house, various corrals, and a fenced area that looked like a ring used for breaking horses. He sat up in the seat, lowering his window to sniff the air. *It felt like coming home. Lord, how he missed the horses he'd been so close to in his former life.* Jane was almost jumping up and down in the seat, and he had to smile at her enthusiasm as she pointed.

"There! Drive down to the stable. That's Mick. Ellen said she'd ask him to have the horses ready for us at ten, and"—she looked at her watch—"it's straight up, ten."

He pulled up to the left of the driveway, away from the horses. Jane bounded out of the vehicle almost before it stopped, grabbing her Stetson from the back seat.

"Come on, Mark, I'll introduce you." She waited for him to come around the car, before continuing. "Mick has been with Ellen's family forever. He started out as a cowboy, but he's too old to ride the range any longer. Now he works around the stable area, cleaning tack and looking after the horses. He has help when there are more horses here."

Mark got out, settled his black Stetson low on his brow, and stood looking around. His eyes sparkled, and a wide grin split his face. He let out a soft whistle. "*Nice.*"

Jane could see that he was impressed with the horses Mick had saddled for them, and she was as proud as if they had been her own. As they walked toward the man holding the reins of two horses, she smiled.

"Mick, this is my friend Mark Vail. Thanks for

tacking up for us."

"No problem." He stuck his hand out, and Mark shook it firmly, hardly taking his eyes off the tall black horse shaking his head and pawing the ground impatiently.

"Ellen said you were a champion bronc rider."

Mark's cheeks reddened. "Amateur . . . and it's been a while."

"I can tell you know horses. Ellen was right when she told me to saddle up Prince John here. He needs a strong hand, but he'll give you a good ride . . . and a challenge."

Jane was almost laughing at Mark's excitement. He looked like a little boy about to meet Santa Claus.

Easing up to the horse, he slowly put out his hand and began to stroke the horse between his ears while talking to him softly. She couldn't understand the words, but the horse pricked his ears up as if he did.

Mark looked back at Mick. "He's a real beauty. How old is he?"

"Four. He was born here. His Daddy is King John, the pride of the ranch."

Mark was easing his hands down over the big horse's chest, all the while continuing his soft talking. He had totally forgotten about Jane for the moment, but seeing his pleasure, she didn't mind at all.

After a few minutes he turned back to her. "You ready?"

She handed him the saddle pack filled with their lunch.

Mick had saddled Golden, her usual mount. The beautiful Palomino gelding knew her, and whickered softly at her approach. When she stood next to the horse, Golden leaned his head over and nuzzled the pocket of her long-sleeved shirt, looking for the sugar she always carried. She laughed. "Just hold on, Golden. You know I wouldn't forget." She reached in her pocket and took out two cubes of sugar, giving one to the waiting horse and handing the second to Mark who immediately placed it on his palm and held it out to Prince John. The horse's velvety soft lips moved over his hand until they found the sugar cube. The horse wasted no time in licking it up.

Mark loosened Golden's reins and turned to Jane, cupping his hands to give her a leg up to the high stirrup. Once she was on the horse, he handed her the reins, then turned and easily put his foot in the stirrup and swung lightly into Prince John's saddle. Watching him, Jane knew she would never look—or feel—as comfortable and at ease on a horse as he did. He looked perfect. Still, she <u>had</u> come a long way.

Mark looked down at the old man watching them.

"Thanks again, Mick. I'll do the untacking and make sure they're rubbed down when we get back. I assume Jane knows where they go?"

"She does, but I'll be here. Y'all have a good ride now." He continued to watch as they rode away from the stable and headed out to the faint trail leading across the grass towards the mountains in the distance.

They rode in comfortable silence, and Jane felt no compulsion to speak. It was a perfect day for a ride. Spring had come to the area, and a light breeze ruffled her hair where it hung below her hat. Suddenly Mark reached up and gave his Stetson a firm push down on his head. Then he turned to her, his expression again that of an excited little boy.

"Do you mind if we step up the pace? Prince here is just itching to let go—I can feel it."

166

She laughed. "And so are you, if I know anything."

He shrugged and then grinned.

She gripped her reins more firmly, and took off, calling over her shoulder. "Let's go. We're headed for that clump of trees just over the next rise."

He laughed delightedly, already giving the big horse his head. "You're on."

Racing across the lush green grass, the sun warm on her shoulders, and Mark closing in on her, Jane didn't think she had ever been happier. *So what if it was only temporary? Today was perfect.*

Mark and Prince soon passed her and Golden, but she didn't mind, and it wasn't long before Mark reined the big horse in enough so that they didn't leave her too far behind. The horses' long strides ate up the distance, and soon they could see the sun's glint on the stream winding its way beneath the trees in the clump where they were headed.

Mark pulled up and dismounted to wait for her. After dropping Prince's reins over his head, he reached up to lift her down. She stumbled slightly and fell against him. He leaned forward and kissed her lightly, then immediately released her.

"Thank you for this, Jane. You can't know how much it means to me. It's been forever since I've ridden, and I didn't know how much I missed it. I . . . thank you."

"I know how much you love horses; you always did— and I wanted to surprise you."

Unwilling to let Mark see her feelings for him, she quickly grabbed the blanket she had fastened behind her saddle, then turned and spread it on the grassy bank of the stream. Here, the shade from the trees would protect them from the rays of the sun, already strong at mid-day even though it was still early spring.

Mark unfastened the saddle bag that held their lunch, and handed it to her with a grin. "This is heavy. What did you pack?"

Smiling as she unpacked it, she hauled out several bottles of water, two apples, a plastic bag filled with man-sized sandwiches, a bag of cookies, and a container of potato salad. Mark's eyes lit up, and she was thankful she had packed a big lunch.

"Those wouldn't be *chocolate chip* cookies, would they?"

"They would. I didn't have time to bake, but I had these in the freezer."

Mark rolled his eyes. "I never forgot your Mom's chocolate chip cookies. I can still remember the five of us coming to your back door. Your Mom knew only Kit would be staying to play with you—the rest of us would be off on our own pursuits—but she always got that blue cookie jar down and handed out those wonderful cookies to every one of us."

His eyes were not seeing her, but the past, and she stilled, not wanting to interrupt his thoughts. Suddenly he shook his head, and looked at her, a funny half-smile on his face.

"Long time ago. . ."

"Yes. It was so great that you all lived next door. I never minded being an only child because I had 'Kit and her brothers.' Did you know that I used to pretend you were my family?"

"That's because you didn't know the real us." He grinned as he met her gaze. "I'm sure Kit told you all the traumas we put her through."

Jane was thoughtful, as she continued to unwrap and

168

set out the food. "I guess . . . but sometimes you used to let us play with you, and that was *wonderful*."

He grinned wryly. "As I recall, usually when we let you play with us it was because we needed an Indian captive, or someone to kidnap, or an assistant to hold the tools while we were building a fort."

She laughed. "It was still fun."

"But then you and Kit grew up, and the boys started noticing—"

"You never did."

"No?"

"Don't look like that. You know I was never anything but your kid sister's pesky friend. By the time I was grown up enough for the boys to notice, you were a rodeo champion, brushing the girls away like flies."

"Maybe. Still . . . I noticed."

Jane's eyes widened, and she just looked at him. Before she could think what to say, the moment was lost as he reached for a bottle of water, unscrewed the cap, and took a long drink. She watched the movement of his throat as he swallowed, and was overcome with a hunger for this man she had dreamed about for so long. Forcing herself to look away, she busied herself with the food.

"I made ham and cheese, and roast beef. Which do you want?"

He reached for the roast beef, and she handed him a plate with potato salad, pleased that everything was still cold from the freezer packs she had stashed with the food.

Both of them became silent, eating and just enjoying being together. The horses grazed contentedly on the plentiful grass, a light breeze stirred the warm air, and dappled shade fell on their blanket. Jane sighed softly. *If things could just stay like this forever . . . but of course they wouldn't—couldn't.* Deep in thought, she was startled when Mark spoke.

"What's your commitment to the Reserves?"

She frowned at him, surprised by the sudden change in topic. "I signed up for four years."

He nodded thoughtfully. "I have twelve more years . . . if I stay for retirement."

"Are you thinking of getting out? I thought you loved flying?"

"I probably won't get out before I have my twenty years, especially if I make Major. Hawk and I should make it the next go-round. But . . ."

"But what? Are you having second thoughts?"

"I'm not sure. Maybe I realize there are other things I want to do in my life, and I'm not getting any younger." Her laugh rippled over him, and he realized he loved the sound.

"Yes, Grandpa."

He grinned back at her, and then regained his serious expression. "Flying fighter jets is a young man's occupation. I still love it, but—"

She tipped her head and looked at him in surprise. "But what?"

"Remember earlier when I started to tell you something, and didn't?"

She hadn't forgotten a thing he said, but didn't think she wanted to tell him that. "When you insisted it was 'nothing'?"

He nodded. "I have a small ranch in Wyoming." He waited anxiously for her reaction. At first she seemed stunned. Her mouth almost dropped open before she

170

controlled it.

"Mark Vail, when did you buy a ranch! Does Kit know about this? How do you take care of a ranch when you're in the Air Force—you're not even close to . . . where in Wyoming is it?"

He laughed out loud. "Now you sound like that pesky little kid who used to accompany Kit—trailing behind me asking forty million questions about what we were doing and how come?"

She reddened, remembering that little girl too, and how, even then, she had adored him. "Well? How?"

"I bought it about three years ago. And no, no one knows about it. I didn't intend to keep it a secret—it just never seemed the time to mention it. And you're right, I don't get out there very often."

"But then who takes care of it?"

"I ran into a mechanic—Sergeant Frank Mason—just after I got to Luke. He was from Wyoming, and we used to talk some about growing up out here. When he found out I was crazy about horses and used to ride broncs, he asked me what my plans were after the Air Force. Up 'til then, I didn't have any plans—I was too into jockeying planes around the sky."

Jane was spellbound by this surprising revelation. Not wanting to interrupt his story, she quietly opened the bag of cookies and set them on a napkin, uncorked the thermos of coffee, and poured two cups, setting one in front of him. When he grinned and reached for a handful of cookies and the cup of coffee, she resettled herself and looked up at him.

"So, go on. Tell me the rest."

"Frank was in the hangar most days when I was getting ready to fly. One day I noticed he was missing. I

171

asked around, found out his Dad had died, and he had gone home on thirty-day leave. When he came back, he cornered me and asked me if I had thought any more about what I was going to do when I got out. Since it was obvious I was a long way from retiring, I told him I hadn't. I was surprised he had even asked."

"And why had he?"

"Well, the family ranch was going up for sale. Apparently, there were several other siblings, but none of them had any interest in ranching. Frank said he wasn't financially in a position to buy them out, and wasn't sure he even wanted to, but it had occurred to him that I might be interested. I was amazed that he would think I would be interested in buying a ranch."

"So, what did you tell him?"

"He had obviously expected my reaction and came prepared to convince me why I <u>should</u> be interested. He said even though retirement seemed a long way off to me, due to the current market, the asking price was reasonable. He told me retirement would come around before I realized it, and since I was such a horse lover, this was perfect."

Jane's forehead wrinkled as she tried to understand.

"Yeah, that was my reaction. I thought he was really full of it; but he kept right on talking, and I started seeing possibilities. He said it was a small horse ranch, and would be perfect for someone who wanted to raise horses for the rodeo circuit—"

Jane's mouth curved up into a grin. "And that's where he had you."

"Yep! I was beginning to see, but I still had a lot of questions like, who was going to take care of this ranch, assuming I did buy it, and how did he know I could even afford it, when I wasn't even sure I could?"

His eyes were full of excitement, and she loved seeing him so happy.

"He had answers to all my questions. Seems he was due to retire within the year—the guy was almost old enough to be my father. I don't know why we ever struck up a friendship, but I really liked the man. Anyway, the upshot was that he'd be willing to live on the ranch and act as caretaker until I was ready to move out there. Said there was some stock that went with it, and if I wanted to run some horses, he could keep his eye out for good buys. Since he was willing to live there, I asked him why in the hell he didn't just buy it himself. He had an answer for that too. Said in the first place, he couldn't afford it; and in the second place, he didn't want the responsibility long-term."

"Wow! In a way I'm totally surprised . . . but you know what, Mark? I can really see you on a ranch. Actually, I can see you more as a rancher than I can as a fighter pilot."

She saw him raise his head and frown, and hurried to clarify what she meant. "Not that you aren't a good pilot. I know you are; you were always good at whatever you did. You have that single-minded determination to be the best. It's just that horses always seemed . . ." She trailed off, not sure how to explain.

Mark shrugged his shoulders, "Now you know."

"Is Frank still there? Did he retire? And do you have horses there?"

He grinned at her questions, glad she hadn't changed in all ways. "Yep, he did retire; and he's still there. We have about fifty horses now, some good breeding stock. I get out there about once a year, and he sends me

173

monthly reports. I call periodically. It's worked out well, better than I would ever have imagined."

"I just can't believe that your family doesn't know."

"I'll tell them eventually. Just . . . not yet."

He wanted to ask her if she could see herself living so far from all the conveniences she was used to, but it was too early.

Jane, meanwhile, had been watching the sky and noticed thunderclouds rolling in from the distant mountains.

"I wish we could stay longer, but I don't like the look of that sky."

Mark had been facing the trees, away from the mountains, but after a glance behind him he agreed with her.

"You're right. If we don't want to get wet, we'd better pack up and head back right now."

They both stood, and in minutes everything was picked up, the saddlebag and blanket lashed behind their saddles, and they were ready to leave.

As Mark stooped to pick up Golden's reins, Jane reached out and touched his arm. "Thank you for telling me, Mark. It means a lot that you trusted me enough. I'll keep your secret, I promise." His eyes locked onto hers, and the flicker of emotion she saw in them made her tremble.

He spoke softly, "I wanted to tell you before, but I was afraid it might . . . might. . ." Instead of finishing the sentence he grabbed her around the waist and pulled her close into a hard embrace. This time his kiss was not merely a friendly peck, but a deep promise. Her hands slipped around his neck, and she pressed close against him, feeling as if she had come home. She wanted the kiss to go on forever, but suddenly he leaned away, released her, and turned to pick up the reins.

When he turned back to give her a leg up, his expression revealed nothing; it was as if the kiss had never happened. Within minutes he had mounted his horse, and they were headed back to the ranch, the storm chasing them.

Chapter 8

The rain began to fall as they approached the barns. No sooner were they inside than it turned into a downpour. Before they could remove the saddles and rub down their horses, Mick appeared out of the gloom, grinning.

"That's what I call cutting it close. You almost got wet."

Both Jane and Mark began to speak, but Mark stopped and let her talk. She smiled at him, then turned to Mick.

"I wasn't paying close enough attention. When I noticed the clouds coming out of the mountains, the storm was already moving toward us. We raced the whole way back and still, as you say, just made it."

Mick grinned again, and Jane could tell he had his own ideas about what had distracted them. "Want me to do that?"

This time Mark spoke up. "No. We rode them, we'll take care of them. Thanks."

"Okay, I'll just go finish cleaning the tack." Mick walked off toward the little room at the end of the main corridor of the barn, leaving an uncomfortable silence behind.

Jane kept her eyes on the currycomb she was using to make long sweeps across Golden's withers. Eventually she dared to peep at Mark. He was just as carefully brushing Prince John, his eyes also fully on the job at hand. When he suddenly looked up, his eyes met hers.

"Mark . . ."

He continued to watch her, raising one eyebrow.

Her mouth got dry. She had started to ask him what happened, what was wrong, but the words wouldn't come. She wasn't sure if it was because she was afraid of the answer, or afraid he might realize how important this week was to her. Eventually, when he continued to watch her without speaking, she looked back at her work, mumbling softly.

"What, Jane?"

"Nothing."

"You're wondering why I pulled away back there, hmmm?"

Again, that raised eyebrow. *How did he know her thoughts so well?* Realizing her expression gave her away, she looked up at him from beneath her lashes, and nodded. "I guess I was."

"Let's finish up here and head back to your place. Then we'll talk."

His expression revealed nothing. Afraid she knew what the talk would encompass, she felt a sense of dread.

They finished their work in silence, and by the time the horses were back in their stalls with full feed boxes, the rain had tapered off to a quiet drizzle.

Mark gave Prince's nose one last pat and turned to face Jane. "You ready? I think this is the best chance we're gonna get," he said, nodding toward the quiet rain falling outside the open stable door.

A sense of foreboding settled over her, and she was unable to answer. Instead, she took off for the car in a mad dash, diving into the front seat while Mark was still standing in the barn. When he finally stepped out into the rain, he walked slowly, appearing to be in deep thought and totally unconcerned about getting wet. *What was he thinking so hard about?*

He opened the car door and slid in, turning as he did so to study her, his eyes warm. "Thank you, Jane, for a wonderful afternoon."

She nodded. "You're welcome."

Her mind still on the upcoming talk, she could think of nothing further to say. Mark put the car in gear and began the drive home as she stared fixedly through the windshield.

"Jane. . ."

She didn't look at him, and when she spoke, her voice was soft. "What?"

"Jane, what's wrong? Did I say something to upset you?"

She glanced away from the road long enough to look at him. When she turned back without saying anything, he reached over and lightly touched her arm.

"Jane?"

She shook her head. "Nothing is wrong."

"Then why did I see fear in your eyes just now . . . and why are you so quiet?"

Surprised that he had noticed the fear in her eyes, and

178

unable to deny that it was there, she bit her lip, unsure what to say. Risking another look at him, she saw him frown and knew he was trying to figure out what he might have said to upset her.

The rain suddenly stopped, and the sight of the sun peeking through scattered clouds raised her spirits. She wanted to defuse his obvious worry, but she didn't know how.

"Jane, please tell me what's wrong."

She forced a smile. "It was what you said back there. I thought everything had been so perfect . . . and then you said . . ."

"Said what? What did I say?"

"You said, 'We have to talk.'"

Mark's eyebrows raised in surprise at her answer. "But, we do. Why should that upset you?"

"Because . . . when I was growing up, whenever my Dad said, *'We have to talk*,' it always meant I was in trouble, and I knew I wasn't going to like what he had to say. I guess I'm afraid of what you're going to say."

"Oh, Jane."

He was trying to keep from smiling, and she knew she had sounded foolish.

"I'll try to remember never to use those words—even though this time I hope you'll like what I plan to say."

He grinned mischievously, and her heart lightened as she gave him an answering smile.

They pulled into her driveway, and she used her remote to open the garage door, and he pulled the car inside. The car had barely stopped before he spoke.

"You go on in. I'll get the picnic things out of the trunk."

She opened the door into the laundry room and went

into the kitchen, unable to free herself from the sense of foreboding, foolish though it might be. *Mark had said she would like what he was going to say. How could he be so sure? In four days he would return to his base—and in less than a week leave for Afghanistan. How could any kind of relationship survive that—the two of them at opposite ends of the earth?*

She was washing her hands when she heard Mark in the laundry room returning the picnic gear to its place. A few minutes later he was in the kitchen, right behind her.

"I put the blanket and backpack on the shelves. Do you want me to empty the picnic basket?"

"No, just leave it here; I'll take care of it later. I feel like a cup of tea. How about you?"

"I think I'd rather have a beer, but don't you want to get out of your wet clothes first?" He moved to get the beer, glancing over his shoulder at her.

As she filled the blue teakettle, she realized she had been so worried about Mark's upcoming 'talk,' she had totally forgotten she was wet. "I'll change while the water is heating. What about you?"

"I'm on my way—I'll take my beer with me."

A short time later she came out of her bedroom in a pair of sweatpants and much washed t-shirt, and heard the teakettle whistling. *Perfect timing.*

She poured hot water into her favorite china teapot and set it on a tray with a cup and saucer and a second bottle of beer for Mark. She had just picked up the tray when she saw him coming down the stairs; sucking in a deep breath she set the tray back on the counter. A clean pair of faded jeans rode low on his lean hips, and he was barefoot. He held his empty beer bottle in one hand, and was buttoning his shirt with the other. The sight of his six-pack abs and the dark hair covering his chest riveted her attention. At his grin, she quickly looked away. She was still trying to get her mind to work when he set the empty bottle on the counter, picked up the tray, and headed toward the sliding glass doors to the deck.

Shaking her head as if recovering from a dizzy spell, she spoke the first words to come into her mind, "Won't it be wet out there?" He turned to face her, grinning mischievously.

"Don't tell me you're afraid of melting?"

"Of course not, but we *did* just change clothes."

"I got it covered," he smirked as he elbowed the door open, set the tray on the wrought iron table, and pulled a towel out of his waistband.

She couldn't help but laugh at his self-satisfied smile as he began to wipe down the seat of the old-fashioned glider. She wasn't sure she should be sitting that close to him, but she definitely didn't want to mention it—and since all the other seats were wet . . . He finished drying and swept his arm out, flourishing the towel.

"Your seat awaits, ma'am."

This time she really did laugh as she sat down in the glider.

He walked over to the table and poured her tea. He handed her the cup, and she set it on the small end table beside her. As he went back to the tray to pick up his beer, she looked down at her hands, clasped in her lap.

He came to stand beside her. Instead of sitting, he leaned down, grasped her chin in one lean hand and moved her head up until she was staring into his smoky brown eyes, their faces only inches apart.

He studied her for several seconds. She moistened her lips, and he sucked in a deep breath.

"Don't be afraid of me, Jane. I promise, I'll never do anything to hurt you again. Not *ever*."

His dark eyes held hers, and she had the feeling his words were a vow to himself as well as to her. At her almost imperceptible nod, he leaned closer and brushed her lips with a soft kiss. She responded immediately; he abruptly pulled back and sat down beside her. She felt the blush warming her face and looked away from him.

"Jane, please stop. I didn't want to quit any more than you did, but we need to talk first. If I hadn't stopped just then, we both know what would have happened." He leaned back and took a long swig of his beer.

She watched his strong neck as he swallowed. Suddenly feeling the need for her own drink, she reached over and picked up the cup of tea, took a hearty drink, and almost burned her throat. Coughing and sputtering, she was forced to set the cup down lest she spill it.

Mark reached out and touched her shoulder. "Are you all right? What happened?"

"Nothing. I didn't realize how hot the tea would be. It was silly of me." His eyes reflected worry as he continued to look at her.

"Are you sure you're all right?"

"I'm fine." Despite her embarrassment, she had to smile at her use of the familiar word.

Assured that she really was all right, Mark leaned back again which set them gently rocking, then looked out across the yard,

After several seconds of silence, she carefully took another sip of her tea. Mark was still looking out across the yard. He appeared to be miles away, and when she reached out and touched his arm, he jerked.

"Sorry. I was trying to figure out how to say what I want to . . . what I *need* to say."

"Why is it so hard?"

"It not that it's hard, it's just . . . so important. I'm afraid I'll screw it up."

What was he going to say? . . . That they shouldn't see each other anymore?

"You better just say it. If you don't, I'm going to pass out trying to imagine how bad it's going to be."

"Why do you insist on thinking it's going to be bad?"

Now she was getting angry. "Just <u>tell</u> me!"

He stopped the rocking and half-turned in the glider, facing her and reaching for one of her hands where it lay in her lap. Enclosing her small hand in his large one, he absently rubbed her palm with his thumb, and she had to force herself to concentrate on what he was about to say, instead of on what he was making her feel.

"Jane, this week is going by too fast. I realize a week is not enough time for me to show you that I really have changed, that I'm not the same young kid who treated you so badly. I know it's too soon, that I shouldn't say anything at all."

She held her breath as he gripped her hand even tighter, his eyes stormy and troubled.

"Mark—"

"No, please let me finish before you say anything."

He took a deep breath and looked away. When he looked back, he seemed to have made up his mind.

"I shouldn't say this now, but I can't leave—not with so much time and distance between us—I have to tell you."

"Mark, say it. Whatever it is you want to say, *please*, just say it."

183

He looked down at their clasped hands, then met her eyes. "Okay, here goes. I know it took courage for you to agree to have dinner with me after the wedding. As I said before, I knew you wanted to say no. I also felt your mixed feelings about my coming to visit you in December." He hesitated, but when she started to interrupt, he put a finger softly to her lips. "Please . . . let me finish while I still can." He took a deep breath and continued, "I want to thank you for having the courage to give me a second chance; it means . . . it means—"

"Mark, I told you—"

"Jane, wait, let me finish. We still have a couple of days left, and I hope by the end of this week . . . by the time I leave . . . you will feel we've gotten to know each other again, gotten closer."

He leaned in until their lips were almost touching. She knew he was going to kiss her, and she wanted him to. Instead he spoke even more urgently, and she didn't know how to react.

"Jane, I don't want us to drift apart again. I'll call you whenever I can, and I'll email you, just like I did while you were in COT. Will you do the same?"

This was so not what she had expected—*it was so much better*—and her heart soared with hope. She realized he was waiting for her answer.

"I promise to answer every email I get."

"And *I* promise you'll get lots of them, maybe just a line or two, but you will get them."

Relieved to have the 'talk' over at last, she smiled up at him, glad that it hadn't been as bad as she had feared. "You're right, I do like it."

He looked nonplussed for a minute, then grinned. "I told you." Then he leaned forward, gripped her waist and, picking her up carefully, swung her over onto his lap, where he hugged her tightly before placing his lips against hers in a kiss so tender she felt like crying.

All sign of the earlier rain was now gone, and the sky around them reflected a beautiful sunset. She felt as if it were a sort of benediction, a sign of hope. Mark kissed her lightly on the back of her neck, then dropped his arms and leaned back. Surprised, she turned to look up at him, a question in her eyes. "I was so comfortable."

"Me too, but I thought we were having dinner tonight with Ellen and her friend?"

Letting out a groan, Jane stood up and sighed, wishing she hadn't set up the double date. "I had forgotten, good thing you didn't." After a quick glance at her watch, she spoke again. "Wow! We're going to have to hurry. I told Ellen we'd meet her and Dennis at six at the Golden Spurs Restaurant—it's less than an hour to that now!"

"No problem, we're already showered. I can be ready in twenty minutes."

Jane laughed and, determined not to be outdone, started running for her room, calling over her shoulder.

"Bet I can be ready before you—I'll meet you at the door in fifteen minutes."

Fifteen minutes later when he came out of his room, still sliding his belt through the loops, he was surprised to see Jane standing in front of the door, grinning like a Cheshire cat. Even more amazing was how she looked—he swallowed hard—*wonderful*. His fingers stilled on the belt as he took in the picture she made. Her short blonde hair, normally windblown into a halo around her face, was slicked into short wisps across her forehead and behind her ears. Her usual scrubbed look was not in evidence tonight. Instead she had highlighted her green eyes with shadow, and dark eyeliner extended their length at the corners enhancing their feline appearance. Her mouth—her mouth was simply made for kissing, and he knew that it was going to be a pure struggle to keep his vow from flying out the window tonight. As he watched her, Jane's smile disappeared, and a look of concern appeared in her eyes. Obviously, he had been staring, and it had unnerved her.

"Sorry, I didn't mean to make you uncomfortable, but when you hit a man with a look like that, you have to expect to bowl him over."

"I bowled you over? Wow! And it only took me fourteen minutes too," she said smugly, glancing at her watch. "You, on the other hand, aren't ready yet, and you're, umm, three minutes late."

Still stunned by her appearance, he was unable to respond to her teasing. Instead, he finished with his belt, then reached out and put his hand on her arm and headed them toward the door. "Well, I guess we'd better get moving then."

"We still have ten minutes."

She stopped outside the door and turned to watch as he pulled it closed and checked to ensure it was locked. Puzzled by the change his attitude since he'd come out of his room, she thought back over what he had said. *Had she really "bowled him over?" She had assumed he was teasing, but what if he wasn't? What if he wasn't!* She hugged the thought to herself and determined to pursue the possibility further as the evening progressed.

When he turned around, Mark took another few

186

seconds to scan her body from head to toe, then grinned at her before grabbing her hand. "Come on *femme fatale,* let's get this show on the road."

Jane's mouth dropped open. What had gotten into this man? She shook her head. Whatever it was, she wasn't complaining. This evening was going to be fun!

"What did you say Dennis does?"

"He's the ranch foreman. He's a Texas Aggie, and he always had a thing for Ellen. The problem was, she'd known him forever and sort of took him for granted."

"And he *let* her? Doesn't sound like any Texas Aggie I've ever known."

"Apparently he was just 'giving her enough rope.'"

Mark threw back his head and laughed. "How'd that work?"

"Pretty well, I'd say; they got engaged over Christmas vacation."

He laughed again. "I'll have to remember that." When the comment earned him a questioning look, he winked.

Within minutes, they were at the restaurant. Jane leaned forward to look out the windshield. "Hey! There they are! How about that—we got here at the same time!"

She lowered her window and leaned out to hail her friend. "Ellen! Over here!"

Ellen waved, and headed toward them. Mark parked, but before he could get out, Jane bounced out of the car and began talking excitedly with Ellen and Dennis.

"Ellen, this is my friend, Mark Vail. Mark, Ellen Whitaker and her fiancé, Dennis Martin."

Mark leaned forward to shake hands with Dennis, and immediately revised his earlier opinion of the man. Dennis's firm grip and friendly smile told him that this

187

was a man he was going to like. Noting Dennis's eyes on Ellen, he recognized the man's feelings for Ellen duplicated his own for Jane.

Ellen turned to him and spoke. "Well, Mark, how did you like your ride?"

"It was fantastic, Ellen. Thanks for setting it up."

"Dennis, you've got some nice horseflesh out there. Jane tells me you're a feeder ranch for—"

Jane and Ellen looked at each other and shook their heads. "We've lost them for the night, Ellen."

"I know. What were we thinking, putting two cowboys together?"

Jane leaned closer to Ellen and whispered, "Does Dennis know Mark is a former rodeo rider?"

"No, does Mark know Dennis was too?"

She groaned. "No. Now we're really in for it." She laughed. She wasn't really upset, just glad that the two men would find common ground.

★　★　★

As they left the restaurant several hours later Jane smiled to herself. It had been a fun evening. She was happy that Mark seemed to like her friends and, even happier that the feeling seemed to be mutual. It would be fun to get together again . . . except there was no more time. As she thought of how quickly the time was flying by, the smile faded from her face.

They reached the car and Mark opened her door, but instead of helping her in, he turned her to face him, clasped her face in both hands and spoke softly.

"What just happened, Jane? What were you thinking of to turn that lovely smile into sadness?"

She hadn't realized Mark had been watching her, and

188

now that he'd caught her, she was unsure whether or not to let him in on her thoughts. "Nothing special." As she spoke, she looked away from him, but he pulled her face back, and kissed her lightly on the forehead.

"I think it was," he said. "Tell me, please."

She hesitated and took a breath. "I . . . all right."

Satisfied that she would tell him, he helped her into the car, then went around to the other side. Once inside the car, he fastened his seatbelt, then turned to face her. "I like both of your friends, Jane. Tonight was fun; I'm glad you set it up. I could tell you had fun too. So how come your face went from happy to sad just now?"

She looked at him, amazed that he was so perceptive.

He smiled. "You may as well realize you can't hide things from me. Your face reflects your emotions as soon as you have them."

Flustered that he was able to read her so well, she put her hands over her face, but he reached out and removed them.

"Don't! I'm glad. We should never keep secrets from each other."

Her heart seemed to stop, and she lowered her eyes again, remembering the huge secret she kept from him. She had known for some time she had to tell him; she just couldn't imagine how she was going to do it.

"Don't you agree?"

She had to think—*what had he said? Secrets, right.* "Uh, yes. I mean, no. No, we shouldn't."

"Good. We agree! So, what were you thinking?"

"I had a good time tonight. Ellen and Dennis like you, and you seemed to like them. I was thinking it would be fun to do something else with them . . . and then I remembered—we *can't* do anything else with them. We

189

can't do anything else at all. You're leaving at the end of the week. I guess I'm just sad that it all has to end."

"It's not going to end, Jane! That's what I was trying to tell you earlier. Didn't you understand? I'm not leaving forever; we'll still be able to talk and write to each other. In no time at all—"

"Six months is not *no time*, Mark! You say we'll keep in touch . . . but a lot can happen in six months."

"Hold that thought. I'm not going to continue this conversation in the car. Fasten your seatbelt."

Surprised at his abrupt command, she did as he asked. He looked over at her before starting the car, his expression worried, but he made no further comment; neither did she.

They were on River Drive approaching Gibson Park. He drove into the park, pulled up at a clump of picnic tables along the shore of the Missouri River, and turned toward her. "Come on, let's go watch the moon come up over the river."

They got out of the car, and he took her hand and walked toward the tables. Once there, he lifted her and carefully set her on a table, then climbed up to sit beside her, his feet on the bench. Leaning forward, elbows on his knees, he silently contemplated the river. Unsure what to expect, Jane waited for him to speak. Eventually, he leaned back and turned to face her, concern evident in his eyes.

"Jane, where did those thoughts come from? I thought we understood each other."

"We do, *I* do. It's just that I thought . . ."

A light came on in his brain. *How could he not have realized?* Suddenly everything was clear to him. She couldn't forget that once before she had believed him;

190

once before she'd expected him to call, to write. That time he had done neither. Naturally, she would be afraid the same thing would happen again. *He knew he wouldn't let her down again, but how could he make her believe? What could he do?*

"Mark . . . I'm sorry. I believe you, I do. I guess I'm just afraid—"

He put his fingers on her lips and softly stroked them. "Don't be sorry, Jane. You have every right to feel the way you do. That's what I meant when I said earlier that our time was too short, that I hadn't had enough time to show you I'll never do that again. I'm sorrier than you know about what I've put you through, and I know there's no way to abolish the doubts you rightfully have. Just promise me that you won't give up on me—that you'll write as often as you can while we're apart. Then we'll have this conversation again when I get back. Can you do that?"

His velvet brown eyes bored into her own, as if he could compel the promise he was asking her to make. She smiled slightly, knowing that, despite her fears, she'd never even considered not writing. She was older and wiser now, and she intended to make sure he couldn't forget her . . . *even if he tried.*

"Does that smile mean yes?"

His eyes were still on her, and his expression had turned hopeful. "It does! And you let me tell *you* something Mark Vail. I also promise you, I won't <u>let</u> you forget me. You'll get so many emails they'll clog up your server, so many letters they'll weigh down the mail sacks, and your squadron will ask for relief."

She tried to glare at him, but giggled instead, and a rush of thankful relief flowed through him. He stood and

191

pulled her against him, hugging her for all he was worth. He kissed her slowly and tenderly, then hopped off the table and helped her down with a laugh.

"Don't worry, you couldn't send too many emails and letters. The more the better. I may not be able to do quite as well—" He leaned away from her, and looked into her eyes, "—but I promise to write whenever I can. You can count on it."

"Oh Mark, I lo—" She stopped abruptly, horrified at what she had almost said. No way did she want him to know that she loved him, at least not yet.

He gripped both of her arms to keep her from turning away. "What did you start to say, Jane?"

She shook her head. "Nothing. I . . . nothing." She lowered her eyes to avoid looking at him.

He knew there was no use in asking her again. She had made up her mind, but it was all right. It was enough for now. He could be patient, but he would hold that almost said word in his heart until they were together again. He put his fist under her chin and raised her head as he pulled her against him. "You can't see that beautiful moon if you're looking at your lap."

There was amusement in his voice as he said it. She gave him a tentative smile and relaxed against him, thankful that he wasn't going to press her further.

Chapter 9

Two days later Mark woke early, unable to sleep. He donned a pair of jeans and slid his feet into moccasins. Entering the kitchen, he put on a pot of coffee then let himself quietly out the back door. The early morning air was crisp as he stood on the deck and watched the sun rise over the mountains and thought about his ranch in Wyoming. He was glad he had bought it. He wouldn't be able to spend much time there for a long while, but it would be completely paid for by the time he retired, "the good Lord willing, and if the creek don't rise," as his Dad used to say. The thought made him smile. Dad would have approved, and it gave him a sense of satisfaction knowing it was there—especially now that he knew how well Jane could ride, and how much she loved it!

The aroma of fresh coffee told him it had finished brewing. He went back inside to pour himself a cup, listening for any sound that Jane was awake. Reassured that she was still asleep, he took his coffee and went back outside. Taking a sip, he savored the strong brew, then set the cup on the railing. Leaning forward, he put his foot on the lower rail and braced his elbow on his knees. He watched the sunrise, and reflected on the past week.

Today was his last day of leave; he'd catch an early flight back to Luke in the morning. He regretted that their time had been so brief, knowing Jane still had doubts that she could depend on him. The thought brought him up short. It was ironic that she felt that way, since everyone else in his family had depended on him for as long as he could remember. Still . . . she had promised to write, and he felt she would. He knew for damn sure he would. It was a beginning, and the second chance he'd hoped for.

It was probably a good thing their time together was running out. Jane needed to be sure of him, more than she was now, and if they weren't forcibly separated by distance, he doubted he could keep his vow to give her all the time she needed. He smiled, remembering what she had started to say last night. *She'd almost told him she loved him. For now, that was enough.* He laughed out loud. Life was good . . . and Jane had slept long enough!

He headed purposefully into the house and climbed the stairs to her room, where he raised his fist and banged on the door. He heard the rustle of bedclothes and then Jane's voice.

"What! Who's there? What happened?"

"You planning to sleep all day, woman? This is our last day. Breakfast will be ready in fifteen minutes." A loud thump told him she had thrown her pillow at the door. He laughed and headed for the kitchen.

Before getting out of bed, Jane leaned back against the remaining pillow and pushed her tousled hair out of her eyes. She hadn't wanted to wake from her dream—in which Mark had told her he loved her, even asking her to marry him. He was just about to give her a ring when she had been so rudely awakened . . . by him. *Would it ever be more than a dream?* She sighed deeply, then kicked back the covers, slid out of bed, and headed for the bathroom.

Ten minutes later she descended the stairs, after swiping a washcloth over her face, brushing her teeth, and donning faded jeans and a sweatshirt. She'd brushed her hair so quickly static electric had it standing out in a fluff around her face. Trying to beat Mark's deadline, she hadn't even donned shoes but padded downstairs on bare feet. He hadn't heard her approach, and she stood in the kitchen doorway and watched him. He seemed happy this morning, she thought, noting his smile as he slid eggs and bacon from the pan to a plate and set it on the small table. When he turned to reach for the coffee pot, he finally saw her.

"You're in a good mood this morning," she said, trying to smooth down her hair.

"I'm always in a good mood."

"Right," she said dryly. "Your whole family used to complain about what a bear you were when you woke up. I've seen it myself when I used to stay overnight with Kit."

"Untrue, all untrue," he replied, grinning. "Besides, *one* of us has been up long enough to enjoy a beautiful sunrise over the mountains. That's enough to put anyone in a good mood. Anyone who saw it, that is."

His eyes taunted her, but she didn't take the bait.

"I was having too good a dream to wake up. Besides, I can see a gorgeous sunrise anytime." She walked into

195

the kitchen and leaned against the counter.

"Mmm hmm. You'll appreciate these Montana sunrises once you can't see them anymore. The sun coming up over the beautiful Bearpaw Mountains can't help but start a man's day off right." He gave her a sidelong glance.

"I guess." Suddenly he was standing right in front of her, his dark eyes staring into hers. She felt her heart pounding and took a deep breath.

Mark leaned forward and kissed the tip of her nose, his eyes still holding hers as he whispered softly. "What were you dreaming about that was worth missing a Montana sunrise?"

For a minute she was mesmerized. Then she shook her head, gave a small laugh, and moved away from him. "I'll never tell. Didn't you ever hear that dreams don't come true if you tell them to anyone?"

He picked up the coffee pot and moved to fill the two cups on the counter. "You're just making that up because you're afraid to tell me. Did you dream about me?" He grinned at her, one eyebrow raised.

Darn it all, he knew he was making her uncomfortable. She blushed, but her answer was flippant. "You wish."

Instead of taking it the way she'd intended it, he stepped closer and looked at her seriously. "You're right. I do wish." He didn't elaborate. Retrieving the toast, he set it on the table, then pulled out her chair for her and sat down beside her.

She waited for him to continue, but he bowed his head and offered the silent grace he knew she had grown up with. She quickly followed suit, raising her head when he did.

"It's nice to see you still do that. I'm surprised." He flushed, and she knew she'd embarrassed him.

"Actually, I don't. But I didn't even think about it this morning. It just seemed right. I guess being back here reminds me of my parents—we never sat down to a meal without offering grace."

"Well, I think it's nice. I'm glad you did it."

"This is our last day. How shall we spend it?"

She shrugged unhappily. "I wish I didn't have to go to work. I even tried to see if I could pull a double shift for one of my friends tomorrow instead."

"I take it you didn't have any luck."

She shook her head, toying with the slice of toast she had taken before realizing she couldn't eat anything.

He reached out and put his hand on top of hers, stilling it. "Don't. It'll be fine. I'll use this morning to wash my laundry and pack. How about I meet you for lunch? You have to eat, don't you?"

She looked up and smiled. "Of course. My lunch hour is from 11:30 to 12:30, but there's not really enough time to go anywhere."

"That's okay. I can eat in the hospital dining room with you, can't I?"

"Sure, but the food's not all that great."

He grinned and pushed her chin up. "Stop worrying. I'm not coming there for a wonderful meal, but for the wonderful *company*." At last she gave him her lovely smile.

"You're right. I promise to stop complaining about the time we don't have and cram every minute we *do* have with special memories. And now I have to get dressed, or I'll be late for work."

He rose with her, and set his dish in the sink. "I'll

drive you to work, so I'll have your car and can meet you for lunch."

"Oh . . . I never even thought—"

"I'll warm up the car while you get dressed," he said. I'll be out front."

"I'll be out in a few minutes."

She dashed for the bathroom while he headed to the garage.

That afternoon, Jane stood on the front steps of the hospital anxiously scanning the parking lot as she waited for Mark to pick her up. Lunch had been fun, and she had enjoyed introducing him to her friends. She sighed. It had been such a wonderful week, she couldn't believe it was over. She would miss him . . . so much . . . even more so after this visit.

The sound of a horn roused her from her reverie as Mark pulled up in front of the hospital. She ran lightly down the steps and caught the door as he reached across the seat and thrust it open.

"You looked as if you were daydreaming."

"Maybe."

He raised a questioning eyebrow at her attempt to hide a smile. She didn't answer, instead asking a question of her own.

"Did you get everything done today?"

"Laundry and packing, all done. And I have a surprise for you."

Her expression brightened as she looked at him, eyes glowing. "What is it?"

He shook his head and looked pointedly at her seatbelt, waiting for her to fasten it. When she did, he put the car in gear, looked in the mirror, and pulled into traffic.

"What's the surprise, Mark?"

"Nope, not telling. It's a surprise, and you'll have to wait. We're going home so you can change clothes, and then . . ." He looked over at her, his eyes full of mischief.

"Darn it, Mark. If you don't tell me where we're going, how will I know what to wear?"

"Jeans and running shoes will be just fine."

He was wearing his usual faded jeans and dark tee, but instead of the ever-present worn cowboy boots, he wore jogging shoes. Hmmm. That had to be significant.

"It's killing you, isn't it? Don't you like surprises?"

"I guess . . . but I'd rather know!" He burst out laughing, and she found herself grinning back at him. He pulled up in front of her house, and motioned for her to get out with a wave of his hand.

"Hurry up. The sooner you get back the sooner you'll know what the surprise is."

"Aren't you coming in?"

"He looked down at himself. Nope. I'm ready. Now move, woman, move. Time's a wastin'."

"Okay, okay! I'm moving."

She slid out of the car and dashed for the house, fishing in her purse for her house key as she ran. Inside the house she stopped, taken aback by the sight of his packed bag sitting in the living room. Even though she knew he was leaving in the morning, it was a reminder that she didn't want to see.

Fifteen minutes later she ran out of the house, slamming and locking the door behind her. She had left her room in a total mess, her uniform just where she had stepped out of it, taking only enough time to scrub a washcloth over her face and apply fresh lip gloss before sliding into a clean pair of jeans and long-sleeved tee. As an afterthought she had grabbed a sweatshirt, just in case. The late May weather could be cold at night . . . if they were going to be outside.

She was out of breath when she opened the car door and slid into the seat beside Mark. He looked at her, nodded his head as if in approval of her outfit, then leaned over and kissed her lightly.

"What was that for?"

"I couldn't resist," he said, then turned abruptly and backed out into the street. Neither of them said anything as he concentrated on his driving. She looked out the window, curious about their destination. They weren't dressed for dinner in a restaurant, nor for riding or hiking.

She was still speculating when he turned at the sign for the park—the same place he'd brought her the night before. As before, the place appeared deserted—it was a little early in the season, she supposed. This time Mark drove past the picnic tables and right down to the dock, where she noticed a dark green canoe on a trailer tied to a tree.

Mystified, she watched as Mark stopped the car, then came around to open her door.

"Well, are you ready for your surprise?"

She looked around, seeing nothing but the canoe. "What? The *canoe*? How did it get here?"

"I put it here earlier—it's part of the surprise."

He went to the back of the car, opened the trunk and took out a paddle and a large picnic basket. Setting them on the ground, he reached back into the trunk and retrieved a blanket and two jackets. She realized one of them was hers. He seemed to have thought of everything.

Enchanted with the idea of a canoe ride, she clapped her hands. "Mark! What a great idea! How did you think of it? And where did you get the canoe?"

"I wanted our last evening together to be special . . . and private . . . and quiet. I borrowed the canoe from Jack."

She nodded, recognizing the name of his long-time friend who was a game warden.

He smiled and pointed at the pile of supplies. "Get the blanket."

She grabbed it, as he picked up the lunch basket and canoe paddle, setting them both on the dock. Together they lifted the canoe off the trailer and set it on the sand at the water's edge. He got in and carefully stowed the picnic basket in the bow of the craft, then used the paddle to push the canoe out into the water. Holding it steady against the dock, he helped her step down into the canoe, continuing to hold it close to the dock until she was seated in the bow.

Mark settled himself on his knees in the stern, and reached in the pocket of his tee and pulled out a bottle of insect repellent, which he handed her. "It's good you wore long sleeves, but you might want to put some of this on your hands and face. The mosquitoes will make a meal of you this time of day."

"I can't believe you thought of everything. And you're not even a Marine." Jane laughed, remembering Luke and his "Semper Fi" answer to everything.

Mark's raised eyebrow told her the reference wasn't lost on him. He shoved off from the dock, and the canoe moved silently out in the water.

She leaned back against the pillows he had thought-fully placed for her comfort and breathed a deep sigh. *It was all so perfect.*

"Well, what do you think?" His grin told her he was pleased that he'd surprised her.

She dropped her fingers into the slowly moving water and watched the wake they left behind. The canoe skimmed silently along, and sparkling drops fell from the paddle each time Mark lifted it out of the water. The sun was just beginning to lower in the western sky, turning the water to molten gold. Jane felt a lump in her throat as she tried to put together an answer to his question. When she looked up, he was watching her quietly.

"This was how you spent your day, wasn't it?" she asked.

"I wanted our last evening to be special, and I—"

"Oh, Mark . . . *it is.* I'm speechless with the beauty. I haven't been in a canoe in years, and all this . . ." She threw out her arms to encompass everything in sight, causing the canoe to wobble wildly before Mark used his paddle to stabilize it. "Oh!"

"It's fine." He smiled at her exuberance. "You just can't make sudden moves in a canoe. You were saying?"

"Thank you for all this, Mark. I'll never forget it, never." She studied him thoughtfully.

"What?" he asked.

"Either you've really changed . . . or I never knew you at all. You're so different from what I remember."

"I should hope so"

She heard the disgust in his voice and frowned. "I was fond of the old Mark."

202

"Even though I let you down?"

"We all do things we regret," she said softly.

He saw the compassion in her eyes and wanted to ask her if she could ever forgive him, but just then the tremolo sound of a loon calling its mate drifted across the river, and Jane's head snapped around as she searched for the bird. The moment was lost, and he decided to let the past stay in the past . . . *for now.*

As they rounded a bend in the lake, he began maneuvering the canoe in toward shore. Jane felt the subtle change in direction and grasped the sides of the canoe as she tried to turn in order to see their destination. Mark shook his head.

"No. Don't turn around! We'll be there in a few minutes. You can see then."

"You've planned everything so perfectly this far, I can't wait to see what's next."

He smiled, hoping things worked out the way he had planned. The canoe scraped bottom; he jumped out and pulled it up on the shore, then offered Jane his hand. As she stood and stepped out of the canoe, she drew in a deep breath of the spicy pine air.

Mark had really been busy today. There in front of them was the makings of a campfire, just waiting to be lit, with logs pulled up for seating. While she stood taking in the scene, he busied himself spreading the blanket atop pine boughs already in place on the ground. He took a coffee pot from the basket and filled it from a large jug of water. Kneeling, he struck a match to the waiting kindling. In minutes a cheerful fire blazed, and he set the coffee pot on a stone close to the flames.

"What can I do to help?"

"Not a thing." He looked over at her and smiled. "This

is my surprise. Get the cushions from the canoe if you wish, and make yourself comfortable on the blanket. I'll start dinner."

She moved toward the canoe, and then turned back to face him. "When is the last time you camped out in the woods? I remember you and your brothers used to do it a lot when we were growing up—"

"And you and Kit always pestered us to take you along—"

"And you never did."

He was thoughtful as he spoke. "Did it ever occur to you that your parents wouldn't have agreed to it if we had?"

"I guess not . . . Have you done any camping since then?"

"Only a few times as part of my military training."

"How come?"

Mark finished putting a chicken on a rod, propping it on two forked rods he had taken from the seemingly unlimited supply of items in the basket. He rolled two foil-wrapped potatoes into the coals, then cleaned his hands with water from the jug and dried them on his handkerchief before coming to sit down beside her on the blanket. "Now, what was your question?"

"How come you stopped going camping?"

"No reason. I guess I just never thought about it. It was a part of growing up with my brothers . . . and we all have different lives now."

He was looking out over the river as he spoke. The sun was almost gone, its rays no longer reflecting in the water.

"So how come you thought about it now?" she asked as she studied his face.

He continued to stare out over the still water until she was almost certain he wasn't going to answer. She was about to repeat the question when he turned toward her.

"How come all the questions?"

"Just curious, I guess. I really did hope and pray that you all would take us with you just one time when we were growing up. I guess I wondered if you remembered and . . . and . . ."

He grinned at her, and touched a long finger to her nose. "And you wondered if this was my way of making it up to you?"

"I guess."

"I can't say it was. I really had forgotten what pests the two of you were back then."

He laughed and dodged her fist as she leaned over to punch him in the arm. Grabbing her arms, he held them at her sides, still laughing. "I was *teasing*. I never thought you were a pest. In fact, I thought you were cute. I just had too much sense, back then, to take you where you were too young to go."

"Oh." She wrinkled her forehead and frowned, trying to decide whether to be mollified or angry. The pot on the stone beside the fire began to bubble, and the aroma of coffee filled the evening air. "Mmm, that coffee smells wonderful."

He moved over to the fire, picked up a barbecue mitt and gave the sizzling chicken a few turns, then removed the coffee pot from the fire and began filling two mugs. Setting the pot back in the fire, he again rummaged in the basket and came up with a small container of milk, which he poured in one mug before handing it to her.

"Even milk for my coffee. Wow! Thank you."

"You're welcome."

She set the mug on a nearby flat stone to cool, remembering the last time she had taken a gulp of hot liquid with disastrous results.

He sat back down beside her, also setting his mug aside before turning to her and taking one of her hands. "Jane . . . I did want to give you an evening to remember, but I also wanted us to have a chance to talk with no distractions, to explain some things, and . . ."

Her glance flashed to his face, and he saw a worried look come into her eyes.

He smiled at her, touching her lips with his finger, then putting his palm on her cheek. "I can see you're already apprehensive. The word 'talk' really does scare you, doesn't it?"

Her smile was rueful. "I guess. So . . . what did you want to tell me?"

"I think you might be thinking I brought you out here for another reason." He felt her hand go rigid, and although she didn't withdraw it, he knew his assumption had been correct.

"What?"

There was that worried look again. "Jane, I'm not going to make love to you . . . not tonight."

Totally surprised, she felt her cheeks heat up, as hurt shot through her. "You're . . . not?"

He reached up and ran his hand over his mouth and chin. *Damn, this was even harder than he'd thought it would be.* He shouldn't have started it, but he sure as hell owed her some kind of explanation.

"Because, back at Hawk and Kit's wedding, when I asked you to have dinner with me, I <u>knew</u> you were going to refuse. When you agreed to go, I couldn't believe it! Right then and there, I thanked God for

206

giving me another chance with you. I vowed that I wouldn't screw up this time, that I would convince you that I was a different, a better person. I also promised myself that I wouldn't rush you into anything, that I would give you time to get to know the person I am now, and make up your mind whether you could take a chance on me again. And that's what I'm doing."

"But Mark, I know you're different. I already told you—"

He didn't let her finish, but put his finger over her lips again, then leaned forward and softly kissed her. When she went to put her arms around his neck, he carefully removed them, and placed them in her lap. "Don't, Jane. This time I'm doing the <u>right</u> thing. And please don't think I don't want to make love to you, because I do. So much so that it's killing me."

She leaned toward him, but he pushed her back again.

"I can't, Jane. It has to be this way. When I come back from Afghanistan—if you want me then—nothing will stop me."

A lone tear rolled slowly down her cheek as she looked at him. "But Mark, what if . . . what if you don't <u>come</u> back?"

He reached out and brushed the tear away with his thumb, then took her face between both of his hands. "Don't even think that way, Jane. I *will* come back. I will."

This time when he kissed her, it was everything she could have wished for, and when her hands went around his neck, he left them there. When he finally pulled away, both of them were breathing hard. He left her to check the chicken, which was dripping sizzling drops of fat into the fire. He pronounced it done, then proceeded to move it onto a plate and cut off several slices.

Neither of them spoke, and Jane silently watched him prepare their meal. *Darn him. Now he has to prove he's "worthy" of me. Why couldn't he let me be the judge of that?* Even as she thought it, she knew she had to let him do this. It was important to him. She already knew she loved him, had always loved him, was ready to promise him anything, but she could be patient. She would wait . . . until he came back . . . but no longer. He set a plate of food in front of her and, despite everything, she realized she was hungry.

"It looks and smells awesome! I guess all that camping—that you didn't take me on—taught you something."

He grinned. *Whew! She wasn't angry—and, apparently, she was accepting his decision.* "Ya think?"

She nodded and took her first bite of the succulent meat.

He did the same. "Yep, I think I'm a pretty good cook." She rolled her eyes, and he laughed.

After they had devastated the chicken, he emptied the bones and scraps into a plastic bag and put it into the basket, then reached in and came out with two wrapped items, one of which he passed to her with a grin.

"Dessert?"

"Twinkies!"

"A chef I may be, but a baker I'm not. If you want dessert, this is it."

"It's perfect." Jane said as she took a bite. "Mmmm." She licked her fingers, savoring the last bit of the sticky cake. The loons were calling to each other again, and it was almost twilight. They would have to leave soon. The evening hadn't turned out the way she'd hoped, but it had been very special, and she hated for it to end.

Mark reached for the plastic wrapping and handed her a moist towelette. She took it and cleaned off her sticky fingers, shaking her head at his thoughtfulness.

"Mark Vail, you're too good to be true. No one is that thoughtful."

"It's about time, don't you think?"

When she opened her mouth, he silenced her with a raised hand. "It's time for us to leave if we want to get back before dark. You have all of my surprises, except one."

"One more? What?"

He rummaged in the seemingly inexhaustible basket one more time and came out with a tiny, ribbon-tied package, which he tentatively handed to her. "I hope you like it."

Her hand flew to her mouth, and she stared at the small gift. "What is it?"

Mark's smile was gentle. "Why don't you open it and see?" He waited nervously as she carefully untied the ribbon and slowly removed the paper. He had thought a long time before coming up with the gift, had almost missed his flight when he went to pick it up before coming here. He held his breath as she finally finished unwrapping it and slowly lifted the lid of the box. She drew in a long breath, and her eyes grew wide.

"Ohhh, Mark . . ." Her voice trailed off.

"Do you like it?"

Her eyes filled with tears as she looked up at him. "It's your lucky piece. I remember your grandfather gave it to you on your sixteenth birthday. We were all so enthralled when he told us how he got it—in France during World War II—from a girl in the French

Underground who rescued him."

Mark smiled, remembering too.

"But, Mark, you can't give it to me."

"Why not?" His brows knit in confusion.

"Because you've always considered it your lucky charm. Kit said that you never go anywhere without it in your pocket."

He smiled as he met her gaze. "Take it out of the box."

As she did so, she saw that he'd had it attached to a long silver chain. "Oh, Mark, it's lovely. But I can't take it. What if . . . what if . . ." Unable to complete the thought, she just looked at him.

"Jane, don't be silly. I didn't carry it for luck. I carried it because I knew my grandfather had to love me deeply to give me something that meant so much to him . . . and I want to give it to you . . . I want to think of you having it. I hope you'll wear it—and that it will remind you of me. The chain is long enough that it won't show under your uniform."

Jane studied the medal for a long time. *Could it possibly . . . just maybe, mean that he loved her?* She closed her fingers tightly around the medal, then reached out to Mark and opened her palm.

"Thank you, Mark. I'll wear it all the time, and it <u>will</u> remind me of you." She smiled at him. *As if she needed a reminder.* "Here, could you put it on for me?"

He took the piece from her palm. As she leaned forward, he clasped it around her neck, before he lightly kissed her and said softly, "You're welcome, Jane." He stood quickly, took her hand, and pulled her up. "Now we really do have to leave."

★　★　★

Since Mark had arranged for his friend Jack to pick up the canoe the next morning, he and Jane were able to leave for home immediately. They arrived at her house much too soon.

While Mark unloaded the car, she went inside and began to empty the picnic basket. It had been an evening she would never forget, but now it was over. She heard the door from the garage open and close, and then Mark was behind her, his arms around her waist, his chin on her head.

"Jane . . ."

Without turning, she rested her hands on the counter to steady herself. "What?"

"I don't want you to take me to the airport tomorrow. I want to say our goodbyes tonight. That way I can remember you here."

Her heart dropped. *Even though she understood, she selfishly wanted every last minute of time together. She made a desperate effort to steady her voice.* "I had planned to drop you off on my way to work. I'll have time."

"I know, Jane, and I appreciate it, but. . .this is better. I've already made arrangements for a cab to pick me up at 0630."

She didn't answer, and he turned her slowly in his arms until she faced him, staring into his chest. He put his fist under her chin and pushed gently, forcing her to look up at him. "Are you all right?"

She nodded, blinking rapidly to ensure that the tears that had welled in her eyes didn't fall. His arms were around her, and hugged her tightly. She laid her face

211

against his chest and breathed in the smell that was uniquely his—fresh air, tangy aftershave, and . . . just him.

"You don't have to get up in the morning. Sleep in."

"No way! I'll agree to the taxi and not taking you to the airport, but you're *not* sneaking out of here while I'm still asleep. Don't even try! I'll get up at 5:30 and have breakfast ready when you get out of the shower."

He started to object, but she put a hand over his mouth. Her expression told him not to argue, so he simply nodded. "Okay. But nothing big. I don't eat much when I'm traveling."

Now it was her turn to nod. *If she spoke again, the tears would come.* "Well, I guess that's it then. I'll see you in the morning."

She turned to go, but he reached for her again and pulled her close, his lips nuzzling her soft hair. "Jane, don't be sad. It has to be this way—I couldn't handle it any other way." He kissed her softly on the forehead, then let her go.

Her eyes shimmered with tears as she turned toward the stairs. He watched her go, murmuring under his breath, "Good night, sweetness." He squeezed his eyes shut. *He was doing the right thing.* He knew that, but it was the hardest thing he'd ever done. He walked over to the buffet and poured himself a stiff drink of Scotch, hoping it would help him get to sleep, knowing it wouldn't.

She arose at 0430, before the alarm went off. She made her bed out of habit, and ran downstairs to turn the coffee pot on before showering and putting on her uniform. Her hair was still damp when she walked into the kitchen. Mark was leaning against the counter with a mug of coffee in his hand. He immediately set it down and reached for another mug which he filled and handed to her.

His bags had been moved to the front door. Seeing them there gave her a lonely feeling.

Neither of them had any appetite for the doughnuts and juice she had bought the day before, but they both pretended. When the clock struck the half-hour, they both stood. Mark leaned over and kissed her quickly, but otherwise didn't touch her. He strode into the front room as the cab honked outside. He picked up his bags, looked at her and smiled, then opened the door.

"Goodbye, Mark."

"So long, Jane. I <u>will</u> call."

He hurried down the walk, turning once to wave as he got in the cab, and then he was gone.

She had to be at work at seven. There was no time to think about how much she was going to miss him. She put the few dishes in the dishwasher, made a quick trip to the bathroom to brush her teeth, then hurried out the door, leaving the silent, empty house behind her.

Thankfully, her day was very busy, and eventually, it was three p.m. She drove home slowly. She dreaded entering the empty house, knowing she would see Mark everywhere. She should have gone shopping, or asked Ellen to go out for dinner, but she didn't feel like doing either. She hoped Mark would call, but was afraid he wouldn't.

Once inside the house, she quickly changed out of her uniform, emptied the hamper, threw a load of clothes into the washer, and vacuumed the living room. She heated up a can of soup, which she didn't eat. She turned on the TV, and almost immediately turned it off. By nine p.m., she couldn't take it any longer and decided to go to bed. After laying out a clean uniform for the next morning, she headed for the shower.

Minutes later she came out of the bathroom in her pajamas, and stared at the phone on the nightstand, willing it to ring. When it didn't, she walked over to the bed, grabbed the spread and yanked it down. As she did so, a white piece of paper flew up into the air. Puzzled, she picked it up. It was folded, and when she opened it, her name sprung out at her.

Jane—Miss me? Someday I hope it will be my head lying beside yours on this pillow. 'Til that time, dream of me . . . Mark.

She stared at the note, speechless, then closed her eyes and put it to her lips. As she stood there, trying to figure it all out, the phone rang. She grabbed for it, falling across the bed as she said, "Hello?"

"Hi."

"Mark!"

"Where are you?"

"In bed."

"Did you find my note yet?"

"I just did . . . and I do . . . miss you."

"Good."

She heard the smile in his voice. "When did you put it there?"

"Before I came downstairs this morning. You were still in the shower, but your bed was already made. I snuck it under the spread and figured you wouldn't find it until tonight."

"I didn't."

"Did you miss the picture from the mantel?"

"No." She sat bolt upright. "Which picture?"

"The little one of you in your nursing uniform. I took it. I hope you don't mind."

"Of course not . . . but now I want one of you."

"I'll see what I can do."

"Don't forget."

"I won't."

"Where are you?"

"I just got home about five minutes ago, and decided to call you before I unpacked . . . as a down payment on my promise to keep in touch."

She felt her lips curve up in a smile. "Thank you. I'll mark it down." The sound of his laughter came over the phone.

"You do that. Now, I really have to go. I'm beat, and I have to work tomorrow."

"Me too."

"Take care Jane, I'll be thinking of you."

"'Bye, Mark. Mark!"

"Yes."

"Thank you for calling."

"Just wanted you to know I meant what I said."

She heard him replace the phone, and slowly put down her own, smiling as she crawled beneath the covers. She reread the note, then folded it carefully and laid it on her nightstand. In the morning she would put it in her wallet. She wanted to have it with her all the time, to read whenever she needed reassurance. As she laid her head on the pillow, she wondered if he knew how much the note meant to her. *He'd said to dream of him*

. . . and she would.

★   ★   ★

He put the phone back in its cradle and walked over to stare into the darkness outside the window, his mind on the woman he'd just talked to. He couldn't help the smile that creased his face. *The visit had turned out even better than he'd hoped, and he knew Jane was beginning to trust him, and—*

The ringing of the phone surprised him, and he looked at his watch—2230. He frowned, wondering if it was the base calling him in for some emergency. He picked up the phone and held it to his ear; his younger brother Jon, was already talking.

"Boy oh boy, Bro! And everyone says *I'm* hard to catch up with—I've been trying for two days to reach you."

"Well, you've got me. What's up, Jon?"

"Nothing much. I just wanted to tell you goodbye before you headed for the sandbox. You're leaving next week, aren't you?"

"The thirteenth."

"So, how's the romance progressing? I hear Jane's in the Air Force. "

"I'm ignoring the first part of that statement, but yeah, she just graduated from officer training. How did you know? Never mind—Kit again, right?"

"You know our sister."

"I do, too well."

"I also know that's where you've been! Visiting Jane!"

"All right, that's where I've been. I just got back today."

"Listen Bro, all kidding aside. I'm really happy for

you, and I hope it all works out. Everyone in the family has known for years that you've been carrying the torch for Jane Brewer. None of us could figure out why you never did anything about it. I don't suppose you want to enlighten me on that?"

"No, I don't. A man has a right to some secrets."

"Okay, okay. I'm was just yanking your chain. By the way, isn't that great news about Kit and Hawk? They deserve it."

"Kit and Hawk? Deserve <u>what</u>? What are you talking about?"

"You didn't know?"

Mark could hear the smirk in Jon's voice, and knew he was enjoying this. "All right, spit it out. What do you know about Kit and Hawk?"

"Come November we're both going to be uncles."

"You're kidding! That's great! But how come I'm hearing it from you? I can't believe neither one of them mentioned it. I just talked to Hawk last week . . ."

"And the light comes on." Jon chuckled. "You're getting the message."

Mark groaned. "They're mad about Jane and me."

"They're <u>happy</u> about the two of you, just like the rest of us. They're mad because they just found out about it two weeks ago when Jane called to tell Kit she was graduating from training. Kit said she still wouldn't know about the two of you, except Jane sort of let something slip—"

Mark ran a hand through his short hair, knowing he had some fences to mend as he finished Jon's thought, "—and by now the whole family knows." He groaned again.

"That they do brother, that they do. I'm just giving

217

you a heads up."

"Thanks, Jon. I'll call everyone." *After he called Kit.*

 "Right. And Mark . . ."

"Yeah."

"You take care over there."

"Always. Don't suppose you can say where you are, but you take care too, Jon."

"I can't, and I will."

Chapter 10

Jane treasured the fact that Mark continued to make good on his promise, calling her each night. She missed him as much as she had expected, and his calls were the highpoint of her day. But as the date of his deployment neared, it became more and more difficult to say goodbye to him each night.

The evening of May 12th, she sat with her phone on the table, waiting for it to ring. *I won't cry. I will not cry,* she promised. Even as she thought it, she knew it was impossible. *Well, I won't let him know I'm crying. Surely, I can do that.*

When the phone finally rang, she let her hand rest on it for several seconds before steeling herself to pick it up. *She could do this. She would do this. She was in the Air Force herself. Deployments were a fact of life. Right?* She took a deep breath and answered just before it went to voice mail. "Hello, Mark."

"Ah, breathless again. You rushed to get my call?"

"Always, Mark. Always." Feeling her eyes begin to water, she spoke brightly. "Are you all packed? Everything ready?" The quiet in his voice when he answered told her he was aware of what she was doing.

"Packed and ready. We board the aircraft at 0600."

"That's good then. How long is the flight? What time will you arrive? I looked it up, Afghanistan is twelve-and-one-half hours ahead of us. At least it's easy to remember, basically six in the morning here, six at night there." She tried to laugh but failed miserably, barely choking back a sob.

"Jane, please stop. You don't have to pretend. It's just as hard for me as it is for you. Goodbyes are never easy . . . so we learn to never say them."

"And that helps?" She brushed away a tear, glad he couldn't see.

"Not so much."

In her mind, she could see him smile. "Have you talked to Kit and Hawk?"

"I talked to all of them last night—Hawk, Kit, Matt, Luke—everyone but Jon."

"I know you talked to him last week. We should have known Kit would get even with us. Is your family still upset with you?"

"No, everything's good. I'm thrilled for Hawk and Kit—they'll make wonderful parents . . . and I told them that."

"I know you get aggravated at your 'family grapevine,' but you're so lucky to have such a close family . . . and one that cares so much."

"I know it—that's why I called everybody."

"That couldn't have been easy—saying goodbye over and over."

"No, but it's an unwritten code in our family—we always call before . . . we always call."

"But you never say goodbye. So what do you do, just

220

hang up?"

"Ah, Jane." The line was silent for a moment, and then he began to sing softly, "I'll be seeing you . . . in all the old familiar places—"

"That's a song from World War II! I've heard it lots of times, but I don't think it ever sunk in to me what it was saying—now it does."

"I have to go Jane . . . don't forget me."

"I won't. Safe flights, Mark."

"I'll be seeing you, Jane."

Despite what she had expected, the weeks flew by. Mark emailed about once a week, although there were no more calls. His emails were always brief, but she was thankful for them because they reassured her that he was all right.

Her emails to Mark were much longer. She wrote to him each night before she got in bed, telling him about the funny, sad, or irritating incidents that happened in her days. He'd told her they were the highlight of his day, and that he looked forward to the time during the day when he could take a few minutes to check his email. To make sure he was never disappointed she made sure there would always be at least one email waiting for him.

June came, and with it, Ellen's wedding. Anxious to begin their lives together, she and Dennis decided to forego a big wedding and were instead married in a small ceremony in the tiny church they both had started attending. Ellen's parents and two of her brothers had flown up from Texas, and Jane had kept her promise and stood beside Ellen as her maid of honor. As she watched

Ellen and Dennis recite their vows, she hoped with all her heart that the next wedding she participated in was her own—hers and Mark's.

Mark had been gone two months, and the coming weekend would be Jane's second active-duty weekend with the aeromedical evac unit at Malmstrom. Saturday was a routine training day, but early on Sunday morning their CO—Lt. Colonel Dotson—entered the briefing room carrying a sheet of paper. He headed immediately for the front of the room, said "Good morning people," and proceeded to read a memo from headquarters requesting volunteers for TDY at two bases, one in southwest Asia and one in Germany. The mission to southwest Asia would be leaving almost immediately; the other had a departure date of August 7 and required four personnel. Her mind working, Jane figured that would be time enough to alert the hospital and get her personal affairs in order. Without any further thought, her hand flew up, "Sir, I'd like to volunteer, please."

The colonel looked taken aback at her quick answer but smiled at her. "That's what we like to see Lieutenant, enthusiasm. Are you volunteering for either of them, or do you have a preference?"

She hesitated, looking around for other hands in the air. "Sir, the Germany assignment would be my first choice because I could give the hospital where I work more notice, but I'm willing to take the Asia assignment if that's where you need me."

By this time, several other hands were up, and the colonel nodded his head. "Okay, people. I appreciate your willingness. All volunteers, see Sergeant Foley at

222

the back of the room, and sign up with your preferences. I'll evaluate them immediately and get back to you ASAP. Dismissed."

After the CO left the room, the lieutenant next to Jane spoke up. His nametag said he was 'Fritz Redfern', and she thought they'd met on her first Reserve weekend.

"Are you crazy? Don't you know the first rule in the military is, 'Don't volunteer for anything'? You don't even know that you'll get Germany; they may send you to southwest Asia—probably Afghanistan."

Surprised by his outspoken comments, she didn't know what to say. When she did speak, her puzzlement was evident. "I thought this was why we joined up—to help. I've been praying for an opportunity—and now it's here. How come you don't want to go?"

"I'm willing to go, if the whole unit gets called up, but I'm not *volunteering*.

"Well, I'm excited, and I hope I'm selected."

That evening she called Ellen as soon as she got home. Since their marriage, she and Dennis lived in a small house on the ranch.

"Ellen, keep your fingers crossed for me. I may be going to Germany! I'm so excited! I never dreamed I'd have an opportunity so soon. I just hope I'm lucky enough to get this duty."

"To Germany?"

"Specifically, Landstuhl. I've been reading up on it—it's a staging hospital for wounded. Most of the medical evacuation flights originate from there to pick up injured in—"

"Afghanistan. Oh, Jane, what have you done?"

"What do you mean, what have I done? This is exactly what I signed up for. I thought you'd be excited

223

for me."

"I am. I'm just surprised. I didn't think you'd be going anywhere so soon. Have you told Mark yet?"

"I'll tell him as soon as it's firm." As soon as she said it, however, she realized Mark would not like it. And she'd have to tell Kit. She and Mark had both gotten the message about leaving Kit out of the loop. And then there were her parents. She'd have to tell them all soon—but not until she actually had the orders.

★ ★ ★

Two days later Jane got a message at work telling her that Colonel Dotson wanted her to call him at the base. At her first break, she did so, quivering with excitement.

His voice sounded harried when he picked up the phone. "Lieutenant Brewer?"

"Yes, sir."

"I've decided to submit your name for the Germany mission, despite your newness to the service. Your civilian experience in the ER will stand you in good stead." She heard papers being riffled. "According to your file, you did well in COT, another reason I'm selecting you."

"Yes, sir. Thank you, sir. Is anyone else from our unit going?"

"The levy calls for two non-com med-techs and two nurses. Lieutenant Fritz Redfern will be the other nurse. Sergeants Jacque DeVeau and Susan Meredith the NCO's. You'll receive your orders within the week. Reporting date is 8 August. Do you have a passport?"

"Yes, sir. We were advised to get one while we were at COT."

"Good, good. As soon as you get your orders, check

with the hospital to be sure your shots are current. Any questions?"

"How long is this assignment, sir?"

"Medical missions like this are usually from sixty to 120 days. You can expect to be gone ninety days this time."

"Thank you, sir."

"Lieutenant, you do know this is medevac duty? You won't be staying in Germany. You'll be going into combat zones to fly the wounded back to Germany for eventual return to the CONUS—Continental US."

"Yes, sir. I expected that. It's the duty I was hoping for."

"Right. I'll see the four of you before you go. And Lieutenant, I appreciate your volunteering. Thank you."

"Yes, sir."

Jane hung up the phone and let her head fall back, exhaling a deep breath. She was going; she was actually going. And so was Lieutenant Redfern—that was a surprise after his comments on the weekend. She looked at her watch—*fifteen minutes of break time left. Good.* Needing a few minutes to let it all sink in, she decided to go to the break room for a quick cup of coffee. Her mind began to reel with all the things she would have to do in the next several weeks. Her supervisor should be given a heads-up today, and advised she'd have her official orders in a few days. Then, in addition to shots, she'd need to check uniform requirements, arrange for her house . . . *and phone calls.* Jane stopped dead in the act of pouring coffee. She'd have to call her parents; they would be upset. And now that she had the details she had to call Kit . . . and Mark. As soon as he heard she was going to Germany, he'd know what was involved.

That was where Kit had been after she'd lost her leg in Iraq. She rubbed her hand through her hair. *She was not looking forward to any of the calls.*

Jane sighed again, and took a drink of the strong coffee in her cup. As she looked up, Ellen was just coming through the door.

"Hey, Jane." Ellen stopped, tipping her head as she looked down at her. "You look sort of shell-shocked. What's up?"

"I just had a call from the Medical Group Commander. I'll be getting my orders within the week."

"Whaat? You got selected?"

Jane nodded. "I leave for Germany in thirty-one days. It's a 90-day assignment, medevac duty."

Ellen looked stunned. "Wow! I guess I just didn't believe it would happen so soon." She peered down at Jane's face before continuing. "I can see you're happy about it."

"It's what I wanted to do."

Ellen looked at her searchingly. "You still haven't told Mark, have you?"

"Tonight. I'm going to try to call him tonight. If I can't get through, I'll email him. I'll be making three phone calls."

"Oooh boy. Mark, your parents, and . . .? "

"My friend Kit, you know—"

"The one who just got married . . . the one who lost her leg—"

Jane nodded again, then looked at her watch. "I've gotta run. I used up part of my break returning the call to Colonel Dotson. On my break this afternoon, I have to tell Mrs. Kohout I'll be getting orders." Grimacing, she threw her paper cup in the trash and headed for the door.

Ellen called out after her, "Let me know if there's anything I can do to help."

"Will do," she said over her shoulder as she left the room.

Telling her supervisor hadn't been as bad as she'd anticipated, Jane thought, as she left the hospital that evening. Mrs. Kohout had said she would definitely be missed, but there were usually people looking for part-time work, and they'd try to fill her position with several of them. *One down, three to go*, she thought; the hardest jobs were still ahead.

She walked slowly toward her car, her mind on the calls she had to make—and how she would phrase the news. Her Mom and Dad first, she decided. Then Kit, which would leave Mark for last. Kit would understand, even if the others did not.

In her car, she fastened the seatbelt and then sat staring out the windshield, her thoughts on Mark. She missed him so much. This Temporary Duty would put her closer to where he was, and maybe—just maybe— she'd get to Bagram and be able to see him. It was a long shot, but it *was* a possibility. She shook her head, forcing herself to stop dreaming, and started the car.

Once inside her little house, she went immediately to her bedroom and changed into an old pair of jeans and a loose sweatshirt. Then she remembered she hadn't gotten the mail, so she went back outside to check the box. Finding nothing but bills, she threw them on the desk in the living room. That reminded her—another task she'd have to take care of, changing her mailing address.

She looked at the telephone, but headed to the kitchen

for a tall glass of milk and a handful of Oreo cookies. She was procrastinating; soon her parents would be at dinner. She took a gulp of the milk, picked up the portable phone, and headed for the living room. Setting the glass of milk on the end table, she settled on the couch while she finished off the cookies.

Refusing to delay longer, she punched in her parents' phone number. Her mother answered on the second ring.

"Hi, Jane. I was hoping it was you. You're so good about calling, but the calls still seem too far apart."

"Hello, Mom. Actually, I'm calling this time because I have some news."

"Oh, what news, dear? Are you okay?"

"I'm fine, Mom. But you might want to get Dad on the other phone so I can tell you both at the same time."

She waited while her mother called her father, still unsure of the best way to tell them.

"Hello, Baby. What's up?"

There was no way to do it but to just . . . do it. "Mom and Dad, I wanted to let you know I'll be getting orders any day now."

"Orders?"

That was her mother. Then her Dad chimed in.

"What kind of orders? You mean *military* orders?"

"Yes. Military orders sending me TDY—that means temporary duty—to Germany. I'll be leaving in a little over three weeks, for ninety days."

"But how come? You just got back from Alabama! I thought you would just be doing military duty one weekend a month." said her Mom.

"Normally, I would be, but they have a need for two nurses and two med-techs in Germany. I'll be one of the nurses."

Neither of them said anything for a moment, and Jane knew they were absorbing what she had said. Her Dad was the one who asked the question she had been dreading.

"What will you be doing in Germany, Baby?"

She forced herself to take a deep breath and speak slowly, when she wanted to just blurt it out quickly. "I'm going as an air-evac nurse—"

Her Dad interrupted. "Flying into battle areas and picking up wounded?"

"It's what I signed up for, Dad. It's what I want to do. There's a real need . . . and I have the necessary training. I'm excited about this. Please tell me you're proud of me." She breathed in, realizing that she had ended up speaking the last sentence in a rush.

"Oh, Jane."

There was a hint of a sob in her mother's voice, but she continued bravely. "Jane, of <u>course</u> we're proud of you. But—"

Her father interrupted before she could finish. "You'll be a wonderful medevac nurse, Jane. You've always made us proud. I . . . I guess we won't see you before you go . . . will we?"

"I'm sorry, no . . . there's no way I can get away. Mrs. Kohout was really nice when I told her today, but they're going to have to advertise for part-time people to replace me while I'm gone. Until they find my replacements I can't leave them in the lurch—especially since it hasn't been that long since I was away at training school.

"We understand, but Germany seems so far away."

"I'll call as often as I can, Mom. You said you were going to take computer classes. Did you?"

Her Dad spoke up. "We both did . . . at the Senior

229

Center. Can you believe your old Dad is now what they call 'computer literate'?" He chuckled.

"That's really great, Dad. In that case, I can email you. I email Mark all the time, and I'll do the same for you, as often as I can."

"We'll look forward to that."

"Mom, Dad—I have to go now. I have to call Kit and tell her . . . and then Mark."

"Mark doesn't know yet?" her Mom asked softly.

"I told you, I just found out. You're the first ones I've told."

Her Dad spoke, voicing her own concerns. "I can't see Mark being pleased about this. I always had the feeling he didn't want Kit to go to West Point, and then after what happened to her . . ."

His voice trailed off, and Jane heard a sound from her mother that sounded suspiciously like a smothered cry.

"Don't worry about me, I'll be fine. I really have to go, but I'll call again in a few days to update you on what's going on." She paused to try and get rid of the lump in her throat before continuing. "Bye, Mom and Dad. Thanks for always being such wonderful parents. I love you."

"Goodbye, Jane. We love you too."

She replaced the phone and brushed her hand across her eyes to remove the dampness, then slumped back on the couch. The two calls other would have to wait. This was harder than she'd thought. She'd wait until after dinner.

An hour later Jane was back on the couch, phone in hand. Dinner hadn't taken long. With no appetite, she had ended up throwing out most of the frozen pizza she'd fixed. Trying to settle her mind, she'd cleaned out the refrigerator and started a load of wash, which was now in the dryer. She'd even debated waiting until tomorrow before making the remaining calls, but knew she wouldn't get a wink of sleep for worrying about what she would say. Nope; best to get it over with.

She had reordered her priorities however, deciding to make the call to Mark first. Hopefully, she'd reach him. Hard as it would be to tell him on the phone, it would be even harder to put it in an email—*although that way he wouldn't be able to talk back!*

She knew his cell phone number by heart—not because she called him, but because she thought about doing it so often before convincing herself it wasn't the thing to do. This time she had no such doubts. He deserved to have her tell him in person . . . or as near to in person as she could get.

She punched in the number and sat up on the edge of the couch listening to the ring. One, two, three, four—*he must be busy, maybe flying*—five, six—*what time would it be there?* She glanced at her watch—1800. She added the twelve and one-half hours. *Midnight!* She should have called before dinner. *Oh dear.* The phone continued to ring, and just as she decided to hang up, he answered.

"Captain Vail."

"Mark, I . . . how are you? I'm sorry to call so late. I forgot about the time difference."

"Jane? This is the first time you've ever called me. What's wrong? What's happened? Are you all right? Is it your parents?"

"Nothing's wrong. Everyone is all right. I . . . I just

231

have something to tell you."

He breathed a sigh of relief. *She'd scared him to death. He'd often hoped she'd call, but while she emailed faithfully, she had never called.* "Must be important."

"It is to me. I—I hope you'll be happy for me." She crossed her fingers in her lap as she said it.

"Well, tell me. The phone service is unpredictable here. We could get cut off at any time."

"Okay. I have orders for Germany. I'm leaving in thirty-one days for a 90-day assignment."

When Mark finally spoke, his voice was very soft with no expression.

"Your unit's been activated already? That's awfully quick. Usually you have more notice."

"No."

"No what?"

"No, my unit wasn't activated." His voice came through the phone line like thunder.

"You *volunteered*! Damn it all to hell, Jane. What's <u>wrong</u> with you?"

He stopped, but before she could answer, he spoke again, this time his voice quietly ominous.

"*Where* in Germany?"

She hesitated, knowing the minute she said it he'd know what she would be doing.

"Where, Jane?"

"Landstuhl."

"Medevac duty! This has to be the <u>dumbest</u> thing you've ever done."

Tears welling, she rubbed her hand across her eyes. *So much for him understanding.* "Stop! Just . . . just stop, Mark." Suddenly the tears were replaced by anger, white and hot. *How <u>dare</u> he? How <u>double</u>-dare he?*

232

"Mark Vail!" Anger kept her from forming the words. She cleared her throat and tried again. "In the first place, nothing is wrong with me. Not a gosh darned thing. This is what I joined to do. You knew that. You say one more thing about how dumb I am, and I'll hang up this phone right now, and you can just forget—"

"Jane, wait a minute—" He slammed his fist into the wall. He'd gone too far, he knew it . . . but no way was he going to apologize. It was his own fear talking, but he wasn't going to tell her that either. Why in the hell did she have to volunteer? He knew the answer. Because she was just like Kit . . . his sweet little Kit who was now minus a leg. And now Jane . . . He blinked to clear the moisture from his eyes.

"Mark?"

He cleared his throat. "Yeah."

Her anger was gone as quickly as it had come, and when she spoke, her words were quiet. "Mark. I know you're scared for me. You're afraid because of what happened to Kit. But there's no reason to assume that because it happened to *her* it's going to happen to *me*. And besides . . . I worry about you, too. You're in danger every day. Did that ever enter your mind?"

"All right. I won't say anything more. You're sure it's Landstuhl?"

"Yes. There are four of us going, two NCO med-techs and another lieutenant, Fritz Redfern."

"Fritz, sounds like a guy?"

"It is, why?"

"How long have you known him?"

"How long could I have known him, Mark? I've only been in the outfit a couple of months."

"Um—"

233

Suddenly all she had was a dial tone. The connection had been lost. She tried several times to call him back, but none of the calls went through. *She had really messed up.* He didn't understand. He was angry with her . . . *and he thought she was dumb.* Common sense told her he didn't really think that, nor would he stay angry with her, but right now common sense was in short supply. All she wanted to do was cry.

With tears in her eyes, she rose from the couch and headed for her bedroom, where she threw herself down on the bed and let the tears come. She had a fleeting thought of Kit, but no way could she talk to anyone now. Eventually the tears stopped, and she fell asleep.

Mark stared at his cell phone in disbelief, then hit his palm against his forehead. *Damn, damn, damn! What a time to lose the connection! Or even worse . . . had she hung up on him?*

He dialed her number, and got the hated "All circuits are busy." Without even thinking, he dialed Hawk's number. He had to talk to somebody about this. Good thing Hawk's number was in his directory; his hands were shaking so much he'd never be able to punch in the number. *Jane didn't know what she was in for—she couldn't. Damn it all. Why couldn't women be content to stay home and let men take care of them?* He realized how stupid that was the minute he thought it, but right now it was the way he felt.

Miracle of miracles, the call went through. Hawk was home, and picked up.

"Captain Hawkins."

The thought went through his mind that Hawk and Kit must have gotten quarters on base.

"Hawk, does Kit know that Jane's got orders?"

"No, I'm sure she doesn't since she didn't say anything."

"Is she there with you?"

"No. She's not home yet. She has an hour commute from Bragg."

Although he wanted to scream his frustration at Hawk, he forced himself to make small talk. "You didn't get the same installation then?"

"No, at least not yet. After Kit gets final word from the board on whether or not she can stay in, we'll try to renegotiate. Why are you calling, Mark? What's this about Jane getting orders? Where is she going?"

"Landstuhl—"

"Medevac duty. And you're scared to death; I can hear it in your voice."

"I guess there's no use in denying it; I am. Even worse, she called me a few minutes ago . . . and I . . . I screamed at her. I told her she was dumb."

"So it's finally happened. Kit was right. The Bronc has fallen in love—and he doesn't like it."

"I'm not in love! I'm just worried. The girl doesn't have idea one of what she's getting into, not a clue. She volunteered for God's sake. How could she be so dumb?" The muffled sound that came through the phone sounded suspiciously like laughter. "Are you *laughing* at me?"

"Of course not! I . . . I've got a cold."

"Uh huh. Well, what am I going to do, Hawk?"

"Did you really tell her she was dumb?"

"Uh, yeah, I did. I was just so mad—I wasn't

235

thinking."

"I guess not. Even *I* wouldn't think of saying something like that to Kit . . . and you should know better."

"I do know better. Of course I don't think she's dumb. I was just so . . . so—"

"Worried, scared, shook up."

"All those."

"Is this the first you knew of it?"

"She told me right after she signed up for the reserves that she wanted to be a flight nurse. I told her she should have done more checking, but she got angry, so I let it go."

"And hoped she'd never get the assignment."

"Yeah, I guess."

"Only she did, and there's nothing you can do about it. No more than you could dissuade Kit."

"And look what happened to Kit!"

"Listen, buddy, if you ever hope to have a future with Jane, you better suck it up and sound supportive. You think I don't worry about Kit? Not a day goes by that I don't, but I fell in love with her bravery and optimism and daring. I can't make her change—and she wouldn't let me if I tried. Are you listening to me, Mark?"

"I hear you . . . and I already know all that. I just . . . I'll fix it . . . somehow."

Hawk laughed. "Believe me, friend, love ain't easy."

"I told you, I'm not in love. I just . . . care about her— she's like a sister." Hawk's laughter rolled through the line before he spoke.

"Right. This is me you're talking to."

"Well . . . I don't want to be in love with her." That drew a snort from Hawk.

"Like that makes a difference. Just don't hurt her, unless you want Kit to be all over you like fur on a bear."

"I'm not going to hurt her. You and Kit can rest assured; I won't hurt her . . . not ever again." The line was quiet for several seconds. He groaned when he realized what he'd said. When Hawk spoke, there was suspicion in his voice.

"Again? What do you mean, 'not ever again'? When did you hurt her before? You better start 'splainin'."

Mark knew his groan was audible. *Why had he said that?*

Hawk pressed for an explanation. "What happened, Mark? Kit never said anything about you hurting her friend <u>before</u>, and she would, believe me, she would. Hell, you hadn't even *seen* Jane for years until our wedding . . . uh oh."

"Forget it, Hawk. You don't know anything—and you're not going to, so stop prying." *Damn it all, Hawk was on the scent, and nothing would stop him now.*

"It was that time you went on Christmas leave, right after flight school, wasn't it? Kit invited Jane to go to Matt's with her. I knew <u>something</u> happened while you were there. You were a different person when you came back. And whenever I asked you what happened you closed up like a clam. I'm not going to let this go, Mark, so you might as well start talking."

"Not this time, Hawk. I can't. I won't, so just don't go there."

"Fine buddy, I'll leave it, for now, but whenever you decide to talk, I'm here. And I don't *necessarily* have to tell Kit, either."

"Hah! You forget, I know her. I bet you don't have

<u>any</u> secrets from my sister."

"Not many. I'll tell Kit about your call . . . but not about the hurting Jane part."

"Thanks, Hawk. I <u>won't</u> hurt her again, I swear. Thanks for listening . . . and DO NOT TELL KIT."

"Yeah, yeah, I got it. Be careful, Bronc."

"Always. So long."

★   ★   ★

Okay! He'd just told Hawk he'd fix it, and he would, but how? He was here, and she was there, and a telephone call just wasn't going to do it this time. There weren't enough words in the English vocabulary to convince Jane to forgive him for calling her dumb.

He paced back and forth, discarding one idea after another. Finally, it came to him. He examined his idea from all angles until, convinced it might work, he reached for his cell phone again, and punched in Hawk's number. As he waited for it to ring and his friend to answer, he almost groaned at the idea of what he was going to ask.

"Captain Hawkins."

"Hawk! Thank God you're still there."

"Two calls within an hour—after not hearing from you in months!"

"I need your help."

"Anytime, buddy. What do you need?"

"I need you to . . . order some flowers for me."

"You want me to send you flowers! Have you flipped, Mark?"

"Not me, you idiot! Now, listen up. I want you to call the florist and order two dozen yellow roses and have them sent to Jane. Ask them to deliver on Saturday so

238

she'll be home. Can you do that for me?"

"Two dozen! Don't you think—"

"Two dozen. And make sure they're yellow."

"Two dozen yellow roses, deliver on Saturday. Got it."

Mark sighed. "Do you think it'll work? It's all I could think of. Ya think it's enough?"

"Well, I'm not a wronged woman, but it sounds good to me. Want me to check with Kit, and—"

"No! I definitely do not want you to ask Kit. Listen man, it's humbling enough having to ask you to do this, without having my sister put in her two cents."

"Is this another one of those things I'm not supposed to tell my wife?"

"I'd appreciate it . . . please."

"Okay, I won't tell her, but man, are you going to owe me."

"And I'll pay, Hawk—in blood if necessary. Now, if you can take care of that for me I better go."

"Hey, Bronc! Wait a minute. Aren't you forgetting something?"

"Oh, damn. I forgot the most important thing. Tell them to include a card with the words, 'I'm sorry'."

"No name?"

"She'll know."

"Okay, Bronc. It's done."

"Thanks, Hawk."

Saturday morning Jane got up early, determined to keep so busy there would be no time to think about the disastrous phone call two days before. She'd gone over the words each of them had spoken again and again. If only they hadn't gotten disconnected. Maybe then Mark would have apologized. Maybe she could have . . . maybe, maybe, maybe. Being interrupted in the middle somehow made it all worse. She grimaced. They seemed doomed never to finish a phone call.

She was in the middle of sorting laundry in the bedroom when the doorbell rang. *Who in the world would be at the door this early on a Saturday morning?* She dried her hands, stepped over the pile of dirty clothes on the floor, and hurried to see.

When she opened the door, she was amazed to see a florist truck in the driveway, and a young man standing in front of her holding a long, slender florist's box tied with a green ribbon.

"Good morning! Are you Jane Brewer?"

She nodded mutely.

"Then these are for you." He smiled as he pushed the box into her hands. "Have a nice day".

She slowly backed up and pushed the door shut behind her, remembering the last time she had gotten a box like this. *Mark had sent her roses on Valentine's Day.* She held the box close to her heart, hope careening through her. She carried the precious box into the kitchen and set it on the table, then carefully slid the green ribbon off. She smoothed her fingers over the box, holding her breath as she lifted the lid. There, nestled in green waxed paper lay the most roses she'd ever seen in one place—yellow roses, her favorite. She carefully removed the white envelope with her name on it. For a minute she just held it, imagining what it would say inside. She opened it and slowly slid the card out. As she read what was written on the card, tears filled her eyes. Only two words were carefully centered on the small card—"I'm sorry." She began to cry in earnest. *Oh, Mark. How can you be so frustrating, so stubborn? How can you make me so mad . . . and then be so wonderful?*

She pulled out a chair and sagged into it, touching the card to her lips before laying it on the table beside the box. Then she removed each flower, one by one, from its resting place in the box. There were twenty-four. *Two dozen roses! It must have cost him a fortune! . . . And to send them from Afghanistan.* She wrinkled her forehead in puzzlement. *How in the world had he managed it? It couldn't have been easy. But, oh how much it meant to her. If he only knew.*

She jumped up from the chair. *She would email him right away!* She turned toward the den and her computer, then remembered the flowers. It wouldn't do to leave the lovely things laying there. She searched the closet until she found a beautiful cut-glass vase that had belonged to her mother, and filled it with water. Cutting each of the stems diagonally with a knife, she arranged them in the vase. Finished, she breathed in the wonderful aroma before carrying them into the den. She set them on the desk beside her laptop, unable to refrain from gently touching the petals.

After opening the laptop she stared at the screen for several seconds before she began typing. *Dear Mark— Thank you for the roses, and for remembering yellow roses are my favorite. They arrived this morning, along with the card. I knew in my heart you didn't mean what you said. Your apology means . . . it means everything to me. I'm sorry, too. I didn't mean all the things I said either. I tried to call you back after we were disconnected. Thanks for being so wonderful. —Jane.*

Chapter 11

Jane had gone to bed early, knowing that since she was on call there was a good likelihood that she wouldn't get a full night's sleep. Sure enough, the phone beside her bed roused her before dawn. She reached for the phone and looked at the lighted dial of her alarm clock—0330.

"Lieutenant Brewer here. Right! Thirty minutes."

Completely awake now, she sat up, a sense of excitement and anticipation filling her. *Her first flight to a combat area!*

She hurriedly washed her face and donned a clean flight suit. Her thoughts flitted back over the past three weeks since she and her squadron-mates from Malmstrom had arrived here at Landstuhl. Their days had been fully occupied with checking in, becoming familiar with the layout of the big hospital, and learning to navigate the local German community and its customs. She and Mark had exchanged regular emails since his amazing rose-accompanied apology, although there had been no more telephone calls. She told herself it was understandable—with both of them having such haphazard schedules, it was almost impossible to know when to call.

In the meantime, she and Fritz had been eagerly welcomed by the other flight nurses—who had been so desperately short-handed they'd had almost no free time, being either on-call or in the air most of the time. She grinned as she thought of Fritz. He'd volunteered for this duty despite his comments to her back at Malmstrom, and was now a good friend. So far, her flights had all been to Andrews AFB, near Washington, DC, the offload point for wounded going to Walter Reed Army Medical Center. Fritz had drawn the flights to Iraq and Afghanistan. But now it was her turn.

Ready to go, she grabbed her always-ready flight bag, zipped her wallet into the pocket of her flight suit, and ran out the door. Ops was sending a crew bus for her, and it should be here anytime—*and here it was!* She ran the last few feet and swung aboard the bus that would take her to Ramstein Air Base, their take-off point for Bagram, Afghanistan.

Jane heard a cheerful "Mornin', Lieutenant!" and peered through the early morning dark. Sergeant Susan Meredith, one of the two noncoms who'd accompanied her and Fritz from Malmstrom, was sitting halfway back in the bus, an empty seat beside her.

"Good morning, Sergeant Meredith. Is this your first flight to Afghanistan?" Jane moved down the aisle of the bus toward the seat beside the diminutive sergeant.

"No, ma'am. I've been to Bagram once before. My other flights have been back to the States. You?"

"My first time."

Someone yelled, "Good morning, Jane!" from the rear of the bus, and she turned, recognizing Fritz. "Morning Fritz! What is this, old home week? Is Sergeant DeVeau here too?"

She glanced around before sliding into the seat beside the Sergeant, who answered her. "No ma'am. He left yesterday on a flight to the States."

Turning in her seat, Jane looked to see who else was on the bus. The basic crew complement on an air evac mission was five—two flight nurses and three med-techs. She could see a number of people, but in the low light was unable to pick out anyone else she knew. "So who else is on this flight?"

"Sergeants Bronson and Boulder."

She knew Boulder, but had never flown with Senior Master Sergeant Bronson—although she knew of his reputation. He was almost a legend, and would undoubtedly be the senior medical technician on the flight, all the rest of them being relatively new.

It was a thirty-minute drive from Landstuhl to Ramstein Airbase. They were scheduled for an 0530 lift off. They would be using a C-17 aircraft that had been specially configured for medevac. During the special AE briefing, they would learn what equipment and supplies would be needed, and the Senior Med Tech would insure everything was aboard.

After the briefing, Jane reasoned that should leave enough time for a quick breakfast at the 24-hour cafeteria in the Terminal Building where Ops was located. Breakfast was available around the clock due to the number of incoming and outgoing crews passing through from so many different time zones. It was a seven-hour flight to Bagram, and she'd just as soon not

244

have to eat an in-flight lunch if it could be avoided.

Dawn was beginning to streak the horizon as they neared the airfield. Jane could see the maintenance team swarming around the aircraft doing final checks. The C-17 Globemaster was the primary plane used for air evac duty. Its large cargo bay could hold as many as seventy patients. The fact that it was quieter, vibrated less, and had more temperature control than the C-141 it had replaced had earned it the affection of the evac crew members who flew it.

When the bus stopped in front of Flight Ops, Jane quickly stood and grabbed her bag, grinning at the young woman beside her. "Let's do it, sergeant," she said as the bus door opened, and she stepped down onto the tarmac. The early morning air was cool, and she shivered in her flight jacket.

Fritz spoke from behind her. "Are you thinking the same thing I am?"

They spoke in unison: "Breakfast!"

The rest of the group got off the bus, and Fritz introduced Sergeant Bronson. Both of them already knew Sergeant Meredith, and the four of them headed for the Terminal. Breakfast was quick. Thirty minutes later they exited the glass doors from the terminal onto the flight line, and headed across the tarmac toward the aircraft which was already running up its engines. As they neared the huge plane, the pilot came from behind the plane after completing his own pre-flight check. Jane recognized him from previous flights.

"Good morning, Jake. You our chauffeur this run?"

"Yeah, you got lucky."

Fritz nodded his head and grinned as Jake turned to speak to the sergeant next to Jane.

"Sergeant Meredith. What do they do—give you all these flights?"

"No sir—just the ones you're flying." She grinned at him.

Jake laughed, and Jane hoped she'd soon be a part of the easy camaraderie.

Fritz introduced Jane and the other two sergeants to Jake, then asked, "Who's in the left seat?"

"A newbie, Lieutenant Logan McCallister. This is his first trip to the sandbox."

As Jane started up the crew ladder, she turned. "What's our ETA, Jake?"

He shrugged. "Noon, under normal conditions."

She knew what that meant.

As they settled themselves in the jump seats and strapped in, she looked down the length of the plane's cavernous belly. It was rigged with racks to hold the stretchers they'd be carrying on the return trip.

They were soon joined by the loadmaster and the flight engineer, both of whom Sergeant Meredith seemed to know. Their jobs finished, the loadmaster strapped into a seat across from her and settled back against the webbing, while the flight engineer continued forward to the cockpit.

She could see Jake and his co-pilot, the newbie Logan, running through the pre-flight check-list, and then the plane began moving down the runway. *They were on their way!*

The noise of the engines precluded conversation, so Jane leaned her head back, her thoughts immediately going to Mark. Although he was based at Bagram, she wouldn't be seeing him. Their patients would already be waiting for them when they arrived. Once their own crew performed essential maintenance and the aircraft was refueled, they'd load the patients and head back to Landstuhl where the injured would be hospitalized for treatment and, if necessary, later transported to hospitals Stateside.

Still, she couldn't keep her mind from wondering. It had been four months since she'd seen Mark . . . *and fallen in love with him all over again.* She could admit that fact to herself, but was glad she hadn't let him know. Despite the noise, she dozed off.

She was roughly awakened by the plane's mighty shudder and the screaming of its engines in response to . . . *what?* She looked over at the flight engineer who had jumped up from his seat and was making his way forward. She wondered where he was going, but he didn't give her time to ask. The loadmaster, who had remained in his seat, answered her unspoken question.

"We've been hit by groundfire—probably a rocket launched from a shoulder-held weapon."

The plane was still shuddering but didn't seem to be dropping as ominously as it had at first. Still trying to get a grasp on what had happened, Jane reached over and touched the loadmaster to get his attention. "Are we going down, Sergeant?"

He grinned reassuringly at her. "Nah. Captain Bellamy's a great pilot. He's got things under control. We're only about five minutes out of Bagram. We'll make it. Maybe on a wing and a prayer, but we'll make it."

She wondered if his seeming disdain for danger camouflaged a fear like hers. The flight engineer had disappeared through a hatch in the floor of the plane, and she assumed he was checking out the condition of

247

the landing gear. Minutes later she felt the plane vibrate sharply.

Jake yelled back from the cockpit. "You all right back there?"

She found herself yelling "Okay" along with the rest of them, and realized she had just survived her first near miss. *Now, if they landed in one piece . . .*

Minutes later the flight engineer, whose name she learned was Deke, passed by, and the other sergeant spoke to him.

"Everything okay down there?"

"Could be worse, John, but we won't be making an immediate turn-around this time. The rocket damaged our landing gear. I had to lower it manually."

"But it did go down?"

Deke frowned. "Yeah. Can't tell if it'll hold though."

"Are you trying to cheer me up?" He grinned slightly. "So they'll be foaming the runway?"

Deke nodded. "Could be dicey. Good thing the Captain's flyin' this trip."

John nodded. "Yeah, he's gettin' good at this."

Jane couldn't keep from asking, "You mean this has happened to him before?"

Susan answered her question. "Last week—but they missed us that time."

"You mean you were there?" Susan nodded, and Jane found herself looking at the petite sergeant with new respect.

It was one thing to board the plane with no idea of what could happen, but something totally different to have experienced an attack on the plane and know it could happen again . . . as it just did. *God, Mark would die if he knew—but he didn't . . . she hoped.*

248

"Okay guys, batten down the hatches—we're going in."

Deke answered for all of them. "All set, Captain. Go for it."

Jane gritted her teeth, shut her eyes and found herself praying. In less time than she would have believed possible, she felt a rough bounce, and the plane was rolling down the field. The landing gear held; they were down . . . safely. *The landing gear had held!* She breathed a sigh of relief and murmured, "Thank you, God."

John grinned at her. "Nothin' to it."

She grinned back at him weakly. "Right."

Feeling under the seat for her bag, she remembered Deke's earlier comment and turned to speak to him. "You said we wouldn't be making an immediate turn-around. How long will we be on the ground?"

"Don't know, ma'am. I'd say we'll at least have to RON. Depends on what we find when we check her out. May have to wait for Ramstein to send another bird."

Jane's heart gave a lurch. *RON—that meant remain overnight. They'd probably be here at least one night. Maybe Mark*—she refused to finish the thought. She wasn't going to look him up. She so wasn't.

★　★　★

As it turned out, she didn't have to. Mark was standing in front of the terminal building as she descended from the aircraft. *How had he known?* As she walked toward him across the black tarmac, she could see him watching her—arms crossed, body rigid, eyes . . . angry? *Was he still mad at her from their argument on the telephone?* Her footsteps slowed. She didn't even

249

notice the pilot's approach until he spoke to her.

"Check with Ops after 1800 to see what our status is. They'll have already advised the hospital."

She acknowledged him without turning around. "Call at 1800. Right. I'll do that. The flight engineer said we might have to RON?"

"I'd say it's likely. Looks like you're being met." He tipped his head in Mark's direction, and raised an eyebrow.

Before she could answer, he strode away, calling over his shoulder, "See you later."

He disappeared through the doors of what she guessed was the Operations Building. She was still standing there when the three noncoms passed her. Sergeant Meredith spoke. "John and I are gonna get some chow. Deke needs to talk to the Maintenance people about the plane. He's pretty sure we won't be going anywhere today. If you need me, here's my cell number." She handed over a slip of paper, looked at Mark, then back at Jane, before running to catch up with the departing loadmaster.

Fritz caught up with her and when he spoke, she realized he'd also noticed Mark waiting for her.

"I see you have unfinished business," he said as he glanced toward Mark. "I spoke with Jake, and it's for sure we're going to be here at least a couple of hours. I'll check in with the hospital and give you a call—I've got everyone's cell number."

"Thanks, Fritz. I owe you one."

He shrugged. "It's fine." He grinned before continuing. "I'll see you later; looks as if your *business* is getting impatient."

Mark was no longer standing in front of the building

but was striding across the tarmac toward her. She looked at Fritz, knowing her cheeks were red, but the man was already walking away. His comments floated back to her.

"Go on. I'll meet the captain later."

She was alone on the flight line, and Mark was descending on her like an avenging angel. Unable to move, she watched him approach. When he stood in front of her, he grabbed her arms tightly, and for a minute, neither spoke, their eyes riveted on each other.

"Mark . . . I was afraid . . ."

"You were afraid!"

Seeming to realize where they were he dropped his arms; but then, as if unable to help it, he reached out and gripped one of them again.

"Come on, let's get out of here."

Suddenly it was all too much for her—the hit to their aircraft, the rough landing, the shock of finding Mark waiting for her. She stumbled and would have fallen if he hadn't firmed his grip on her arm. Her eyes filled with tears, and she turned her head, trying to brush them off on her shoulder before he could see them.

He noticed anyway, and stopped their progress. With his thumb, he gently wiped away a tear that was making its way down her cheek, as he gave her his first smile. "It's okay, Jane. You just need to unwind."

She looked at him searchingly, trying to figure out how to take him. "You aren't mad? I thought . . . you looked so . . . fierce. I—" The emotions visible in his dark brown eyes made her heart pound.

"I just had the worst scare in my life, Jane. A guy doesn't get over something like that in an instant," he said, his voice tight.

"Oh." It was all she could think of to say as her eyes rested on him in wonder.

Once through the double doors of the building, Mark headed for the counter marked "Ops." He had dropped her arm, but she followed him as if he still held onto her. He called out to a captain who stood behind the other end of the counter.

"Hey, Gip! I'm taking Lieutenant Brewer to get something to eat. She's the nurse who just came in on that medevac flight." As the captain approached, his eyes rested first on her and then on Mark.

"So, your gut feeling was right—she <u>was</u> on the plane." Gip's gaze moved back to her as he continued. "He came storming in here, said he just landed from a reconnaissance flight when he heard them clear the runway for an emergency landing of a medevac flight that had taken enemy fire and had uncertain landing gear. He demanded—"

"Shut up, Gip. TMI." Mark spoke gruffly, his eyes boring into Gip's,

Gip only grinned and looked back at Jane, bowing slightly, "Welcome to Afghaniland, where life is never dull."

There was no doubt that Gip's sharp eyes had caught her shaken state, but thankfully, neither of them could know it was as much from the shock of seeing Mark so unexpectedly as it was from the attack on the plane.

Her smile was more wavering than dazzling as she tipped her head, "Thanks, but I'll settle for a little less excitement the next time, if you don't mind."

Gip laughed and turned to Mark. "I take it Lieutenant Brewer's a friend of yours?"

"She is."

At the possessive tone in Mark's voice, Gip raised his chin speculatively and Jane knew he had gotten the message Mark intended—*she belonged to him.* The interaction between the two men gave her a warm feeling, and she began to relax for the first time since they had been hit. She had wondered how Mark had known she was on that flight. She smiled slightly at her thoughts, and realized Mark was speaking to Gip.

"You've got my number, Gip—call when you know what's going on with Jane's flight."

"Captain?" Jane asked.

"Call me Gip."

"Gip, do you know how many wounded are scheduled for the return flight to Germany?"

"Um, let me take a look at the manifest." He reached into a pile of papers on the desk behind the counter, pulled out one and frowned. "Six—it says here two ambulatory and four on stretchers."

"Does the hospital know we're here?"

"They do. They also know the aircraft was damaged incoming. We'll keep them posted. You can check in with them for more details."

"Do you have their number handy?"

"Sure do." Gip riffled through his papers again and handed her a list with the number for the hospital prominently highlighted.

She reached into the breast pocket of her flight suit, produced a small notepad with attached pencil, copied down the number, then handed the sheet back to him. Even though Fritz would be checking, she wanted to contact them herself.

"Thanks." She tucked the note pad back into her pocket.

"No problem."

As they turned to leave, Gip spoke again, this time to Mark. "You flying tomorrow?"

Mark shook his head. "Not scheduled to." He shrugged, and she knew that didn't mean he wouldn't be, but she hoped they would be able to have at least the rest of the day and the evening together. They needed time to discuss some things—she had to know where she stood with him. Their whole relationship had been a roller coaster ride.

Mark turned away from the counter without looking at her. In fact, if his demeanor was any clue, he didn't even seem to be aware she was there. By the time they had walked the entire length of the building without one word from him, she couldn't stand it any longer.

"Is Gip a friend of yours?"

"We know each other."

Still the straight-ahead stare. Her worry was turning into anger. "Where are we going?"

"To eat."

Mark pushed open the door, and the brightness of the now mid-morning sky nearly blinded her. She reached for her sunglasses and put them on, noting that Mark did the same, while continuing to stride toward some destination he didn't seem inclined to share. When his pace increased until she was nearly running in order to keep up with him, she'd had enough. She stopped dead in her tracks.

He was so intent on not looking at her that it was several seconds before he realized she was no longer with him. When he did, he stopped and looked back at her, a puzzled expression on his face. "What's the matter? Come on."

"That's it, Mark Vail. I've had enough. I've had *more* than enough. I'm not taking another step until you tell me what the heck is the <u>matter</u> with you. You haven't spoken more than two words since we left Gip back there, and then only because I asked a direct question. You won't even look at me! You won't tell me where we're going, but you're in such an all-fired hurry to get there I've been practically <u>running</u> to keep up with you. That's <u>it</u>!" She raised her chin and crossed her arms across her chest.

Mark stared at her in disbelief. He'd been so shaken by his reaction to her being in danger—and angry with Gip for letting her know about his concern—he hadn't realized what he had been doing, let alone how she would take it. She was definitely angry—looked like a setting hen whose eggs were being stolen—all ruffled feathers. He smothered the grin he knew would be disastrous.

He walked back to where she was standing and took her hands in his, speaking earnestly as he looked deep into her clear green eyes. "I'm sorry, Jane, really sorry. I was trying to straighten some things out in my mind. There's a lot we need to discuss, and I was so anxious to get somewhere we could do that I didn't think about how it would look to you. I apologize."

He looked so worried, and there was so much concern in his dark eyes she felt her anger evaporating. *Darn the man, all he had to do was look at her, and she melted.* "It's okay. Let's go . . . but a little more slowly, please. I don't have your long legs. I must have looked like a puppy trying to keep up with its mother."

He smiled at the picture she painted. "I'll pace myself. How's that?"

"You do that."

Mark began walking, this time taking shorter steps. Jane easily kept pace with him.

"That's much better," she breathed.

He smiled at her, his mind still trying to come up with a place they could go—somewhere quiet enough that he could say all the things he knew he must.

"If we're going to eat, how come we just left the terminal? All the rest of the crew were eating in the cafeteria."

"And that's why!" His frustration showed in his voice. "We're about half a block from the chow hall. We'll go there."

"Won't it be crowded there too?" Jane frowned in confusion.

"Not with people who know us."

She looked at her watch and saw that it was after 1300—*no wonder her belly was growling.* She quickened her pace as she spoke. "Then, let's get there. I had a breakfast burrito at 0430 this morning. I'm starved."

He laughed. "You're the one who wanted to slow down."

Minutes later they were moving through the chow line in the huge building that comprised the mess facility for the installation. She scooped scrambled eggs, several sausage patties, home fries, and fried apples onto her tray, and then reached for several slices of toast.

Mark looked at her tray, clapped his hand to his chest

and pretended shock.

She shrugged. "I love breakfast—and I <u>told</u> you I was hungry." She noticed he was also getting breakfast and realized he probably hadn't eaten in some time either. He filled a cup with coffee and set it on her tray, then filled another for himself, as he motioned toward several empty tables near the wall.

"I'll get this; you find us a table."

Nodding, she picked up her tray, and moved away from the line. After setting her tray on one of the empty tables, she sat down. As she waited, she selected a few packets of creamer and sweetener from the container in the middle of the table and fixed her coffee. She took a sip and then a long drink from the heavy mug before setting it down.

As Mark sat down, she picked up her fork and began to eat. She looked over at him. "Sorry, but I'm starved." After several mouthfuls, she wiped her mouth with her napkin. "Mark, I need to check in with the hospital. Is there a telephone here?"

"You can use my cell, but the hospital's only about a block from here. If you want, we can just walk over."

"That's fine, but if you don't mind I'd like to call them now—just so they know."

He pulled the phone out of one of his pockets and handed it across the table.

"This'll just take a minute." She already had her notepad out and proceeded to punch in the numbers. He watched her whole demeanor change into that of a serious medical professional.

"Yes. This is Lieutenant Jane Brewer. I'm the nurse from the medevac flight that came in this morning from Landstuhl." She nodded several times as she listened

257

and then spoke again. "Right. I'll be checking in with Ops later, but the general consensus seems to be that we won't be getting out today. Do you need me to come by now?" Again, she waited and then spoke. "No problem. I'll be there." She looked at her watch, then closed the phone and handed it back to Mark.

"They'd already gotten the word, and were expecting my call. The briefing on the patients being transported is at 1500. Fritz is calling the rest of the team."

"Fine. That gives us several hours." He looked at her steadily with the hint of a smile, then shook his head. "I still can't believe you're here."

"Aren't you glad to see me?"

"You know the answer to that. We need to talk, Jane. I just wish I could come up with some place a little more private." Suddenly his eyes lit up at something he saw over her shoulder. "That's it!"

"That's what?" She frowned, confused.

"Excuse me, Jane. I need to speak to Gip about something. Be right back." He stood abruptly and strode across the large room as she watched. *What was so urgent that he had to speak to the Captain now?* They had just seen him, and it hadn't seemed to her they were all that friendly.

As Mark hurried across the room, the irony of what he was doing struck him. Asking Gip for a favor was the last thing he would normally do, especially when the man already suspected . . . but these weren't normal circumstances. *Whatever it took.* He was waiting when Gip came through the chow line. "Gip! You're just the person I need to see."

"Yeah?" Gip arched an eyebrow, then his eyes scanned the room. "You got a table—I'll join you."

Mark's cheeks reddened. "Um, yes . . . uh no . . . uh. Look, I don't want you to sit with us. I just need—" He stopped in mid-sentence as he watched Gip look around the crowded room, then look back at him with laughter-filled eyes.

"Ah so. Well, if you don't want my company, what is it you want from me? I see the lovely Lieutenant sitting over there."

"Look, Gip, I need a vehicle, just for a little while. Can I borrow your Humvee?" At Gip's expression, he raised his hand to stop him from interrupting. "I know . . . I'll owe you big time."

"Well—"

Damn it all, the man was grinning. "Come on, Gip—I wouldn't be asking . . . wouldn't be putting myself in your debt if it wasn't an emergency."

Gip looked over at the woman watching them curiously. "What if I need it? What if a *real* emergency comes up?"

"Like what? We'll drop you off back at your office. Your emergencies will be on the flight line—where you'll already be. You can do this, Gip. Please. I won't forget it."

Gip chuckled. "Don't worry—I won't let you forget it." A wide grin spread across his face. "Hmmmm . . . okay, you can have it. But, you can't go far . . . on the off chance that I do need it. You have to be close enough to get it back in—"

"Five minutes. I only need it for—" Mark's mind scrambled to figure out the most time he could bargain for. *Jane had to be at the hospital in ninety minutes.* "For an hour, hour-and-a-half, that's all. I'll have it back and parked in front of Ops. You have my word. Now, is

259

it a deal?"

Gip stuck out his hand and Mark shook it.

"Thanks, Gip. I'll see you in an hour-and-a-half."

Gip raised his eyebrows. "You mean you still don't want me to sit with you, not even after I was so generous?"

Mark's scowl was sufficient answer. "You're only lending it to me for a lousy hour-and-a-half. Now go find your own table . . . and eat fast."

"You're a hard man, Mark, a hard man."

"Right . . . and you're gonna demand blood for this favor."

Gip's tuneless "dum de dum dum" floated over his shoulder as he went to find his own table.

When Mark finally reached their table, Jane was full of questions. "What was that all about?"

"I borrowed Gip's vehicle."

"It didn't look like it was that simple from here."

He shrugged. "Simple enough."

She rolled her eyes. "What's it going to cost you?" she said dryly.

"Don't worry about it. I got it, and we're getting out of here as soon as Gip finishes eating."

She glanced over her shoulder at the man who was the subject of their conversation. Gip caught her eye and winked as he made speed-up motions with one hand while spooning in food with the other. When he laughed, she found herself laughing back at him.

She turned back to Mark. "I got the impression earlier that you barely knew him."

"I didn't say that." He didn't elaborate, and she looked at him suspiciously.

"What did you do, sell your soul for his vehicle?"

He scowled at her. "Not quite. Now, finish your breakfast. We're leaving in a few minutes."

She looked over at Gip's table again, and saw he was almost finished; he'd apparently wolfed down his food. *What had Mark said to him?* She swallowed the last bite of her food and wiped her mouth with her napkin as Gip stood up and headed toward them. Mark was already pushing his chair back, and she quickly stood up too.

Mark didn't wait for Gip to get to their table, but met him in the center of the room. Gip reached in his pocket and pulled out a set of keys, which he dangled in the air. Before he could speak to her, Mark moved between them, grabbed the keys, and reached out in a herding motion. "Come on, Gip. If you want us to drop you off, let's move it."

Gip looked at Jane and rolled his eyes. "I don't see what's the rush."

Mark hmphed. "You wouldn't."

The Humvee was parked in front of the dining hall. Mark got in on the driver's side while Gip held the passenger door for Jane. She slid across the wide seat until she was thigh-to-thigh with Mark. Gip slid in, pushing against her more than was necessary before pulling the door shut. Determined not to let him see she didn't appreciate his action, she stared determinedly through the windshield.

Seconds later, Mark stopped in front of the Operations building, and Gip got out of the vehicle. Once on the ground he stuck his head back in the vehicle, but he'd barely opened his mouth when Mark glared at him and growled, "Don't say anything, Gip . . . just don't."

Gip backed out of the Humvee, looking at his watch

as he did so. "Ninety minutes—from <u>now</u>!" He grinned as he slammed the door, leaving Mark muttering, "Or what, it'll turn into a pumpkin?"

Jane moved unobtrusively and put a few inches between them. "What's going on between you two?"

"We're not wasting any part of this hour talking about Gip Bogart," he said decisively.

"Okay, fine. What *are* we talking about? Where are we going?"

Mark's hands were on the steering wheel of the Humvee, and he was staring straight ahead. "Nowhere!" He turned to look at her defiantly, and she stared back at him as if he had lost his mind. "You went to all that trouble to get this vehicle to go nowhere?"

"I don't want to <u>go</u> anywhere. I want some *privacy,* and if the inside of a Humvee is the only place we can find it, it'll have to do. I need to talk to you . . . and I'm not going to do it in the middle of Flight Operations or a crowded dining hall, or . . . or . . . I'm just not."

He started the vehicle, and she watched him in silence. Whatever he had on his mind, it was very obvious from the way he was acting that it was something big. A frown formed on his face, and his eyes moved rapidly from one side of the road to the other; then he glanced at his watch and cursed softly under his breath.

She reached across the narrow space between them and touched his thigh. He jumped as if she'd burned him.

"Don't <u>do</u> that!"

She yanked her hand back and stared through the windshield.

"Damn it, Jane. I'm sorry. I didn't mean that the way it sounded. It's just that I'm . . . I . . . we just need to talk. If

I can ever find a place to park—ah, I think I've found it."
He slowed down, and she was surprised to see where they were."

"This is the BOQ. Is this where you live?" A hint of a smile was on her lips as she spoke.

He looked over at her, and his voice was firm when he spoke. "Don't worry, we're just going to park behind the quarters. We're not going inside."

"We're not?" Her face fell. "Then, why are we here?"

"Because this lot is always deserted at this time of day. I told you, we need to <u>talk</u>—and that's what we're gonna do."

He opened the door and got out of the vehicle, and she did the same, her eyes puzzled. He motioned toward a covered picnic table and benches in the open court of the buildings. They headed in that direction, just as a truck pulled up. Two airmen got out and walked around to its rear, where they proceeded to unload tool kits and lumber. After Jane and Mark returned the men's salutes, Mark put his hand to his head and huffed out a breath. She recognized his frustration at the seeming impossibility of finding privacy anywhere but in his room. He looked at his watch. She knew he was watching their brief time slowly get away from them. He glanced at her, then shrugged.

"Come on."

"Where are we going now?" She almost giggled—this was beginning to assume comic proportions.

"Inside. The dayroom will be deserted this time of day."

"The dayroom?"

"Yes, the dayroom," he almost yelled.

They were going to the dayroom . . . when this was

263

his BOQ . . . where he had a perfectly good—and surely empty—room. *What was wrong with the man?*

Mark's expression dared her to say anything, so she didn't.

Once inside the building he stopped in the hall and looked around. Silence greeted them. He told her to wait, and walked down the hall to the office. He disappeared inside, and she heard voices. He returned a few minutes later, a look of satisfaction on his face, as he brandished a key.

"Come on. The dayroom's vacant, and what's more it's got a key—and I've got it."

She rolled her eyes before following him down the hall. He unlocked the room, motioned her inside, and then locked the door behind them. She looked around at the empty room furnished with a TV, several comfortable couches and overstuffed chairs, a few tables piled with magazines. The only window looked out over the parking area, where the two airmen were still unloading lumber from their truck. She faced Mark, folded her arms on her chest, and scowled at him. "Now, are you going to tell me what's been going on with you? You've been acting strangely ever since I got here."

He walked toward her until he was right in front of her. Her arms dropped to her side. Mark touched her cheek with one strong finger, then pulled her to him and kissed her desperately. Her heart pounding, she put her arms around his neck and pulled him closer. They were both breathing hard when he stepped back, his eyes studying hers.

"And you don't know why that is?"

Wide-eyed, and under the spell of his kiss, she slowly shook her head.

"You scare me to death, Jane Brewer."

Whatever she had expected him to say, that wasn't it. She opened her mouth, but no words came out.

He grasped her arm and led her over to one of the couches, where he gently pushed her down and settled beside her.

"You scare me. You have since the beginning because whenever I get near you, I lose all common sense." He took a deep breath. "You make me think of a house to come home to at night, white picket fences, and kids and dogs . . . impossible stuff."

He looked away from her, and she could see he was struggling to control himself. Her heart thrilled to the realization that this man she had loved for so long actually loved her back, whether or not he had realized it yet.

She leaned against him and whispered urgently into his ear. "Mark, take me to your room, to your bed."

"No!"

"But that's what you want . . . what we *both* want."

The fire in his eyes said yes, but his voice was hard when he spoke. "I <u>do</u> want it, more than anything, but I won't . . . not until we're . . . not now," he gritted out.

She let out a plaintive wail, "Then marry me . . . today."

He froze, his voice expressionless and his eyes filed with pain. "You know that's not possible."

She seemed to crumple in on herself as he watched. He stood, his hands tight fists, the veins in his forearms standing out, as he tried to keep from taking her in his arms again, an action that would land them exactly where he had forbidden himself to go. When she finally spoke, she sounded defeated.

"You won't. Even though it's what we both want. Even though we may never have the opportunity again in this lifetime."

His eyes flashed at her. "That's not fair!"

She held his eyes. "I'm not playing fair."

He groaned. Tears streaked her pale face as her eyes pleaded with him. She had never looked more beautiful. *God help him, he could not do this.* He shut his eyes and took a deep breath.

Seeing his pain, she stood and moved toward him, but his eyes flew open, and he spoke ferociously.

"<u>No</u>! Don't come any closer."

The words hit her like a weapon, cutting her to the quick. She backed away, arms to her side, watching him.

His eyes beseeched the ceiling. Then, as if receiving strength from above, he stiffened his shoulders. His eyes begged for her understanding as he walked away from her toward the window.

There was only silence until she softly said his name, "Mark?"

He shuddered as if her cry had physically wounded him, but he didn't turn around. She stood for several seconds, staring at his rigid back. Her own shoulders slumped, and she had already turned away when he spoke.

"You'd better go, Jane. This wasn't a good idea."

His voice sounded odd. She knew that this man would always do what he determined was right, no matter the cost, and in his mind this was. She admired his strength, even as it frustrated her.

"Goodbye, Mark," she said sadly, the words catching in her throat.

"So long, Jane."

266

He continued to stare out the window, refusing to look at her. Knowing she had lost, she reached for the door. She heard him move, and knew he had turned to watch her.

He spoke just as she reached the door. Her hand stilled on the knob, but she didn't look back. His words were so soft she barely heard them.

"I . . . I love you, Jane."

"I know," she answered, tears in her voice, as she opened the door and walked through. As it closed behind her, she heard Mark's fist slam into the wall. She drew some small satisfaction from the fact that his frustration was equal to hers.

★   ★   ★

She came out of the building and stood indecisively, trying to decide whether to laugh or cry. Refusing to let herself do either, she took a deep breath and looked around. She was on foot, and she had no idea where the hospital was located. *What a mess!* Then her normal optimism came through, and she smiled. *Mark had admitted that he loved her, and that was something. That was definitely something.*

The two men working in the small courtyard had been joined by another man who'd apparently delivered more construction materials. The third man was about to get back in his truck and leave—*and there was her ride!* She'd take it as a sign—things were definitely going to be all right.

She hurried toward the courtyard as she hailed the man. "Airman!"

He turned curiously, then straightened and saluted her. "Yes, ma'am."

"Airman, I need to get to the hospital. Do you know where it is, and could you give me a ride?"

He nodded. "It's not far from here; I go by there on my way back to the yard. Hop in, Lieutenant." He gave her a wide grin.

She got in and fastened her seatbelt. As her chauffeur backed up and turned out onto the road, she looked out the window. Mark had come out of the BOQ and stood on the walk looking up and down the street. She knew he must be puzzled that she had disappeared so quickly. It had obviously just occurred to him that she would have no way to get to the hospital, and he'd come looking for her. She was glad he wouldn't find her waiting. Their recent argument had been too emotional, and she didn't want to face him again right now.

Her ride stopped in front of the hospital, and she forced herself to focus on the men and women who would soon be in her care. Hopping out of the car, she thanked the young airman and entered the large building, looking around in fascination. She'd heard that the Craig Joint Theater Hospital was the most advanced in the area, and the 41-bed facility certainly appeared to be.

It was after 1930 when she finally sat down in her seat aboard the C-9 for the return trip to Landstuhl and automatically inserted her earplugs against the inflight noise. The decision had been made to replace their original aircraft—which would be grounded for several days while undergoing repairs. It had been a busy afternoon for her and the rest of the medical crew. She and Sergeant Meredith had taken care of prepping the

268

patients for onloading. Fritz and the other med-techs had arranged for the loading of necessary equipment and medical supplies in addition to configuring the replacement plane for their medical mission. The wounded were all safely strapped in and ready for wheels up. Once in flight, she and the rest of the crew would maintain a close watch over them during their trip. Essentially a flying hospital, the aircraft was equipped with all manner of life support equipment from ventilators to heart monitors. Having meticulously reviewed the PMR—Patient Movement Request—and medical records for each patient, Jane and her team would be able to monitor their condition during the flight. They would help reduce a patient's pain level and continue any necessary treatment. It would be a busy seven hours for the team, but for now—until they were safely airborne—she could take a breather.

Gip, still on duty in Operations, had told her she'd just missed Mark, who'd gone up on an unscheduled reconnaissance flight. When she'd asked, Gip told her Mark knew she'd be gone by the time he returned. He must have asked about her flight. She was glad that he knew, and breathed a silent prayer for his safety.

From the time she had stepped inside the door of the hospital, there'd been no time to reflect on the emotional scene with Mark. Now, her thoughts returned to their conversation earlier in the day—*had it really been today? So much had happened.* She'd been mad when he'd refused to take her to bed . . . but, looking back—it was probably a good thing. What would he do when he saw the ugly scars on her body? She should have told him . . . should tell him . . . but he'd never forgiven himself for leaving her without saying goodbye, for not contacting her again. Once he knew she'd been pregnant—and what she'd gone through when she'd lost the baby—he'd not only be angry with her for not telling him—that she could take—but he'd never get over not being there for her. No . . . it would be better to wait. She remembered his last words, hugging them to her heart until they could meet again.

Mark was devastated when Jane walked out the door, even though he'd been the one to insist upon it. Neither of them could endure another scene like that. It occurred to him that he'd given up the idea that he didn't deserve her. *She was his, and he was taking her.* He loved her, although he certainly hadn't planned to tell her. It had just come out. It was apparently a moot point anyway, since her last words as she walked out the door had been, "I know."

He scrubbed his hand through his short hair. *What was he going to do?* There was only one thing to do. He'd ask her to marry him, as soon as possible. People got married in foreign countries—they'd just have to work out the problems. Somehow. Having made up his mind, he had an urgent need to find her and tell her. He couldn't let her leave without knowing his intentions. He rushed out the door after her, then stood puzzled, staring up and down the empty street. *How had she disappeared so quickly when she was on foot?* Dispirited, he headed for his room. He'd try to call her at the hospital.

His phone was ringing as he entered the room. He had a fleeting hope that it was Jane calling him. His hopes were dashed as soon as he picked it up and heard the voice of the flight scheduling officer from Ops.

Mark was afraid his frustration was evident in his voice. "Now? But what . . . I'm—" He looked at his watch. "—I'm only seven hours into crew rest."

He scrubbed his hand through his hair again as he listened, his voice resigned when he finally spoke. "Yeah. Okay. Understood. I'll be there—" He looked at his watch again. "—in fifteen minutes. I'm in the BOQ."

He put the phone down and looked at himself in the mirror over the dresser. There was no time for a shower; he'd just have to shave and change into a clean flight suit. As he ran the razor over his face, he found himself praying Jane would still be here when he got back. With any luck, they wouldn't be able to get the plane repaired for a while. *Damn it all.* Sometimes it seemed as if he and Jane were never destined to get together at all.

From long practice, he forced his current thoughts into a separate compartment of his brain to concentrate fully on the mission facing him. By the time he finished shaving and donned the clean uniform, his fifteen minutes were gone. Luckily, he still had Gip's vehicle— he could return it at the same time as he reported to Ops.

Chapter 12

It was late afternoon when Mark landed. Although many of the dangerous surveillance and bombing runs were now done by drone aircraft, he and his fellow F-16 pilots were still kept busy flying cover for convoys and troop movements on the ground. Their workload would only increase, and their downtime lessen, with the slow decrease in the number of pilots assigned as the U.S. began the drawdown.

Exhausted, he rubbed one hand over his sweaty face, longing for a hot shower after the long hours in the cockpit. It wouldn't happen soon. He still had to complete his trip report at Operations, and then the debriefing at his squadron. It would be dark before he finished.

Gip wasn't working, so he asked the lieutenant on duty—Jernigan, according to his name tag—if the medevac flight to Landstuhl had gotten off.

"They left at 1930."

Mark nodded and started filling out the report. *He'd just missed her.* He felt disappointment and frustration with the way their relationship was going, but more than anything, he was angry at himself for sending her away like he had. "Damn!"

"What's that, Captain?"

Too late he realized he'd spoken aloud. "Nothing. Just wrote in the wrong block."

The lieutenant returned to his task, and Mark grimaced.

As Mark had expected, it was long after dark when he finished. Outside the ops building, he adjusted his flight cap and looked around the brightly lit area. He glanced at his watch; he still wanted that hot shower, but might as well get something to eat first. As he headed toward the mess facility, the scene with Jane replayed in his head. He needed to talk to Hawk—Hawk would understand after all the complications in his romance with Kit. His mind made up, Mark quickened his steps. He'd eat, go back to his quarters and shower —then he'd call Hawk.

He never made the call. When he got to the dining hall, he ended up sitting with a group of guys from the squadron. They convinced him to go to the movies. It was the last thing he'd felt like doing, but it was better than sitting around his room beating himself up over his handling of Jane's visit.

He rolled and tossed all night. He woke the next morning still wavering between calling Hawk and giving him the opportunity to laugh at his predicament, or working out his problem for himself. He and Hawk had shared everything over the last seven years—well, most things. He'd never told anyone about what happened on that Christmas leave at Matt's . . . although Hawk apparently had his suspicions. Between his indecision about making the call and an operational problem at the squadron, it was mid-afternoon before he got around to making the call to Hawk. He'd already dialed the number in North Carolina before he thought to look at his watch and grimaced. It would be very early in the morning there.

He spoke before Hawk could answer. "Did I wake you?"

"At 0530 in the morning! What do you think?" Hawk growled into the phone.

"I'm sorry, man. I need to talk to you." He could hear the rustle of fabric and knew Hawk was scrambling to sit up in the bed.

"What's so urgent? Why are you calling this time?"

After several seconds of silence, Mark spoke defensively. "I'm . . . I'm in love."

"With Jane, I assume."

"What do you mean, *with Jane*? Of course, with Jane!"

"Well, Hallelujah! You're finally admitting it! Kit and I have been wondering how long it would take you."

"Is she there?"

"At this time of the morning? Of course she's here. You wanna talk to her?"

"No! I need to talk to you . . . in private. Can you—"

"Can I what? Ditch your sister—my *wife*? You know better. She's already awake and knows I'm talking to you, but I'll go downstairs. Why the need for privacy?"

Mark took a deep breath. Although he'd felt the need to talk to Hawk, he hadn't taken the time to formulate

274

what he would say, or how he should say it. In the end he just blurted it out. "I need to marry Jane. Now!"

"Mark . . . Did you get Kit's best friend *pregnant*?"

"<u>No</u>! I did <u>not</u> get her pregnant."

"Then, why do you need to marry her in such a hurry?" Hawk asked logically.

"I just told you—I love her."

"Um hmm. So what's the problem? Isn't the woman willing?"

"I . . . I haven't asked her yet."

"And you have some reason to think she won't say yes?"

"She already asked me." Mark clapped his hand over his eyes as he heard Hawk's shout of laughter and realized what he had said. "Hawk Hawkins, if you tell my sister that, I'll kill you. I swear, I'll kill you."

"Okay, now you've got my attention. So how did 'Mr. Life According to Plan' get himself into such a mess?"

Hawk's laughter again came through the line, and Mark could only hope his sister was no longer within hearing distance as Hawk continued.

"Let's go back to your earlier comment—'she already asked you.' I find that *very* interesting. Care to provide some details?"

Mark groaned. This was not going at all the way he had anticipated. "NO! I don't care to provide <u>any</u> details. And you're not making this easy, man. I called you—at this time of the morning—because I'm desperate. I need *help*. And all you can do is laugh."

"Sorry, buddy, but I gotta tell you this is a momentous occasion—the Bronc has finally fallen. Never thought I'd see the day—"

"Hawk!"

"Okay, okay. Sorry. What do you want from me?"

"What I called for—advice. I need *help*, Hawk."

"Oookay. Well, first of all, when you say 'now,' what does that mean? How soon are you planning to do the deed?"

"As soon as I can. As soon as . . . if . . . when she agrees."

"If? When? I thought she'd already asked you! Why *wouldn't* she agree? What did you <u>say</u> to her?"

Mark groaned again, realizing how this was going to sound. "I—I told her it wasn't possible. I made her leave. And now I don't know how to—"

"How in hell did you—? No, don't tell me. You are in *deep* trouble."

"You are <u>not</u> <u>helping</u>!" Mark could hear Kit in the background. When Hawk covered the receiver and started talking to her, he realized he had made a mistake. No one could tell him how to straighten out the mess he had made of his life—and now everyone would know about it. Things just got worse and worse.

Hawk came back on the line. "Kit's standing here beside me, demanding to talk to you. If I don't give her the phone, she's just going to go pick up the extension."

Mark sighed. "Fine, put her on. Things can't get any worse."

"Mark Vail! What have you done! You got Jane *pregnant*?"

"For the second time, I did <u>not</u> get Jane pregnant. And I am <u>not</u> discussing this with you. It's none of your business. I don't know why I even called. It was definitely a mistake."

"Stop grumbling, Mark, and tell me how you got yourself into this predicament. This is not like you at all!

Tell me how you got yourself into this predicament. If you want help fixing it, you've got to tell me what happened."

What a miserable mess! But he might as well be hung for a sheep as a cow. He resignedly began his story.

"Okay. Kit, I've really botched it with Jane."

"In that case brother, you're talking to the wrong people. Jane's the one you need to talk to. Call her and apologize."

"I can't."

"Why can't you? What's she going to do—hang up on you?"

"She did that last time."

"What *last time*? You mean this has happened before?"

He heard what sounded like a giggle. "Are you laughing at me?"

"Of course not! But I have to admit, there's a certain satisfaction in knowing my lofty brother has at last met his match. I'm glad Jane doesn't let you walk all over her, that she can stand up to you."

"You're not very sympathetic for a sister."

"Nope!"

This time he definitely heard her giggling. "Put Hawk back on."

"Goodbye, Mark . . . good luck. You're going to need it."

He heard her say something to Hawk, and then his friend was back on the line.

"I have to say, Hawk, your wife wasn't much help."

"What did you expect! She's your sister, your *long-suffering* sister I might add."

"Et tu, Brute?"

277

"I am sympathetic, Mark, I just don't know what you expect from me. Kit's advice was the best we have to offer—call the woman and offer your abject apologies. Beg. Maybe she might forgive you."

"Gee thanks, buddy. Go back to sleep."

"It's time to get up now, and you're welcome."

"So long Hawk. Thanks for listening, anyway."

"Any time. Be sure you call and let us know how it works out."

"I'll have to think about it." He hung up. That had gone well—not. Might as well call Jane. *Here goes nothing,* he thought as he dialed the number at Landstuhl, asked the hospital operator for Jane's number and waited for the transfer. In the intervening minutes, he had time to reconsider what he was doing and realize how dumb it was. He had decided to hang up when he heard her voice.

"This is Lieutenant Brewer."

"Jane!"

"Mark?"

"Marry me!" *Well that was cool,* he thought. *What was wrong with him?*

"What?"

"Marry me. Now."

"I thought you didn't want to marry me. 'It's impossible,' I think you said, not twenty-four hours ago."

"I didn't mean it. I was wrong. I've reconsidered." He remembered Hawk's advice. "Please, Jane. I'm sorry. I—I love you. I *need* you. Please say you'll marry me."

"What happened since yesterday? How come you refused to marry me yesterday, and now you want to marry me right away? What's changed, Mark?"

278

"I always wanted to marry you. I just didn't think it was possible logistically, but—"

"And now it is?"

"It *has* to be —we can work it out. Just say you'll marry me. I'll do whatever—"

"I'll marry you."

"—whatever it takes. Please, Jane. You have to forgive me—"

"I said, yes. I'll marry you, Mark."

"Oh . . . you did? You did! Thank God!"

"I've agreed to marry you, Mark, but someday I expect you to tell me what happened in the last twenty-four hours. It must be a doozie of a story, whatever it is."

"Um, all right, some day." As he said it, he knew he wasn't about to let her find out about his phone call to Kit and Hawk. Bad enough they knew how she tied him in knots—he'd humbled himself enough.

"Mark?" Her words jerked him back to the present.

"Yeah. I'll check with the legal types here and see what it takes to marry in Afghanistan. You check it out on your end, and we'll get married wherever it's easier."

"I don't think it's easy to get married in any foreign country."

"It can't be that hard, but I'm sure it's easier there in Germany than it is here. See what you can find out. I'll call you tonight."

"Okay. And Mark?"

"What?"

"I love you." For a minute he didn't answer. When he did, his voice was almost a whisper.

"And I love you. I know sometimes I haven't acted like it, but I do. Someday I hope I can prove it to you.

279

'Til tonight."

"Tonight. 'Bye, Mark."

★   ★   ★

Mark's day was busy. By the time he sat down to call Jane that night, he knew it would be easier to marry in Germany than Afghanistan. He'd talked at length with the chaplain who had laid out all the difficulties he'd face, and all the hoops he'd have to jump through to comply with the local requirements.

After his discouraging talk with the chaplain, he'd gone by the squadron and talked with his commander, who had offered him a three-day leave to get married in Germany. Now, if only Jane had been able to learn what it would take to get married there. He dialed her number, anticipating just hearing her voice, as he settled back to wait for the connection,

"Hi, Mark. I just finished dinner. Hold for a second."

He could hear her voice as she excused herself, and then she was back on the line.

"Okay, how did your day go?"

"I sure hope the results of your research are better than mine. Getting married here is just NOT possible. Not realistically anyway."

Mark sounded discouraged. She sighed. "Well . . ."

"Ah, Jane, don't tell me—"

"It's not all that good here, either. It *is* possible, but it won't be quick, and it won't be easy. I went by the chaplain's office as soon as my shift was done today. I've got all the info, but we have to have recent copies of our birth certificates, military ID card, an affidavit from the Legal Office, and income statements. And everything has to be translated." She sighed again. "The chaplain said it takes from four to six weeks."

"You're kidding! Four to six *weeks*!"

"Mark, we'll both be back in the States in two months. Wouldn't it just be easier to wait until we're back in the States to get married?"

He groaned. She was right—both of their tours were up in November, within days of each other—if they didn't get extended. "I know. You're right . . . but I don't want to get married in two months, I want to get married now." *Dammit! He sounded like a spoiled child. What was happening to him?* He pushed his hand through his hair and tried to calm himself down.

"I don't want to wait either, Mark. I'm trying to be realistic."

This time he took a deep breath before speaking, and when he did his voice sounded calm and reasonable. "I know, I know. I'm sorry if I sound angry. I'm not, at least not with you. I'm just frustrated."

"Now, aren't you sorry you didn't take me when I offered?"

He could hear the laughter in her voice, and he had to see the humor in the situation.

"If you were here right now, I'd reconsider."

"Mark!"

"Good thing you're not here. Okay, I guess we'll plan a wedding for two months from now. Tell your parents, and I'll ask Hawk and Kit to take care of the logistics for us."

"All right . . . but do you think . . . that's a lot of work for them?"

"This isn't going to be a big wedding . . . is it?"

"No, of course not, but still."

"If we get married there, Hawk can reserve the

chapel, and the club for our reception. Kit can order flowers, and whatever. You can talk to her about the other stuff."

Mark was back in his usual take-charge mode. He had decided this was the best they could do, and he'd make it work. She breathed a sigh of relief. He'd had her worried there for a minute.

It was finally dawn. Jane had only slept in snatches and was actually relieved to get up. As soon as Mark hung up last night, an idea had popped into her head. She had pushed it out, but it had persisted, and she had rolled and tossed all night, examining it from all angles, poking holes in it, and then refilling them.

Her decision was made. *It was the right thing to do, and she was going to do it.* She could be every bit as plan-oriented and determined as Mark Vail when the occasion called for it. And it did! She bounced out of bed, grinning, and punched her fist in the air.

Waiting until she returned to the States to marry Mark made sense. She'd go ahead with her plans and let him go ahead with his. But as he had said, there was no way they could be sure it would happen then, not given their situations. So, she'd put her own plan into operation.

There was no reason they had to wait to consummate the marriage to be. They could have a "pre-wedding" honeymoon, as it were. Mark wouldn't object because he wouldn't know; she wouldn't tell him. Not until she was standing right in front of him, all tied up in ribbons. He had refused her once, but she knew—he'd admitted as much—he wouldn't be able to do it again.

And she'd better get in the shower or she'd be late for

work despite having risen so early. She wrapped her arms around herself in a hug, happier than she'd been in a long time. There'd been one stumbling block after another in their romance; it was time, and this felt right.

Two weeks later her confidence was slipping. She'd gone online, found a posh lingerie store back in the States, and ordered the most gorgeous, sexiest nightgown they had. It had arrived last week, and was everything she could have wished. It was in the bottom of her lingerie drawer just waiting to be stashed in her flight bag. Now, all she needed was a trip to Afghanistan, which hadn't happened yet.

She'd certainly been busy— several Stateside and Iraq evac missions, even a flight to Kyrgyzstan. She loved her work. She had never felt more useful or needed in her life. Mark had called several times, and they emailed regularly. It was getting harder and harder to keep her secret though, and she was going to burst if something didn't happen soon. The regular weekly evac trip to Afghanistan was tomorrow, and once again—she wasn't on it. That meant another week would go by. It had to be the regular mission, because emergency flights never remained on the ground long—just onloaded the patient, or patients, and began the return flight within hours. It had to be the regular mission because that one always stayed overnight.

She had just returned from a flight to Andrews AFB and wasn't scheduled for duty until tomorrow at 0700, so she might as well do some laundry. Her phone rang as she headed out the door with her bundle of dirty clothes. She dropped the laundry to grab it, hoping to hear

283

Mark's voice. Instead she heard the hospital duty sergeant.

"Lieutenant Brewer, this is Sergeant McKinney."

"Yes, sergeant."

"Ma'am, I know you just got back from CONUS, but we've got a problem. Captain Nicholas was supposed to take the weekly evac run to Afghanistan tomorrow, but she's down with the flu. You're the only flight nurse available. You'll be crewing with Lieutenant Redfern, and Sergeants Bronson, DeVeau, and Barksdale. Sergeant Bronson will be the Charge Medic Technician."

It was difficult to keep her voice calm as she replied. "Got it. Departure time is when?"

"At 0700, with a scheduled arrival time of 1400. Return departure time is 0700 the following day. Manifest indicates six patients for the return flight. Any questions, Lieutenant?"

"No. I've got it." She replaced the phone and picked up her abandoned laundry, her mind definitely not on dirty clothes. As she walked down the hall to the laundry room, she went over in her mind all she had to do. First and foremost was make sure that sexy nightie was in her flight bag. Then . . . *should she call Mark . . . or not?* She'd love to surprise him, but it was too much of a risk. She didn't want him to be somewhere else when she got there. She'd have to call and let him know. It would be surprise enough when he found out what she planned to do.

She dumped the laundry in the washing machine and hurried back to her room. Now, if she could just reach Mark. Looking at her watch, she quickly calculated the time difference and decided this was as good a time as any. Thank goodness for cell phones. Luck was with her, and Mark answered on the second ring.

"What are you doing tomorrow about 1400?"

"Why?"

She could hardly contain her excitement. "We've got a scheduled evac flight tomorrow at 0700—and I'm on it! We should get to Bagram around 1400."

"I'll be flying . . . until late afternoon probably."

Trying to keep the disappointment out of her voice, she spoke quickly. "No problem. I'll check in with the hospital, verify the patient load, look over the manifests, then get a room." *She almost giggled. Getting a room would definitely not be necessary if things went according to plan.* "Why don't you call me when you land. You can go by your room for a shower, then we can meet for dinner."

"Sure . . . sounds great. See you tomorrow. Look, Jane, I have to go. Take care."

"I will. Love you."

"Me too. See you tomorrow." The line went dead.

She pocketed her phone and frowned, puzzled. Mark had sounded weird—almost as if he weren't glad she was coming. Surely, she was wrong. He was probably with a bunch of his friends and didn't want them to know who he was talking to . . . or something. But she couldn't put it out of her mind. The rest of the evening, as she folded laundry, packed her flight bag, and prepared for bed, she replayed his conversation over and over in her mind. It wasn't what he had said exactly, more what he hadn't said. Maybe she ought to reconsider her plan.

Once in bed, despite an awareness of her early rising time, it was a long time before she fell sleep,

★   ★   ★

This time, the flight to Bagram was uneventful. So far, everything had gone according to plan. After a late lunch with the other members of her team, she and Robyn, the other nurse, had gone by the hospital to get briefed for the next day's return flight to Landstuhl. At 1700 she had begged off from seeing a movie, and had gotten a ride to the quarters.

Instead of getting a room for herself, she had prevailed upon the billeting clerk to let her into Mark's room. Which had not been easy. But it had worked, and she was taking that as a good sign. Mark had just called from Operations and said he was going to his room for a quick shower and would meet her in the day room—ah yes, the infamous day room. Now that the moment was almost upon her, her whole body shivered with nerves. But this was no time for second thoughts. *He was on his way—here!* She had to hurry.

In the bathroom, she stripped out of her flight suit and stepped into the shower. Minutes later she was donning the filmy nightgown. It really was lovely . . . and barely there. As she stood in front of the mirror, she slowly gripped the hem of the short gown and pulled it up to shoulder height. She smoothed one hand over the long scar running from just below her breasts to her lower abdomen. *What would Mark think when he saw it?* It wasn't too awful looking . . . although maybe she was just used to it. It <u>had</u> faded considerably in five-and-a-half years. She let the sheer gown fall and smoothed it down over her hips. *Definitely still there though. Mark would notice it.*

She put a hand over her eyes and then ran it up

286

through her hair. *And just what was she going to say?* She'd always planned to tell him . . . someday. But she'd been unsure of him for so long . . . and there'd been no point in telling him if they'd never be together.

The sound of a key in the lock startled her. *Mark was here!*

He stepped inside the room, and came to an abrupt halt. His mouth dropped open when he saw what she was wearing.

"Jane? What are you doing—?"

"Please say you're glad to see me." She took a tentative step toward him. "You sounded so strange on the phone—like . . . like you didn't want me to come."

His heart in his throat, Mark couldn't utter a word. *His favorite dream had come to life and was standing there in front of him.* He could see the hope—and worry—in her eyes and knew he couldn't push her away again. He simply couldn't do it; he'd known it as soon as she said she was coming. His eyes met hers, and he opened his arms. "You better be sure about this . . . because I'm not strong enough to walk away this time. I want you too much."

"Just tell me you love me," she said, slowly walking toward him.

He enfolded her in his arms and buried his face in her bright hair. Seconds later, he leaned away and let his eyes rake her from head to toe. "The nightgown is beautiful; such a waste though, since it definitely has to go." He grinned, fingering a strap of her nightgown.

"I need a shower. You won't disappear, will you? I'm half afraid I'm dreaming."

"Just hurry."

"You're kidding, right? This'll be the fastest shower in

287

history." The heat in his dark eyes warmed her as he kissed her tenderly. "Get in bed and wait for me."

As soon as the bathroom door shut, she closed the blinds and turned off the ceiling light and the lamp beside the bed, leaving the room in shadow. She yanked the sheets down and climbed into the bed, pulling the covers up to her chin as second thoughts began to bedevil her.

Suddenly, the door opened and Mark stood there—one glorious male—*fully aroused, judging by the protrusion of the towel loosely wrapped around his lean hips.* Her mouth suddenly dry, she tried to swallow.

"How come it's so dark in here?"

He strode to the bed, stopping beside it to flip on the lamp. She shut her eyes. "Mark, can we do this in the dark? Please. Turn the lights out." He stopped, and his eyes locked on hers.

"In the dark? Why?"

"Just . . . just this once. *Please.*"

Unable to understand her obvious panic, he decided to go along with her request—for now. He reached over and turned out the lamp on the bedside table, and the room fell back into shadow.

"Thank you."

He leaned over and slowly pulled the covers down and let his hot gaze roam over her from head to toe. He sat down on the edge of the bed, reached out and lifted her onto his lap as the towel slipped even lower. The warmth of his body, the strong arms surrounding her, and the clean smell of him all reassured her. This man would never hurt her. She curled against him.

"What's this all about, Jane? What are you afraid of?" He could feel her breath quicken, and he pulled back,

288

took her chin in his hand, and lifted it until their eyes met. Then he kissed her softly. "It isn't our first time, Jane. It may have been almost six years, but I haven't forgotten a single thing about making love to you that night. Did I hurt you so badly; are your memories of that night so terrible that you're afraid—"

"No, Mark, no. My memories of that night are *wonderful*. I never forgot either."

"Then what? What's wrong, Jane? And don't say, 'nothing.' I know you, and this isn't like you."

"It's just that I . . . I haven't told you. I'm not . . . my body's not perfect . . . not anymore."

His heart seemed to jump into his throat. *What had happened to her? Had she been raped? Oh God, no.* He pulled her tightly against him. "Stop worrying, Jane. I love you with all my heart, and to me you're beautiful, will *always* be beautiful. Now, let me unwrap this beautiful package the way I've been dreaming of for so long."

She slowly raised her arms and let him slide the gossamer garment off over her head, thankful for the near darkness of the room. *She could put off his discovery for just a little while longer.* She wasn't afraid for herself, but for him. She hadn't, however, considered his keen aviator's eyesight, or his sensitive fingers.

He wrapped his arms around her, his lips found hers, and she responded with all the love and desire she had hidden for so long. His sensitive fingers explored her body—and found the beginning of the scar just under her breasts. His hand stopped moving, and she sucked in a deep breath.

Mark lifted her abruptly off his lap and stood her on the floor in front of him. His fingers slowly traced the

289

line of the scar from its beginning to where it ended at the bottom of her abdomen. Then he retraced it again, from top to bottom.

"What the . . . what the hell *happened* to you?"

Despite the dim light, she could see the glitter of his dark eyes, and the shock on his face as he looked up at her. She wanted to dive into the bed and pull the sheet up over herself, but knew she could not. *It was his right to look, his right to know . . . and she should have told him before now.*

"The scar isn't new," he said, finally.

"No."

"How long has it been there?" He spoke flatly, and the light in his eyes had gone out.

"Five-and-a-half years."

She felt his body stiffen, and his voice was shaking with emotion when he spoke.

"I left you *pregnant*?"

Slowly one finger gently traced the scar. Then he looked at her accusingly.

"Why didn't you tell me you were pregnant? How far along were you when you lost our baby?"

How did he know she had lost the baby? Then the rest of what he had said registered—"our baby." *He'd said "our baby."* Tears flooded her eyes until she could no longer see his face. He continued, his staccato words sounding like a prosecuting attorney as he rapped out his fierce questions.

"A normal birth, even Caesarean, wouldn't leave a scar like that. What happened, Jane? Tell me—all of it— every single detail."

Her knees were collapsing, and he pulled her back onto his lap, but now he felt stiff and unyielding. She

290

sagged against him, tears spilling down her cheeks. Desperate, she grabbed his face and held it in both of her hands, and looked at him with shimmering eyes.

"All right. But know this—I love you, I have always loved you, and I will never stop loving you. I'll tell you everything, but you have to hold me, *please.*"

His body was rigid, his eyes squinched shut in pain. She thought he was going to refuse her. Finally he nodded, slid back against the headboard of the bed and settled her body against his. She laid her face against his chest and began to speak, her voice expressionless, her eyes staring straight ahead.

"I was so naive. I didn't even know I was pregnant until several months after you left." She felt his body tense at the word "left," and she stopped.

He squeezed her arms and said softly, "Go on."

"When it finally dawned on me I was going to have a baby, I didn't know what to do . . . so I did nothing. I guess I . . . No one knew, and I couldn't tell anyone."

"Didn't it occur to you to call me? Kit knew where I was. After all, it was my fault."

"Not just yours, and no, it didn't. I was four months pregnant when the accident happened. I had already made up my mind that whatever it took, I would have the baby. I could never abort it; never destroy a baby that we had made."

He lifted her face to his. "Jane—"

"No . . . let me finish. It was April, and there was a bad snowstorm, but the snow stopped and the weather cleared. I took advantage of the clearing weather to drive the fifty miles to Conrad for my check-up. I went there because no one would know me. Anyway, my late-afternoon appointment was delayed. By the time I got

291

out of the doctor's office, it was dark.

"I was about five miles from the doctor's office when it happened. I didn't see the black ice on the road. The car went into a skid; I couldn't control it. It spun around, slid off the road, and landed in the roadside ditch. I was wearing my seatbelt, but the airbag didn't deploy, and the steering wheel . . ."

She shook her head, fighting tears. "I knew I was going to lose the baby. I just *knew*. I remember crying and crying. I was lucky a road crew came by because that highway isn't widely traveled at night. They called an ambulance. I must have blacked out because I woke up sometime later in the hospital back in Conrad. When I felt the bandages, I knew they hadn't been able to save the baby. The doctor said they barely saved my life. I asked him if I would be able to have more children, and—"

She stopped, squeezing her eyes shut to hold back tears.

Mark fisted his hands. *Surely not that. Fate couldn't be that cruel.* "What . . . what did he say?"

"That he couldn't say definitely I wouldn't be able to get pregnant again, but it would be unlikely and . . . difficult." Mark tightened his hug and gently stroked her arm.

"No one knew? Not even Kit . . . not your friends? You didn't call *anyone*?"

When she shook her head, he gritted his teeth and shut his eyes. "Oh, Jane . . . you had nobody . . . you went through that terrible experience all by yourself. How can I . . . How can I . . .?"

His head fell forward onto the back of her neck, and she felt the dampness of his tears. *Mark was crying!*

292

She turned in his lap and gently brushed his tears away with shaking fingers, then arched her head up and kissed his closed eyes. "Don't Mark. It was a long time ago. We were both young and scared back then. We aren't the same people now."

"Jane, I would give my life if I could go back in time and do things differently. I've never been able to forget that night . . . or what I did afterward." She dropped her head and her voice was barely a whisper.

"I thought you didn't care."

"Didn't care! I cared *too* much. I was scared to death. I didn't have a clue as to how to deal with it. If you never believe anything else I tell you, please believe this—if I had known about the baby, I would have moved heaven and earth to get there. I would have."

"Oh, Mark . . ." Tears brimmed in her eyes.

"I should have been there for you."

"Mark, there's no way you could have been there, even if I had called you when I first knew I was pregnant. You were in Iraq then . . . but I would have told you when the baby was born—"

"Would you?"

"Of course I would! But . . . but it *wasn't* born. And the loss . . . the loss of our baby was so sudden, so unexpected. By the time I realized what had happened it was all over . . . and there was no need to tell you."

"No need? Jane Brewer—you suffered all alone, with no one to help you get over it, no one to sympathize with you. No one at all. If you couldn't tell me, why didn't you tell Kit . . . or a friend . . . *someone*?"

"I didn't tell them for the same reason I didn't tell you—there wasn't time."

"But afterward?"

"I just . . . I just wanted to put it out of my mind; it was the only way I could get through it. Sympathy would have done me in." His eyes were sad as he looked at her, and he struggled to get his next words out.

"Jane, how can you ever forgive me? How can you still *love* me? I can't love myself, and I'll <u>never</u> forgive myself."

She leaned forward and placed her hand on his cheek, looking deeply into his velvet brown eyes, now filled with tears. "Don't say that, Mark. Don't *ever* say that. It wasn't your fault . . . no more than it was mine. It was meant to be. I know that now . . . and you have to believe it. I couldn't *not* forgive you Mark; there was no choice. I love you; I told you . . . always and forever."

He touched his forehead against hers and murmured her name brokenly. "Jane. I'll love you forever too. I may never be able to make up to you for what you went through . . . but I promise I'll spend the rest of my life trying."

She lifted his chin with her finger and peeped at him through wet lashes. "Can you start *now*, do you think?" she said impishly.

He clasped her face with his larger hands and stared deeply into her eyes. This time he let her see the emotion in them. She sucked in a deep breath as she saw all her hopes, all her dreams fulfilled by the tender emotion she saw in his eyes. He leaned toward her and kissed her softly.

Suddenly he pulled back, raised his head and let out a war whoop. "Yes! *Finally*!" Then he looked at her, his eyes full of mischief. "Starting . . . right . . . <u>NOW</u>!"

He lifted her off his lap and swung her over beside him, snatched the towel from around his waist, and pressed her down into the bed. He leaned down close to her face, wrinkled his eyebrows. Then his mouth curved upward into the grin she loved.

"How long do we have?"

She burst out laughing with sheer happiness as she gave him an arch look. "How long do you need, *lover boy*?"

He hooted with laughter. Then his face turned serious. "I love you, Jane Brewer, with all my heart . . . and I'm about to show you how much right now."

A long time later, moonlight shone through the window, silvering their bodies as she studied Mark sleeping. He was so beautiful, and his lovemaking earlier had been everything she could have dreamed. Tender, caring, and showing his strength. *Where did they go from here?*

She rolled over until her body was touching his. Instantly his arm went around her, and he pulled her against his side, releasing a deep sigh as he did so. She snuggled against him, enjoying the feeling of safety and security just being close to him gave her.

The next morning, Mark watched the med-evac plane lift off—with Jane on it. It felt as if a part of him was going with her. His mind was so filled with memories of the preceding night, he felt he would explode if he didn't tell someone. *But who? Definitely not anyone around here, that was for sure.* He immediately thought of Hawk. He sure missed that guy. *Well, what were cell*

phones for? Half an hour later, he listened to Hawk's phone as it rang, and wondered how to phrase his news. He was still wondering when Hawk answered.

"Hello, Mark. Whenever my phone rings in the middle of the night I know it's going to be you. This better be important, you son of a gun."

Mark laughed. "It's midnight there, not the middle of the night."

"That *is* the middle of the night. What's up?"

"Only the most important thing in my life to date, that's all."

"I can tell from your voice: you asked her, and she said yes?"

"I did, and she did, and last night was—" *Damn! How had that slipped out? He was in for it now.*

"So, you had a good night, hmm? I wonder why." Hawk chuckled.

Mark laughed ruefully. "And you can just keep on wondering, Hawk."

The gruffness in his voice brought a shout of laughter from Hawk, and then Mark heard his sister in the background. *Maybe this hadn't been such a good idea.* "Good grief, Hawk, don't you ever answer the telephone without Kit right beside you?"

Hawk laughed again. "Not in the middle of the night, buddy; not in the middle of the night."

"Okay. I'm sorry I woke you up."

"No problem. So we're going to have a new sister-in-law?"

Kit's squeal nearly deafened him. He heard sounds of movement, and then she was on the telephone.

"Well big brother, you finally did it! I've always known Jane Brewer was the woman for you—"

Hawk interrupted her, his mouth close to the phone so Mark couldn't help but hear. "And . . . he had a *big night* last night."

"Whaat? Oh, wow!"

"And you can tell your husband he's got a big mouth!"

Kit laughed, and then her voice got serious. "I'm really happy for you, Mark. So, what are your plans? Is there a wedding in the offing?"

"Certainly there's a wedding in the offing! That's what I called about. It's impossible for us to get married here in Afghanistan—and not much easier in Germany. Even there, the paperwork would take so long both of our tours would be over first."

Hawk interrupted, and Mark realized he and Kit must be sharing the telephone between them.

"So, what's the plan? When are you getting married? You are getting married, aren't you?"

"Yes, we're getting married! What's wrong with the two of you?"

"I just thought—"

"Well, forget it; we're definitely getting married. Both of our tours are over in early November. The plan is to get married then—"

Kit didn't let him finish the sentence. "Oh, Mark, that's perfect! Then Matt can marry you! Does he know yet? Is it going to be a Christmas wedding? Tell us what you want, and we'll handle all the details. Won't we, Hawk?"

At this point Hawk grabbed the phone from his wife, pretending to be grumpy. "He called me, Kit. How about you let me say a couple of words?"

Mark could hear the smile in Hawk's voice when Kit finally let him speak. "Seriously, Mark, we'd love to help. Have you talked to Matt yet? Mark, you still there?"

"Yeah. I'm here. I just . . . thanks guys. I don't have any details. You're the first ones I've called. I'm going to call Matt as soon as I hang up—"

Kit interrupted. "Maybe you better wait an hour or two—he might not be as gracious as we are about middle-of-the-night calls."

He could hear her giggling and knew she was teasing him. "He's a padre; he ought to be used to it. And I know Jane will be calling you, Kit. Her evac flight left about thirty minutes ago, heading back to Landstuhl—"

"And you're already on the phone? Man, you don't let any grass grow under *your* feet!"

"I've waited long enough." He laughed and heard a groan from his sister. "What was *that* for? Is Kit all right? The baby still on track? Before he could answer, Kit was back on the line.

"I just realized I'll look like an *elephant* at the wedding! Good thing no one will be looking at me—all eyes will be on Jane."

"Are you all right, Kit? The baby . . ."

"The baby's *fine*, and so am I. Seriously Mark, when is the wedding? You could get married at Christmas, then all the family would be there anyway. By that time, I'll have had the baby . . . be able to get into a decent dress . . ."

"Sorry, Sis. I'm not waiting that long. If you have to wear a tent, so be it! I'm not waiting any longer than Thanksgiving . . . Can you set it up for Thanksgiving?"

"Man, you *are* in a hurry."

"We both are; the sooner the better."

"Don't worry about anything, Mark. I'll call Jane, then

Hawk and I will take care of everything, and we'll love doing it."

"Hey, thanks guys. I knew I could depend on you. I gotta go. Sorry about waking you up."

"Any time, Bro, any time."

Mark laughed. I'll check back soon. Take care of that baby, Sis. You'll make a great dad, Hawk."

"You take care too, Mark."

"So long, buddy."

"Hey Mark, wait; don't hang up yet."

"Now what, Kit?"

"Is this a secret? Can we tell people?"

Mark chuckled. "As if you could ever keep a secret. You'll be burning up the phone lines before daylight. Just let me ask Matt to marry us before you tell him, okay?"

"What about Luke and Jon?"

Hawk interrupted his wife. "Kit, it's *his* marriage—let *him* tell them first."

"Oh, Hawk . . . he knows I'm not trying to steal his thunder; don't you, Mark? I'm just so excited. I can't believe you're <u>finally</u> getting married."

"I don't exactly have one foot in the grave, Kit."

"You know what I mean. It's just that you never seemed to . . . every time we saw you . . . you just never mentioned anyone special. Gosh, I wonder who'll be next—Luke or Jon . . . umph—"

Kit's voice was suddenly muffled, as if Hawk had put his hand over her mouth.

"Quit while you're ahead, Kit."

Mark smiled; Hawk was obviously used to the ramblings of his irrepressible sister.

"Oh, all right. I love you brother; be careful."

"Always."

Mark replaced his phone in his pocket, smiling at the thought that he was going to have another nephew. Then a sense of awe came over him as he envisioned a son of his own—with Jane's blond curls and his brown eyes. *Him a dad.* Now there was a thought. And it felt so right—until he remembered Jane's words and realized— it might never happen for them.

When Matt answered the phone, his voice was calm and unruffled, as though he were used to receiving phone calls at one o'clock in the morning.

"Is everything all right, Mark?"

"Sorry about waking you. Hawk just reminded me it's the middle of the night there. But I wanted to tell you my good news—before Kit beat me to it."

Matt's deep rumble of laughter had him joining in. It was good to be able to laugh about Kit again. A year ago none of them would have imagined it.

"So tell me, what's so important you couldn't wait 'til daylight?"

"Have you got room in your busy schedule for a wedding?"

"You and Jane are getting married?"

"Damn! Uh, sorry. What *is it* with this family? How come nobody is surprised? How come you think Jane's the one?"

"You mean she's not?"

"Well, yes, she is, but—"

"Good! I'm glad it finally worked out for you and Jane. It took you long enough to realize she was the one for you."

"What do you mean?"

"I was here six years ago, in case you've forgotten. You were stunned to find her all grown up. I saw the sparks between you two. When you left here, I *knew* you were running scared. I figured you'd eventually realize that you were in love with her. I just didn't think it would take you this long!"

Mark felt his face redden, and was glad his brother couldn't see. "Yeah, well, you don't know the whole story."

"I know it."

"No, you don't."

"What? That you and Jane made love the last night of your leave? I wasn't even surprised; I saw it coming."

Mark was stunned, both that Matt had guessed what had happened, and that he hadn't said anything about it at the time. It did explain his expression when he'd woke him in the middle of the night to say he was leaving, and why Matt had asked him if he'd said goodbye to Jane.

"How in the he—heck did you know?"

Matt laughed. "I'm a minister, not a monk! And besides, I knew you had been on the lakeshore that night."

"Where were you?"

"In my study. I had just finished typing my sermon and turned out the light when you came in the back door and stopped in the hallway—right outside my door. Even thought you were whispering, I couldn't help but hear—"

"You could have let us know!"

"What? And embarrass you?" Matt chuckled. "Not me."

Mark's face flushed as he remembered what Matt

would have heard.

"Sometimes it's hard to remember you're a man of the cloth."

Matt laughed outright then. "Seriously, Mark. I'm happy for you and Jane. I'm glad you're going to wait until you get home so that I can marry you. I always hoped to."

"I wouldn't have it any other way." Mark's voice was gruff with emotion as he spoke.

"Kit told us Jane is in the Air Force too."

"A nurse in the Reserve. She's in Germany right now."

"When are you planning this big event?"

"We don't have a date, but as soon as possible."

"Well, you'll be home mid-November. What about Jane; when is she due back?"

Mark smiled to himself. As usual, Matt kept track of all of them, where they were and when they'd be home. No wonder they called him Information Central.

"She's on a ninety-day tour. It'll be up the eighth of November."

"So you'd both be available for a Thanksgiving wedding?"

"That's what Jane and I were hoping."

"I'll reserve the date and the church. Keep me posted. Elaine and the kids will be thrilled. We'll make sure you and Jane have a beautiful wedding."

"Thanks, Matt. You'll be hearing from Kit. She and Hawk said they'd help too. I gotta go, but I'll be in touch. And Matt?"

"Yes?"

"Matt, could you—I need to ask—would you pray for Jane, and me . . . since it's in your line of work and all?"

"I'm surprised you think you even have to ask. I always pray for *all of you*. I thought you knew that."

"I did know . . . but this is different. I . . . we . . . Jane and I sort of have a problem. It's my fault and . . . well, I just need you to pray."

"Certainly, I will, but it might be helpful if you could tell me what the problem is."

"Matt . . . Jane was pregnant when I left her that time." *There, he had said it.* And once it was out, he couldn't seem to stop—the whole sad tale came tumbling out. "I didn't know, Matt. She never told me. She lost the baby in a car accident . . . and she never told me that either. She went through all of it alone; she never told *anyone.* And that's not the worst of it . . . the doctor told her she might—" He took a breath, "—she might never be able to have any more babies."

"And you feel it's all your fault."

"*Of course I do*. It *is* my fault."

"So you're omnipotent now?"

There was humor in Matt's voice when he said it, and Mark felt a rise of anger. "Somehow, I thought you'd understand, Matt."

"I <u>do</u> understand Mark. You're the one who doesn't. It was *no one's* fault. Things happen . . . but God is always in control. Sometimes we just can't see his purpose at the time, but he's always right. Jane doesn't blame you, does she?"

"No . . . no, she doesn't."

"There you go. And Mark, have faith, trust God. Remember, nothing is impossible with Him."

"Now you sound like Dad." Mark smiled.

"Where do you think I learned it? And don't worry, I'll pray. And it wouldn't hurt for you to pray, too."

303

"Okay. And thanks, Matt. It's really helped to talk to you. No wonder you're such a good pastor."

Matt laughed. "You aren't the only warrior; I just work for a different commander. I love you, Bro."

"Yeah . . . me too."

He shoved his phone in his pocket. *No doubt about it, he'd struck it lucky when it came to family.* He shook his head. Matt had always been different from the rest of them, but there was no doubt, he was one of them, and he had found his true calling.

Chapter 13

Jane left the chaos of the Vail house and walked the short distance across the lawn to the church next door, the frost on the ground sparkling like diamonds under her feet. The building was unlocked, and she went inside. She stopped in the narthex, awed by the beauty of the sanctuary, and the feeling of peace that came over her as she stood there. Early morning sunlight glowed through the stained-glass windows, splashing rainbow patterns on the seats of the old oaken pews and the scarred wooden floor.

Her eyes followed the long aisle to its end at the altar rail. In less than twenty-four hours she would walk down that aisle to meet Mark. It was hard to believe how swiftly things had moved. Once she'd agreed to marry him, the details just fell into place. Mark's wonderful family had taken over, and she had been swept along in the current of their enthusiasm and love.

It might be unusual for the groom's family to arrange the wedding, but she wouldn't change a thing. Everything was perfect. Her parents were arriving from Florida this morning, and she knew they would approve.

She'd always felt a part of Mark's family, ever since growing up next door to them with Kit as her best friend. *Now she really would be a Vail.*

A dust mote floated in a golden beam of light in front of her, and she breathed a sigh of happiness—*she had to be the luckiest woman in the world. All her dreams were coming true.* She heard footsteps, and suddenly Mark's arms were around her.

"Not having second thoughts, are we?"

She turned for his kiss. "Oh, Mark, it's all so perfect I'm afraid . . ."

Her eyes were glistening with tears, and he gently brushed them away with his thumbs. "Afraid of what? We got here; that was the hard part. From now on, no matter what happens, we'll be there for each other."

She saw a shadow cross his face and knew Mark was remembering the time he hadn't been.

"Mark," she said softly, "you *have* to forget. The past is the past." She smiled as she reached up and smoothed his frown away with her fingers. "The moving finger writes, and having writ moves on. Nor all your piety nor wit shall lure it back to cancel half a line, nor all your tears wash out a word of it."

"The Rubaiyat of Omar Khayyam." He smiled back at her.

"You know it!" Jane's eyes grew wide with surprise.

"My mother gave it to me when I was still in my teens. It was a favorite of hers. I always thought it was a strange one for a minister's wife, since it's all about fate. When I mentioned it, she said she simply loved the images and poetry of it."

"How come you're here?"

"Elaine sent me to find you; breakfast is ready. No

306

one knew where you were, but I had a hunch I'd find you here."

He broke into a grin, and she grinned back, shaking her head. "I love your family, but sometimes—"

"They're a bit overwhelming." He laughed. "Yeah, sometimes they are, especially when they're all in one place at the same time."

"Mark, we're so lucky they could all get here—I mean, given the distances they had to come. Just think, Kit and Mark are pretty close, but Luke came all the way from Afghanistan . . . and who knows where Jon came from? And you were able to get a *two-week* leave! And my parents are here. It's . . . it's all—"

"Amazing?"

He grinned, and she frowned at him. "Don't laugh—I mean, even the sun is shining—it's a perfect day for a wedding." That wrinkled brow told her he didn't understand.

"You sound worried? Is something wrong, Jane?"

"*Nothing* is wrong! Everything is *so* perfect I'm almost afraid. "

He leaned forward and kissed her nose. "Don't be—remember what Matt said."

"That 'God's smiling on this event.' She sighed. "I hope He is."

"Believe it—Matt's a man of God, isn't he?"

She laughed as Mark pulled her against his side and kissed her tenderly. She snuggled against him and felt his arm tighten around her waist. Her dream had come true, and she realized that she had nothing to worry about as long as they could face the future together. As they walked down the aisle of the church and stepped through the door into the brilliant morning sunshine, she

307

stopped and turned to face him.

"Mark, I need to tell you . . . I need you to know how very much I love you, how happy I am today, and that I look forward to sharing our life together, wherever it takes us."

She pulled his face down and kissed him. The kiss brought tears to Mark's eyes for he knew that she had given him her heart and soul in that kiss—his past was forgiven. He smiled down at her, murmuring softly, "And I will love *you* forever." He reached for her hand, intertwined his fingers with hers, and they walked out into the sunny churchyard.

Read on for a preview of the next book in:

The Vail Family Series

...and Face the Future

Chapter 1

He stopped jogging to stare out over the endless
expanse of water. He wasn't tired, even though he'd
been running since 0530, and he knew—without looking
at the diver's watch on his wrist—that it was almost
0630. He wasn't even winded; he could continue for
another hour. But he stopped as he always did, totally
awed by the sight of the sun rising out of the water.
Soon it would make a gleaming path across the serene
blue expanse of the Atlantic Ocean. The sight never
failed to calm his soul. For a few minutes he could
forget the terrible sights and awful sounds that were a
part of his normal life.

As he stood at the edge of the ocean, the frothy waves
of the incoming tide rolling over his bare feet, Jon Vail
inhaled deeply and let out a heavy sigh. Last night had
been bad. The nightmare had awakened him every time
he finally fell asleep. Although he hadn't wanted this
leave, his Captain had insisted—had given him no
choice. *And the Captain had been right; he had to beat
this . . . or be useless.*

He looked down at his feet, now covered with sand from the incessant rushing in and sliding out of the waves. As he had countless times before, he wondered why he was still alive; the only member of his team to survive. *Why hadn't he died too?*

He was sorry about the way he'd treated Kit. She was his twin sister, and she deserved better. But he'd been afraid he couldn't hide his problem from her. They'd always been so close they almost knew when each other took a breath. When she'd lost her leg in Iraq, he'd been half a world away, but he'd known immediately that something had happened to her. And when he'd landed at Andrews AFB five days ago, Kit had met his plane . . . and known right away he had a problem. She'd been hurt when he'd told her he wouldn't—*couldn't*—go home with her.

As he thought of Kit and her family, a sad smile flickered across his face. *Kit was Army all the way*, a ring knocker who'd stayed in the service even after she lost her leg. She'd married their brother Mark's best friend, Hawk Hawkins, and now they had a six-month-old daughter, Julia—*a real heart stealer*, he'd bet.

Kit was the reason he was here—here being Fenwick Island, Delaware. When he'd told her he needed to be alone for a while, she'd insisted she knew the perfect place. She'd had refused to listen to any of his protests, and just called one of her friends who had inherited a family cottage here. Before he could marshal his objections, he was handed the key to #8 Dagsboro Street—*and here he was.* As he watched the sun's golden rays reach closer and closer to the land, he admitted that Kit had been right. Although this beach town was nothing like the sleepy burg it had once been, it had never become the upscale tourist haven that its northern neighbor, Rehoboth, was. That town was often called the 'summer capital' due to all the Washingtonians who spent their summers and weekends there. Nor had Fenwick accumulated the tawdry glitz of its southern neighbor, Ocean City. Instead it huddled between the two ocean meccas, insistent on retaining its small-town aura by permitting no buildings taller than thirty feet, and no boardwalk by the ocean. He was glad. Even though most of the shambling cottages that once strung in a line behind the last dune were now gone—replaced by huge birthday-cake homes with porches and balconies and beachy statuary in their yards—it was still peaceful, and somehow, it settled his soul.

Daisy Brennerman strode rapidly along the almost deserted beach, as she did every morning, summer or winter, storm or calm. She got up at five every morning for just that reason, so the beach would be deserted. She loved everything about the place—the sand, the sea, the hot sun, the cold winter gales, everything. But most of all, she loved the early morning peace; the sense that she was the only person in a world washed clean of all the grit and filth and grime she encountered as a crime-scene photographer working for the State Police.

She narrowed her eyes and stared straight down the beach. If she avoided looking beyond the high-water mark on the sand she didn't see the huge edifices—certainly the term "cottages" didn't fit any more—strung along the crest of the beach. If she didn't look, she could enjoy the pretense that this was all hers, and she was the only one on it.

At least she used to able to. Now, every time she came over the last dune and walked down to the edge of the water to begin her jog, she saw a man already there. He was always far down the beach, jogging along as if he could go on forever. Sometimes he was heading away from her. Other times he was returning, but he never looked to the right or the left, never appeared to even see her, just continued jogging along, his steps almost mechanical. She never saw where he came from or where he went, *but he wasn't a man she could forget.*

He was an incredible specimen of God's handiwork on the male species: over six feet tall, with wide shoulders, a broad chest, and a narrow waist. Strong legs protruded from baggy shorts, and his bare feet pounded the wet sand with determination and strength. He was blonde, with hair closely cropped against a finely shaped head, and he always wore a long-sleeved t-shirt.

She stopped dead in her tracks and let out a short laugh. *Daisy Brennerman, you're a fool. You just admitted he never even sees you, and yet you've just described him in incredible detail. How dumb is that! Oh, well.* She shrugged. That's what came from being a crime photographer—*one noticed details.*

She continued her walk along the sand, unable to put the lone man out of her mind. *Why was he alone? Where had he come from? And how long would he be here?*

About the Author

D. K. Taylor worked at Dover Air Force Base for seven years before being transferred to Chateauroux Air Station in France, where she met and married her husband, an Air Force Staff Sergeant. With family members retiring from various branches of the U.S. military, she has an unending source of inspiration for military romances.

Always a writer, Mrs. Taylor began writing in earnest after the death of her husband. Her first book, *Loving What's Left* launched the saga of the Vail family. *To Forgive the Past* is the second book in "The Vail Family Series."

The Vail Family Series

Loving What's Left

D. K. Taylor

The Vail Family Series

Loving What's Left

D. K. Taylor

In the blink of an eye,
                two lives are changed...

Army Lieutenant Kit Vail has finally escaped the loving protection of her older brother, although it has taken a tour in Iraq to accomplish it. Meanwhile, at an Air Force Base several hours away, lone-wolf fighter pilot Captain Hawk Hawkins is yanked out of his perfect lifestyle by a call from his long-time friend, Kit's older brother. Captain Mark Vail calls in a marker and demands that Hawk drop everything and make a trip to Camp Taji to check on his baby sister—a woman he has never met. Despite their initial animosity, there is an underlying attraction, but sparks fly when neither is prepared to give up his or her independence. Then fate intervenes in the form of an IED (Improvised Explosive Device).

Made in the USA
Middletown, DE
09 July 2019